THE JERUSALEM SCROLLS
VATICAN SECRET ARCHIVE THRILLERS
BOOK FIVE

GARY MCAVOY

LITERATI
EDITIONS.

Hardcover ISBN: 978-1-954123-26-7
Paperback ISBN: 978-1-954123-27-4
eBook ISBN: 978-1-954123-28-1

Library of Congress Control Number: 2022923990

Published by:
Literati Editions
PO Box 5987
Bremerton WA 98312-5987
Email: info@LiteratiEditions.com
Visit the author's website: www.GaryMcAvoy.com

BOOKS BY GARY MCAVOY

(In the order written)

FICTION

THE MAGDALENE CHRONICLES Series

The Magdalene Deception

The Magdalene Reliquary

The Magdalene Veil

VATICAN SECRET ARCHIVE THRILLERS Series

The Vivaldi Cipher

The Opus Dictum

The Petrus Prophecy *

The Avignon Affair *

The Jerusalem Scrolls

NONFICTION

And Every Word Is True

* Co-authored with Ronald L. Moore

Map of the Holy Land

PROLOGUE

THE ROMAN EMPIRE – 1ST CENTURY

Gathered somewhere in Rome in their vast underground *mithraeum,* or temple, the forty *syndexioi*—devout initiates "united by the handshake"—chanted in unison as they bound themselves to their pagan deity. One end of the arched-stone chamber featured the vivid hues of a *tauroctony*—a painted scene of their god Mithras slaughtering a sacred bull.

From the first through the fourth centuries, Christianity and Mithraism embodied two rival factions reacting to a similar series of cultural influences. Mithraism flourished for three hundred years before being extinguished by harsh persecution from the more politically powerful Christian population. Comprised largely of Roman soldiers, Mithraists had found a covert camaraderie, a brotherhood of like-minded followers

1

who shared a secret knowledge of the universe, specifically its constellations and cosmic movements.

Little remains of this once-vibrant cult apart from archeological evidence of thousands of their subterranean *mithraea*, or temples, throughout the Roman Empire, many hundreds of them in the city of Rome alone.

~

JUDEA – 1ST CENTURY

Before Titus Flavius Vespasianus, better known to history as Vespasian, became Emperor of Rome in 69 CE, he was a famed and revered Roman legate—the equivalent of a high-ranking general—who, a year earlier, had led an army 60,000 strong through the hot barren deserts of Judea in a years-long war against the Jewish population of the Holy Land.

On orders from Emperor Nero, Vespasian was commanded to suppress the major rebellions of Jews against the Roman Empire in what came to be called the Great Jewish Revolt, a five-year war fought mainly in Roman-controlled Judea. The Jews were greatly outnumbered and suffered devastating destruction of their towns, expropriation of their lands for Roman military use, and widespread displacement of Jewish people from their ancestral homes.

. . .

AT THE BASE of the terraced cliffs on the northwestern shores of the Dead Sea—located in what was then called Palestine—a secluded ascetic community of some twelve hundred mystic Jews called the Essenes could foresee their destiny. The Romans were coming to destroy their community and their ways of life. It was only a matter of time.

Desperate to preserve and protect their life's work—an extraordinary library of nearly a thousand sacred biblical scrolls, the product of their tribe's past two centuries of scribal efforts—they carefully wrapped the parchments and papyri in linen, placed them into tall clay jars, and concealed them in a series of caves not far from their homes on a dry marl plateau called Qumran. They then fled to save themselves, hoping to return at some later time to resume their lives and continue their work.

But the Essenes never returned to their home, having been vanquished after the Roman Siege of Jerusalem in 70 CE. Their precious scrolls sealed in the nurturing protection of earthen jars lay undisturbed in the arid climate of the Qumran caves for nearly two thousand years.

∼

JUDEA, ISRAEL – 20TH CENTURY

It was in the spring of 1947 when a fifteen-year-old Bedouin shepherd named Muhammed edh-Dhib from the Ta'amira tribe was tending his herd of sheep and goats among the hilly escarpments of the Qumran desert when one of the goats went missing in search of better pastures. Muhammed scrambled up the rocky, sloping hillsides in search of his caprine runaway when he chanced upon one of the many hidden caves in the area.

Hoping to flush out the goat, but wary of entering a dark hole in the desert alone, the young boy erred on the side of caution and tossed in several stones, for Muslim lore decreed that when in the suspected presence of dark spirits, stones must be thrown at them. Muhammed did not want to encounter dark spirits in an underground cave. He only wanted his goat.

But to his puzzlement, each time he threw a stone into the cave opening, he heard the sound of an object cracking and breaking. In a newspaper interview he gave later, young Muhammed was quoted as saying, "*I started throwing rocks inside the cave, and every time I was throwing a rock I was hearing a sound of breaking pottery. At that time I was confused by the sound, and I loved to know what is inside the cave.*" Already apprehensive, though, the shepherd returned later with a friend to explore the source of the shattering sounds.

What the two young Bedouins found that day has forever transformed biblical scholarship and even Christianity itself as it was previously understood. The cave was filled with cylindrical jars of red clay pottery—the same jars abandoned by the Essenes nearly two thousand years earlier. Seven of the jars contained several remarkably preserved parchment manuscripts, written mostly in Hebrew, which came to be known as the Dead

Sea Scrolls—biblical writings from between 150 BCE and 70 CE that largely predated even the Gospels, and which comprised the oldest surviving manuscripts of entire books later included in the biblical canon: Genesis, Exodus, Isaiah, Kings and Deuteronomy.

An antiquities dealer ultimately bought many of the scrolls, which soon found their way into the hands of biblical scholars. Publicity about the sensational discovery spread like gossip in a hookah lounge, and it wasn't long before ambitious archeologists and treasure hunters made their way to Qumran, unearthing some fifteen thousand scroll fragments from ten more caves in the area, ultimately accounting for nearly a thousand Essene manuscripts.

In efforts to prevent the plundering of further scrolls and other rare artifacts bound for the illegal but lucrative black market, archeologists from the Israel Antiquities Authority (IAA) have for years conducted their own excavations of caves burrowed among the steep escarpments and canyons of the Judean Desert.

But the IAA's efforts are often outnumbered by bands of highly motivated antiquity looters, and the fight to preserve the Holy Land's cultural legacy continues unabated.

CHAPTER
ONE

PRESENT DAY

Seventeen-year-old Tamir Pinsky had spotted the cave he sought high on a steep plateau as he and his best friend, Azim Hourani, sped their jeep through the dry wadis—deep ravines and riverbeds cut through the steep rock and limestone cliffs of the Judean Desert. It took a sharp eye to recognize the cave, but Tamir had trained himself to distinguish between shadow and opportunity—for opportunity lay within many of the yet-unexplored caves of the region.

This was a refreshing change from his day job stuck indoors for a security company, installing systems for industries in windowless backrooms. Just days before, he had been here scouting the area by himself when he chanced upon a cave hidden behind desert scrub and a challenging cluster of boulders. Clearly, previous excavators had to have missed this cave in earlier searches of the area—exactly the luck he needed for his cave-raiding mission.

This ancient and storied part of Israel is not far from the neighborhood in which both boys grew up: Abu Tor, one of the few Jerusalem sectors with a mixed, harmonious Jewish and Palestinian population. Tamir was a secular Jew and Azim was an Arab with little religious interest, and both boys became fast friends at Terra Sancta High School in nearby Jabsheh. Their shared passion for caving—or more specifically, cave plundering—was what drew them that morning to the sandy outcroppings of Wadi Murabba'at, some eighteen kilometers south of the more famous caves of Qumran on the northwest shore of the Dead Sea.

Tamir parked his old jeep in the shadows between two towering escarpments to avoid being spotted by the occasional patrols of Israel Antiquities Authority inspectors. The jeep—an older, general-purpose vehicle with camouflaged markings of the Israeli army, from whom he had bought it cheaply at auction—obscured itself naturally in the dappled, variegated desert landscape. The IAA did not look kindly upon poachers of Israel's cultural heritage, so for those in the business, it paid to be elusive.

Scrambling up the rocky hillside with the natural skill of mountain goats, their tactical boots gripping the tangled maquis of the rocky mesa, the boys headed toward the concealed cave above them.

"You will not believe what I found here, Azim," Tamir said with unbridled enthusiasm the closer they got. "Soon we will be rich!"

"But why didn't you just bring it down when you found it?" his friend asked as he panted and grunted his way up the ridge.

"Like I told you," Tamir repeated, exasperated by his friend's complaining, "the pottery was too big for me to carry down the jebel by myself. Don't you ever listen to what I say?!" Azim held his tongue, more interested in getting rich than winning an argument.

When they had reached the summit, they stopped to take a breath, drink from their water bottles, and turn to look at the view from their high perch atop the escarpment: the undisturbed vision of soft, brown, undulating hills, sandy dunes and high plateaus as far as the eye could see, broken only by the occasional oasis with ancient trees of Sodom apples, poplar, jujube and acacia surrounding precious watering holes.

"I never tire of looking out over our beloved desert, Azim. So rich with the history of both our peoples, never mind the conflicts. We are both here today after centuries of struggle and persistence by those who have come before. Are you not moved by that? How can one fail to be in awe of our land and its history?"

"You always were the dreamer, Tamir, with your head in the clouds. It is only a desert to me. Nothing but sand, after all."

The young Jew looked at his friend with dismay. Then, letting judgment pass, he said, "Alright, Azim. I'll show you there's more here than just sand. Let us take what we have come to get."

Pushing aside the brush and bushes, Tamir led his friend into the dark cavity of the cave opening, keeping an eye out for black desert cobras and horned vipers common to the area. Understandably, neither boy was fond of asps, especially those hiding in the relatively cooler caves.

But the attraction of what Tamir had found in this particular cave a few days before was worth the risk. With flashlights in hand, they carefully entered the dark mouth of the tunnel, leading them deep inside the cavern, their beams cautiously sweeping the hidden recesses for coiled snakes.

Reaching the back depths of the underground chamber, Tamir's flashlight shone on a single red clay jar a meter tall, set back inside a natural alcove in the limestone wall. He lifted off the lid of the jar to show Azim the treasure he had discovered.

Inside it were four flat parchment manuscript sheets in superb condition, as if they had been penned only recently. Reaching inside, Tamir withdrew the parchments to inspect them with his friend.

"I think these are written in Aramaic, or maybe even Ancient Greek. I have only seen references to those languages in school. Others will know for sure, but aren't they incredible, Azim?"

Placing them back inside, they also found a rolled and heavily tarnished silver scroll, hammered as thin as parchment and inscribed in some ancient dialect of Hebrew. Even though it was metal, it looked too fragile to remove so they let it be. Then the light of their torches shone on dozens of Nabataean drachmas, an ancient Greek coin currency, along with several Imperial dinars from the Roman period at the bottom of the jar.

"These will all sell well, my brother," Tamir exclaimed. "We will bring them to Ishak Ramzi in Tel Aviv; he will take care of the rest. And the clay jar itself is also of value, which is why I needed your help to get it down the jebel. Here now, give me a hand."

Each taking an end, they gently lifted the ancient crock, the coins inside making rattling sounds as they hustled it from the cavern mouth and carefully hauled it down the hill through the dense maquis. Once they reached the jeep, Tamir opened the rear gate and carefully positioned the jar between several afghan rugs he had brought, securing and concealing it thoroughly so it wouldn't crack during the two-hour drive to Tel Aviv and Egyptian dealer Ishak Ramzi's antiquities shop in Jaffa's *Shuk HaPishPeshim*, one of the largest open marketplaces in Israel.

As the jeep headed toward the city that never sleeps, they passed a sign reading "Entering the Land of Benjamin."

CHAPTER
TWO

The famed *Shuk HaPishPeshim*, the sprawling flea market set in the nineteenth-century Arab quarter of Tel Aviv–Jaffa, extended for several blocks along Olei Zion Street, and was flush with tourists and locals raucously haggling for the best deals on everything from jewelry to fabrics to antiquities. During the summer's annual *Pishpeshuk* festival, street performers and musicians punctuated the night with a lively vibe into the late and early hours, their colorful lights and regional music adding to the delight of bargain hunters and diners alike.

By the time Tamir and Azim arrived, night had fallen, and the market was alive with hundreds of visitors jammed into the narrow streets and alleyways. The rich, airy scents of apple, carob and watermelon tobacco smoke from hookah bars mixed with café aromas of simmering curry and *baharat*—a pungent blend of cumin, coriander, cinnamon, cloves, nutmeg and other fresh and exotic local spices—wafted through the warm night air.

As usual, parking anywhere close to the market was impossible, so while Tamir stayed with the jeep a few blocks away, Azim ran off to borrow a cart from one of the local Arab vendors he knew so they could transport their fragile treasure to Ishak Ramzi's shop.

As ONE OF only sixty-five licensed antiquities dealers in all of Israel, Ishak Sayyid Ramzi provided unique services for an exclusive and discerning clientele. He had his legitimate business, of course: a boutique in the *Shuk HaPishPeshim* that sold rare and desirable Middle Eastern antiques and a prized collection of ancient pottery, bronze and clay figurines, state-registered parchments and papyrus manuscripts, and other scarce antiquities.

But behind the heavy curtain separating his back office from the front shop is where he quietly conducted his most lucrative business: the illegitimate fencing of high-risk, high-demand, high-value artifacts. Israel is one of the few Mediterranean countries that licenses antiquities dealers, so black market artifacts are often permissibly passed on to the international antiquities market, effectively expunging their illegal origins.

A large area in the eastern Mediterranean region known as The Levant, and especially Israel, was a hotbed of activity in the unlawful trade of looted artifacts. The smuggling of pirated coins was an especially large market: rare silver shekels from the Great Jewish

Revolt of the first century, bronze coins from the Roman period, silver coins from the Persian, Hellenistic and Hasmonean periods, and coins bearing the first name of the beloved leader of the Bar Kochba Revolt, "Shimon," were especially coveted by discreet, well-heeled buyers.

But after the discovery of the Dead Sea Scrolls in 1947 and their historically significant impact on biblical scholarship, the most sought-after artifacts were even tiny fragments of such scrolls, not to mention fully intact manuscripts—and thousands of caves were believed yet to be discovered and explored throughout the vast region. With a paucity of official agents dedicated to enforcing Israel's antiquity laws, the IAA did not have sufficient manpower to counter the lively illegal trade.

"AND WHAT TREASURES have you brought for me today, my young friends?" Ishak Ramzi asked Tamir and Azim as they entered his large market stall, pushing their cart toward the back of the shop to avoid nosy passersby.

"Please, keep your voice down, Ishak," Azim whispered anxiously, his eyes scanning both ends of the narrow alley for suspicious loiterers. "Tamir, tell him what you found."

But Tamir held silent, surreptitiously glancing toward the hidden security cameras he had installed for this merchant some time ago.

"I think it would be better if we moved to the back," Ishak said cautiously, now grasping the nature of their visit. "Faisal," he motioned to his assistant, "keep an eye on the shop, you lazy camel. I will return shortly." The young Faisal nodded mutely, then went back to playing Pokémon on his mobile phone.

As Tamir held back the thick damask curtain, Azim wheeled the cart through to the back office. They all took seats in rickety wooden chairs.

"I take it you have something special with you?" Ishak said, his low voice posing the statement as a question.

Tamir smiled broadly with pride. "The other day I was hiking in Wadi Murabba'at and came across a concealed cave on a high plateau, a cave that I suspect had not been discovered before, hidden behind bushes and boulders as it was.

"In it I found this clay jar," he reached over to pull back the rugs, exposing the pottery, "filled with several scrolls I am certain will interest you, especially one made of silver. Would you like to see them?" Tamir's eyes lit up expectantly as his hand nervously raked back the long, dark, curly hair that had fallen over his tanned face.

Ishak's eyes opened wide at the mention of a silver scroll, the holy grail of manuscript artifacts in his line of work. "Yes, yes, of course I want to see them!" he said in an excited whisper.

He had long heard rumors of the mythical "silver scroll" mentioned in the famous Khirbet Qumran copper scroll discovered in the 1950s, reputedly containing not only a duplicate of vast treasure location details contained on the copper scroll itself, but with the addition of new information regarding even more buried riches to be found throughout Jerusalem. The fabled silver scroll had yet to be found, and excavators had been looking for it for years. *Could this be it?* he wondered.

Tamir removed the lid of the jar and reached deep inside, withdrawing the silver scroll and the parchment manuscripts, which he carefully laid on the table between them. He then lifted the jar and tilted it, letting the coins fall out onto the table. Though these were rare enough to have great value on their own, coins were a fairly common commodity in the antiquities markets. But all three of them stared at the scrolls as if they possessed some mystical aura.

"No one saw you take these from the cave? And you were not followed here, I assume?"

"No," Azim replied. "We were very careful. There were no police or IAA inspectors in the desert, Allah be praised, and we took great cautions getting them here to you. Now, it is your job to find a buyer, yes?"

Ishak stroked his long black and gray beard as he pondered what steps needed to be taken. "Leave this with me, young tigers. I must consider many things when moving something so rare and wondrous as this. To get maximum value, I must have the scrolls translated, or at least reviewed by some authority to establish their meaning and origin. Only then will we know what to expect. Do you understand?"

"Yes, most certainly, Ishak," said Tamir, "and I realize this will take time. But we are young, and we have much time!" He laughed and glanced at Azim, who joined him.

Ishak Ramzi did not laugh, for he knew what was at

stake here. If he was caught even having possession of this material, he could not only lose his hard-won license but possibly go to prison.

So, the goal was not to get caught. But first, he had to find a translator. Someone wise and trustworthy. Someone not from this area, who would not breathe a word of this to the wrong person.

And he knew just the right man.

CHAPTER
THREE

S imon Ginzberg and his daughter Rachel lay in teak Adirondack chairs on the sun deck outside the Pyramid Bar lounge onboard the *Royal Egyptian*, enjoying a long-planned one-way Holy Land cruise. Having departed Rome the week before and already called on the ports of Crete, Greece, and Turkey, the ship was now pulling into Haifa, Israel, for an overnight stay. The next day, the ship would cruise down the Mediterranean coast to the port of Ashdod, where they would end the tour in Jerusalem, Simon's birthplace, to enjoy themselves before flying back to Rome.

"I'm so glad we did this, Papa," Rachel said after taking a long sip of her Mai Tai. "You haven't had a vacation, well, since *I've* been an adult, anyway."

"Yes, my dear, I am all too aware of that," the old man said, duly chastened. "I work much too hard, and all the time, it seems. If you hadn't talked me into this cruise, I'd still be toiling away in the Vatican reading rooms, sinking myself into the crusades or some other historical adventure. But it is good to spend more time with you, without such distractions. I am getting on in years, you know, and…well, we'll leave it at that."

"Yes," his daughter agreed, "no need to state the obvious." Pragmatic as ever, Rachel Ginzberg never pulled punches and, like her father, usually spoke her mind with an obliging frankness.

Glancing at her phone, she brightened as she read a text message. "At last, we have cell service again. And good news! You should be proud of your grandson, Papa. Caleb got a new job offer at Rutgers University as a professor of Jewish Studies. He wants my advice on whether to take it or wait for another opportunity. Of course, he should take it, don't you think? I've got to call him." She stood and walked to the railing to phone her son.

"Yes, Rutgers is a fine college," Simon agreed as she walked away. "He should do well there." He reached into his pocket to take out his own phone, checking to see if he had any calls from his office. Two voice messages were waiting, one from his Vatican friend, Father Michael Dominic, and another from an unknown number. He listened to Michael's first.

"Hey, Simon, I wanted to wish you well on your voyage. Sorry I wasn't around to toss streamers for your departure, but I do look forward to your return. Meanwhile, you relax and have some fun with Rachel. You've earned it!"

Such a fine young man, that Michael, Simon mused. Then he tapped the Play button on the second message. The voice was familiar, but it was also adrenalized, even anxious.

"Shalom, Simon. This is your old friend Ishak Ramzi in Tel Aviv. I have come across, um...something of great importance and wanted to get your opinion of it. I would come to Rome, of course, as soon as it is possible for you, since this is not something we can discuss by phone. But I assure you that, uh...you will not fail to be impressed. Please, call me at this number soon, *yedidi*, and until then, be well."

Hmm. What could Ishak have that would be so important, I wonder? And is that fear or worry I sense in his voice? Such curious timing. Tel Aviv is not far from Ashdod...I could surely pay him a visit. But what to do with Rachel?

Returning to the table after her call, Rachel took another long draw on her cocktail before filling her father in on Caleb's decision dilemma, which they discussed at length before exhausting the subject.

"Rachel, I just got a call from an old Egyptian friend, an antiquities dealer in Tel Aviv who wants to meet with me over some important matter. So, I think I'll be going to see him first, once the ship docks in Ashdod. Do you want to go on to Jerusalem and I can meet you there a bit later? Or do you want to join me?"

"I'll go on to Jerusalem and visit with Auntie Zehava while you finish your business, then you can meet up with us later. Okay, Papa?"

"That sounds perfect, my dear. It's a plan, then."

THE TAXI from Ashdod port to Tel Aviv was a breezy half-hour drive along the eastern Mediterranean coast up Highway 4. When Simon had called Ishak from the ship, they had arranged to meet at the dealer's home for more privacy.

"I cannot believe my good fortune, my friend! That you happened to be here in Israel when I most need your advice is a sign from Allah, to be sure. May I offer you some seltzer, or perhaps a nice glass of Slivovitz?"

"Seltzer would be fine, Ishak, thank you." As his host prepared the drink, Simon glanced around the home, noticing discreet video cameras were placed strategically throughout various rooms. *He certainly takes security seriously*, he considered. "So, what is so important that you need the advice of an old man?"

"Ach! You are not much older than I am, Simon, so do not impugn the both of us in such ways. But, more to the point, let me tell you a story…"

Ishak related everything Tamir and Azim had told him about their brief caving expedition in Wadi Murabba'at, south of the famed Qumran caves, and their visit to his shop in the flea market the night before. When he had closed up for the night, Ishak had discreetly transported the clay jar and its contents to his spacious, upper-class home in the village of Neve Tzedek, a quirky but expensive and highly coveted neighborhood located just outside Tel Aviv's city center.

21

"Come…come with me. But leave your seltzer here," he instructed Simon.

Leading him into a large, cozy library, Ishak pressed a button hidden beneath the mantle of the fireplace, and a secret door behind one of the bookshelves suddenly popped ajar with a dull click. Pulling it open, he led his guest into a small, windowless room filled with ancient artifacts which, Simon presumed, were likely a mix of both legitimate and illicit acquisitions—though he asked no such questions and expected no explanations as to the provenance of any.

On one side of the room sat an obviously ancient, tall, faded-red clay jar, and next to that a wide, wooden table on which had been laid out parchment scrolls, each held flat by a brown leather sandbag paperweight on the corners of each manuscript, four documents in all. Next to those on the table was the still-furled silver scroll, which Simon recognized as having early Mishnaic Hebrew letters on it, engraved top to bottom from right to left.

With dismay, however, he also noted that the silver was heavily tarnished by natural sulfuric gasses over the centuries, which presented a problem: attempting to unroll it would undoubtedly cause it to cleave into tiny fragments, potentially destroying any chance of interpreting its all-important contents. This would require very special treatment.

Then he recalled that earlier experts, having dealt with a heavily oxidized copper scroll found among the Khirbet Qumran artifacts discovered in 1952, used a specially equipped circular saw to slice the copper into long, narrow strips, lengthwise. Once accomplished, they could lay the strips down next to each other, brilliantly enabling the linguists to read the scroll more or less as it was written two thousand years earlier. Without the use of more the advanced X-ray technology now available—which would prematurely reveal their ambitions while losing control of the artifact—this tried and true method was deemed best for now. With hopeful anticipation, he turned to Ishak.

"This may be a long shot, my friend, but by any chance, do you possess a circular saw, ideally with a carbide blade?" He explained the earlier successful process used to handle the oxidized Khirbet Qumran copper scroll, and the potentially dire consequences of attempting to unroll his silver artifact in its current tarnished condition.

Ishak thought a moment. "I am afraid I do not, no. But my wife's brother is a metalsmith in the village. Shall I call him?"

"Oh, yes! Please do," Simon said eagerly. "It should be a small handheld circular saw, with a carbide-tipped abrasive cutoff wheel if possible."

"But will this not diminish the value of such a find?"

"I'm afraid there may be little value at all unless we can determine what is engraved on the scroll. The historical content is what brings any measurable worth to the artifact. The value of the silver pales by comparison to the words upon it. So, we must face the inevitable."

While Ishak went into another room to call his brother-in-law, Simon turned his attention to the other scrolls on the table, those written on parchment. Each of the four was slightly larger than the silver manuscript and recorded in Aramaic and Hebrew, easier languages for him to translate. In impeccably straight lines reading from right to left, the small glyphs were neatly and uniformly composed on the thick, fibrous material, seemingly as fresh today as when they were originally penned some two millennia earlier.

To his delight as a biblical scholar, the first scroll contained copies of various parts of the Christian Bible. As he read down the first page of one parchment, he recognized familiar passages from the New Testament, and was deeply moved because he was in the presence of original manuscripts likely written shortly after the time of Jesus. His emotions overtook him as he considered his virtual proximity to history's most prominent Jewish figure after Abraham, the father of Judaism. Before he could read further, Ishak interrupted him.

"My wife's brother is on his way here now," Ishak enthused as he returned to the secret artifact room. "He has exactly the type of saw we need, and he is a master at such things."

"In the meantime, let's get to work removing the tarnish from this," Simon said. "We'll need a large glass or plastic container, some white vinegar, and baking soda. Do you have these things?"

"Yes, my wife keeps a fully stocked pantry here."

Ishak got the required implements, and once both liquids were mixed in their proper proportions, Simon let the silver scroll rest in the solution for two hours, during which most of the tarnish vanished. Now it was only a matter of carefully slicing it into panels.

SOMETIME LATER, after Ishak's brother-in-law had arrived and slowly but expertly trimmed the silver scroll into twelve manageable strips—as Simon looked on, fraught with anxiety should the metalsmith make even one errant cut—Ishak thanked and brusquely escorted his relative out the door.

As he always did when faced with such rare exposure to exquisite historical artifacts, Simon took a deep and focused breath as he reached out, his hands trembling as he touched the reassembled silver scroll, as if assuring himself that, yes, he was surely in the presence of something very special indeed. Respectfully, Ishak let a dramatic silence fill the room as he watched his old friend have his first moments with the silver scribal treasure.

Simon looked up into Ishak's face, his eyes blinking behind thick eyeglasses as he asked in a near whisper, "May I read it?"

Ishak gave a hearty laugh. "Yes, of course! Here, have a seat and make yourself more comfortable." He pulled over two wooden stools and they both sat down. Simon reached out, leaned over the now more-or-less flattened strips of the silver scroll, and began reading.

NEARLY AN HOUR LATER, having translated by degrees the ancient Hebrew to English as he read—made more arduous by bridging glyphs across the seams of each silver strip—Simon sat back, transfixed by what he had just taken in.

"This is absolutely astonishing, Ishak—breathtaking, even. I am at a loss for words."

"What can you tell me, my friend? Does it have much value?!"

"Oh, quite so, yes. I can assure you, this has considerable value..." Simon looked up at Ishak, emotion clouding the old man's rheumy eyes as he held the Arab's gaze, "...for it appears to mention an obscure but once powerful religious sect. And there is something else here, too. Something unexpectedly intriguing..."

CHAPTER
FOUR

F ather Michael Dominic stood off to the side near the arrivals gate of ITA Airways at Rome's Leonardo da Vinci Airport, watching for the familiar face of Aaron Pearce, his old friend and roommate from Loyola University in Chicago.

As the blur of disembarking passengers filed by, Michael thought back to the good times he and Aaron had on the Loyola Ramblers lacrosse team. He smiled at the memories, Aaron being one of the few close friends he had made in his life. Pity they hadn't stayed in touch, he considered, but that would change now that Aaron had been transferred to Loyola's John Felice Rome Center as their new papyrologist and classical studies professor.

Looking up, he saw a tall, dark-haired athletic figure with wolf-gray eyes heading his way, easily spotted wearing a white Adidas track jacket with three black stripes running down the sleeves. Catching Michael's eye, Aaron gave him a wave and a wide grin as he worked his way through the crowd.

Setting his backpack and laptop case down at his feet, he flung his long arms around the priest and gave him a fierce bear hug. "Damn, it's good to see you again, Mikey!"

"You too, Aaron!" Michael huffed, unable to breathe. "Good flight?"

"Well, we got here, that's what counts," he said, releasing his friend. "Customs in Amsterdam was a breeze, thankfully. God, I love that city." Picking up his bags, the taller man threw an arm around Michael's neck as the two headed toward the baggage claim area.

"You got a car? I have two more suitcases to get, and that's it."

"You bet," Michael confirmed. "I borrowed a friend's Jeep. So, where have they got you billeted?"

"They're putting me up in a B&B near campus until I can find an apartment—someplace called the San Pietro Resort Roma."

"Hey, that's only a few blocks from the Vatican!" Michael said. "That makes things easy. When do they expect you to start work?"

"My first class is a little over a week away," Aaron replied. "That gives me some time to settle in and get a lay of the land. You free for dinner tonight?"

"Of course, I'd planned on it. And a friend will be joining us, too. You'll love her."

"'*Her*,' eh? Is she single?" Aaron smiled suggestively, his eyebrows arching.

"No, I'm afraid she's sworn off men, taken a lifelong

vow of celibacy, and could very well be a Wiccan. Besides, she's not your type. Wholly unattractive, dresses like a slob…"

Aaron paused, looking sideways at Michael. "That means she's probably a knockout, you dog. I see through your twisted little game." They both laughed as Aaron's suitcases appeared on the baggage carousel and he hoisted them off. Michael grabbed one of them, then snatched the lighter laptop case from his friend's hand —"You can take the heavy one, pal…"—as they made their way to the garage and the Jeep, then headed to the B&B on Via Tommaso Campanella between the Vatican and the Loyola campus.

IT WAS late evening at the Jasmine Hookah Lounge in Tel Aviv, and Azim Hourani was celebrating his good fortune—not to mention that he and his friends had gotten in using fake IDs with an indifferent doorman. A tall, Byzantine blue glass water pipe sat on a small table surrounded by five beanbag chairs, and the shisha tender had just stoked the coals, adding a few more for a denser smoke.

After taking a long swig from his fourth bottle of Dancing Camel—a local, dark stout beer brewed with toasted carob—Azim reached for his personal hookah hose, took a drag off the wooden mouthpiece, and exhaled the honey-sweetened smoke as he lay back in the beanbag, a broad, satisfied grin on his face, his eyes puffed and glassy.

"Could life be any better than this, my brothers?" he asked his comrades lounging in the other beanbags.

"What are you so happy for, Azim?" asked Faisal, the one sitting next to him. "And what were you talking to Ishak about last night? What was in that cart you and Tamir brought to him?" As the clerk who watched the shop for Ishak when the boys had arrived, Faisal—disinterested at the time when the three had disappeared into the back room—finally found his curiosity had gotten the better of him.

Though Tamir Pinsky had earlier cautioned him not to mention their discovery in the cave to anyone, Azim was just drunk enough to be careless. And soon he would be rich anyway, so what did it matter? Besides, Faisal was a dimwit.

He leaned over toward Ishak's shop assistant, a smug look on his face. The other four friends also leaned in to better hear Azim's response over the DJ's pulsing house music.

"Tamir and I found a cache of ancient scrolls in a clay jar in one of the caves," he boasted loudly, slurring his words. "We are going to be rich! And one of them might be the long-lost silver scroll. Yes, *silver!* The rarest of them all. Ishak is finding a buyer for them now…"

Azim fell back into the beanbag, took another swallow of his beer, and looked around at the others, his head bobbing as he gloated over his big news.

All four of them were wide-eyed at his disclosure. Everyone knew how valuable such scrolls were; whenever one was found by the authorities, it always made headlines in *Haaretz* and *The Times of Israel*.

"You found scrolls?!" they each shouted excitedly over the music.

"Shhh!" Azim said, holding an unsteady finger over his mouth. "Keep it down. I wasn't supposed to say anything about them. You must give me your word that you will not tell a soul."

Everyone nodded dully in reflexive compliance.

Everyone, that is, except for an older boy named Jamal.

CHAPTER
FIVE

Gabriel Obadiah Darwin—founder, president and senior pastor of the worldwide Church of Supreme Divinity—was on a roll as he preached animatedly to his congregation.

Standing on the stage of his gleaming new Diamond Ark Cathedral, a lavish, 18,000-seat stadium built in the assumed shape of Noah's Ark—one that took up a good part of the shore on Lakewood's White Rock Lake in northeast Dallas, Texas—Pastor Darwin spoke passionately to the full house, a ravenous evangelical audience that hung on his every word as he preached the prosperity gospel. His voice echoed throughout the spacious arena.

"...And so I say to you, my friends... *This* is your moment! This is the time to sow your seed, for in doin' so your bounty will be manifest. *God Himself guarantees it!*

"Take out your Bibles right now. That's it, yes. Now

turn to Second Corinthians, chapter nine, verse six, and let's *all read aloud* the good words written there. Are you ready? Can I get an *Amen?!"*

The flipping hiss of Bible pages being turned in the giant arena was broken only by the thunderous response of *"Amen!!"* as people turned to the appointed page. After a pause to let audience members find their places, Darwin began leading them in the bold, charismatic voice he was famous for: a rousing dulcet baritone heard on radio, television and the internet going on fifteen years now in over a hundred countries. Eighteen thousand voices joined him as a colossal pipe organ thrummed its majestic timbres in the background.

"Remember this:" he read, the massive audience following along, *"Whoever sows sparingly will also reap sparingly, and whoever sows generously will also reap generously. Each of you should give what you have decided in your heart to give, not reluctantly or under compulsion, for God loves a cheerful giver. And God is able to bless you abundantly, so that in all things at all times, having all that you need, you will abound in every good work."*

When the reading was over, Darwin paused a few moments for effect, looking out over the vast audience from one side of the arena to the other. Thousands of hands waved silently in the air, eyes closed, heads shaking. Many congregants were weeping, overcome with emotion, assured that the great abundance they so desperately needed was within their grasp.

"Now, I know these are challengin' economic times. But the Lord says we will get through them. Not just *gettin' by,* mind you, but *thrivin'!* Plant your seed now for the harvest that awaits, my friends, for the size of your seed determines the size of your harvest. Keep what we just read fresh in your mind: '...*whoever sows generously will also reap generously.*' Our global ministry *depends* on your generosity!"

The organ music rose as a procession of some two hundred men and women wearing bright red jackets appeared in the aisles, each carrying stacks of small, round, deep wicker baskets which they began distributing to all rows in their assigned areas. Around their necks hung portable Wi-Fi-enabled point-of-sale payment devices.

As baskets made their way up the rows, people reached for their wallets and purses. Everyone gave generously; even parents whose children wore tattered clothing and shoes too small for their growing feet pulled precious five- or ten-dollar bills from their pocketbooks, dropping them into the wicker baskets along with wishful prayers for abundance in return, giving gladly in the name of the Lord for what the good pastor was promising.

The upbeat organ music accompanied a large, robed chorus belting out *To God be the Glory* as Pastor Gabriel Darwin danced on stage, a kind of stiff, awkward foxtrot, his outstretched arms holding an invisible partner as he made eye contact with a cluster of blue-haired ladies sitting in the front row, winking at them flirtatiously.

The enormous jumbovision display behind him on the stage listed various money transfer apps for those who preferred to donate electronically from their seats:

Zelle, PayPal, Venmo and others all were conveniently available; send your donation to the address on display, it prompted. The red-jacketed collectors had their portable payment devices ready, swiping credit and debit cards for hundreds of other donors throughout the stadium.

As the service wound down, Pastor Darwin had one last thing to say to the assembly.

"My friends, I have news. *Big* news. As we reach out to spread the gospel of Jesus to others around the world, my lovely wife Sue Ann and I will be gettin' on our new Gulfstream jet and visitin' the Holy Land! Yep, that's right…we'll walk in the very footsteps of Our Lord on the sacred ground in the land of Israel!

"And on this mission we are hopin' to bring back with us newly discovered fragments of the Dead Sea Scrolls for permanent display in our Biblical Hall Museum right here in Dallas. Our agents in Israel and Egypt have been hard at work findin' bits of parchment and papyrus written some two thousand years ago! And I can think of no better destiny for them than to serve God's faithful here in the Biblical Hall.

"We cannot *wait* to share these with y'all when we return next month, but until then you'll be in the excellent hands of Pastor Pete and his beautiful wife Wanda Rae while we're gone." He raised his arm, pointing toward a debonair couple standing off to the side, now lit by a powerful spotlight—he with a shiny, black-dyed pompadour, she with a lofty platinum bouffant—who waved to the applauding crowd as the organist played a fanciful introductory tune.

"As most of you probably know," Darwin continued, as the organ faded into the background, "we've built a 'fleet' of hundreds of Jewel Ark Chapels in most major countries worldwide, humble extensions of this glorious Diamond Ark Cathedral which your most generous donations have made possible for our ministry. We'll be makin' appearances at many of those on our pilgrimage, bringin' our blessin's to 'em.

"So now I ask that you pray for us and for the success of our ministry in the Holy Land, so that others can hear the Good Word of the Lord..."

CHAPTER
SIX

The Rome Cavalieri Waldorf Astoria's premier restaurant—the Michelin three-starred La Pergola—boasted well-appointed luxuries for its well-heeled diners, with tasteful Venetian art and sculptures, Renaissance oil paintings, and rich mahogany columns supporting an exquisitely inlaid suspended ceiling.

In the adjoining Tiepolo Lounge, the resident pianist was performing a popular jazz tune on his polished ebony Petrof grand piano. As the music drifted into the restaurant, Michael Dominic, Hana Sinclair and Aaron Pearce were taking their seats at a table next to a window overlooking Rome's night-lit splendor, with St. Peter's dome dominating the skyline before them.

"Did you know," Father Michael began, "that by ancient law here, no building in the historic center of Rome can be taller than St. Peter's Basilica? In fact, it's still the tallest building in the entire city."

"Not something I knew," said Hana Sinclair. "But now that I live here, I suppose I need to keep nuggets like that handy for when *I* have friends visiting and can play the tour guide. Speaking of which, how are you enjoying your first day in Rome, Aaron?"

"Not bad so far, but since you've joined us, things are looking up," Aaron flirted, smiling at both her and Michael. "Forgive me, I don't mean for that to sound like a come-on, but one can take being alone with *this* guy only so long..." Reaching over, he gripped Michael's shoulder affectionately. They both grinned, enjoying their companionship.

"It's so good Michael has such a friend in you, Aaron," Hana added. "I enjoy seeing him this way. Apart from me, he doesn't have many close friends."

"What do you mean?!" Michael protested. "There's Karl and Lukas and, well...Marco, in a way. I'm hardly a recluse!"

"You know what I mean. You *work* with those guys, mostly. Aaron has a freshness to him, and it's good to see you two all buddy-buddy-like. That's what I meant."

"So, back to something you said, Hana," Aaron recalled, "that '*now that I live here*' comment. Are you new to Rome, too?"

"Well, not new to knowing the city, which I already do pretty well. I work for the French newspaper, *Le Monde*, and have been based out of Paris for the past several years. But I was transferred to our Rome bureau a couple of months ago. Michael and I have known each other for a few years now. And we've had our share of grand adventures in that time." She glanced at the priest knowingly, and a smile passed between them.

"'Adventures?'" Aaron fished. "That sounds too tempting not to ask for details. What kinds of 'adventures'?"

"Oh, you know," Michael started, "kidnappings, Mafia art thieves, black market artifact fencing... The usual Vatican mischief."

Aaron laughed, then saw that both Michael and Hana were holding straight faces. "You aren't serious...?" he ventured.

"Scout's honor," Hana confirmed, holding up the three-finger pledge salute. "You'd think a reporter and a priest would have fairly boring lives. Not so. The excitement never ends with *this* one around." She gestured toward Michael.

As everyone laughed, the head waiter approached their table, addressing Hana with familiarity. *"Buona sera*, Signorina Sinclair! How have you been? We have not seen you here in a while."

"Buona sera, Stefan. Yes, I've been in Paris and have been traveling for some time, but I now live here in your wonderful city, so I'm sure we'll be seeing more of each other.

"While we look at the menu, could you bring us a bottle of your '95 Valentini Montepulciano d'Abruzzo?"

"Of course, Signorina. I will have the sommelier bring it at once."

As Stefan walked away, Aaron's eyes went wide as

he looked at Michael. "Not only smart and engaging, but she knows her wines *and* the waiters?"

"She's also—to put it bluntly—terribly rich, so don't even try reaching for the check."

Slightly indignant, Hana said with a nod of her head, "Why, Father Dominic...how *rude!* Aaron, pay no attention to him—or to the prices on the menu. But dinner *is* on me. My grandfather has a suite here and we have a house account.

"So," she continued, deftly changing the subject, "tell us about your new job. Where is it? What do you teach?"

"Yeah, Aaron," Michael added. "This all came about rather suddenly, didn't it? You only told me you were coming yesterday."

Aaron paused before replying. "Well...yeah, it does seem sudden, doesn't it? Actually, this has been in the works for, oh...some time," he stammered, fumbling for words, "but I finally got the go-ahead two days ago.

"Anyway, Hana, to answer your question, I'm now a classical studies professor at the John Felice Rome Center, an ancillary campus of Loyola University Chicago, about fifteen minutes from the Vatican. It offers a largely American undergraduate experience in the Jesuit tradition. Since it only accommodates around two hundred and thirty students, classes are fairly intimate, which fosters a superior learning environment. I have a doctorate in classical studies—you know, classical languages and Greco-Roman culture in antiquity. And like Michael, I also have a master's degree in papyrology: Late Antique and Byzantine, Greek, Egyptian, you name it, with an emphasis on biblical studies. I love the work, and being here in Rome now is truly my crowning achievement. This is the center of our historical universe, more or less. But as prefect of the Vatican Secret Archives, Michael has the best job I could imagine, overseeing millions of precious and impossibly rare manuscripts."

"Most of which have never been seen by anyone living," Michael added, "nor have they even been catalogued by my predecessors over the twelve centuries the Vatican has been storing them. It really is an untapped gold mine of history waiting to be discovered, a fact I marvel at daily. I do wish we had more staff to help unearth, transcribe and index the eighty-five linear kilometers of documents the Secret Archive holds. I've been here for a few years now and it's still an overwhelming prospect."

Aaron's jaw dropped on hearing this. "My god, man! How do you restrain yourself from just opening something up and seeing what's inside?! I'd be constantly tempted like a moth to a flame."

"Things aren't that simple here, Aaron. We have very specific procedures for discovery, translation, transcription and registration of inventory. And I only have a staff of some sixty people, all of whom are busy doing the work, much of which goes well beyond the actual Archives material itself, including serving the research needs of a thousand scholars each year. In short, we're all doing the best we can in an all-too-slow-moving bureaucracy. I could use another hundred archivists alone, but we simply don't have the space for them."

"I'd volunteer in a heartbeat if I didn't have other obligations," Aaron enthused as the sommelier brought a bottle of red wine to the table. Standing to Hana's right, he ceremoniously uncorked the bottle, poured a small amount in the silver tastevin hanging around his neck, subtly nodded his head in approval, then poured a small portion in Hana's glass for her to sample. Once she nodded her own acceptance, he decanted the wine in two Bordeaux glasses for the men, then topped off Hana's glass and left the table. Stefan returned moments later to take their orders.

"Do you boys know what you'd like?" Hana asked after they'd toasted to Aaron's arrival.

"It's the John Dory with zucchini leaves and green bean cream for me," Michael said, "and a first course of risotto with baby squid and saffron. Aaron? What sounds good to you?"

"Well, I've never had pigeon before—which, to be perfectly honest, sounds demented—but since this is a fancy restaurant, it must be good, yeah? So, it's the pigeon with corn cream and black elderberries for me. And to start, I'll have the squid risotto, too."

"I'm having the lamb with myrtle sauce and baby Polignano carrots. And a salad for *primo*, Stefan. *Grazie*."

As Stefan left the table, there was a silent pause as all three gazed out the tall windows featuring Rome's nighttime beauty—a pause broken only by Michael's cell phone humming in his pocket. He reached for it, saw who it was on Caller ID, then politely excused himself and left the table to answer the call.

"Does he always take calls in the middle of dinner?" Aaron asked Hana.

"Well, I'm not with him all the time, of course, so I wouldn't really know. But it is understandable since it could be the pope."

"The pope?!"

"Sure. He and Michael are very close," Hana said, not going into specifics. "You must know Michael grew up in Enrico Petrini's rectory in New York and they've known each other his whole life."

"Ah, right. Yes, I'd forgotten about that. I guess I didn't make the connection when Cardinal Petrini became Pope Ignatius. He's one lucky guy, our Michael. And speak of the devil…"

The priest was weaving his way between tables back toward them, an earnest look on his face. He sat down, picked up his wine glass, and took a long draw on it. Hana and Aaron looked at him expectantly.

Michael took a big breath. "That was Simon," he said to Hana, then turned to Aaron. "Dr. Simon Ginzberg is a good friend of ours, a professor emeritus of medieval studies at Teller University who virtually lives in the Vatican Archives' reading rooms doing research in his areas of interest.

"Anyway, he happens to be on vacation in Israel now and has come across something of tremendous importance, he told me. He wouldn't go into much detail on the phone but asked if I could join him there tomorrow for a day or so. It's only a three-hour flight, so it should be a quick trip."

"What could be so important as to require a sudden trip to Israel?" Hana wondered aloud.

Michael paused a moment, then replied, "He said he's discovered a silver scroll mentioning Christianity's main rival in the earliest centuries after Christ, a once-prominent Roman cult called the Mithraists.

"But he thinks the scroll also reveals the location of the legendary treasure of the Essenes."

CHAPTER
SEVEN

"Mithraists? Who are the Mithraists?" Hana asked. "I've never heard the term before."

"You've got to be kidding," Aaron said, addressing Michael. "This scroll your friend has, it actually mentions the *Mithraists?*"

"Indeed, it does. And I was just as surprised as you are when he mentioned the name. And on a silver scroll! Do you realize how rare *those* are?"

"*Who* or *what* are the Mithraists?" Hana pressed again.

"Well," Aaron began, his eyes wide with surprise, "it's not a name one hears very often, that's for sure. Mithraism was a religious cult from around the first through the fourth centuries. In fact, it was a serious challenger to Christianity in its earliest days. Christianity and Mithraism embodied two rival factions reacting to a similar series of cultural influences at the time. It reputedly had its origins among the pirates of

Cilicia along the southern coast of Asia Minor, but more likely had its founding in pre-Zoroastrian Persia before the Common Era. And over the ensuing years, it became a bonding brotherhood chiefly among Roman soldiers who worshiped the god of war and Sun, Mithras. It was very likely that the Roman soldiers who scourged and crucified Jesus Christ were Mithraists.

"The early Roman Empire was teeming with polytheistic deities, each struggling to secure a foothold among those seeking deeper meaning in their lives. Roman soldiers—powerful legions of well over three hundred fifty thousand warriors—believed Mithras to have led them to victory on the battlefield over some four centuries, so it was only natural that he became the god of soldiers. As the cult evolved throughout the Roman Empire from eastern India to the western shores of Spain, it incorporated many secret rituals and mysteries to distinguish privileged initiates from people of Christianity and other faiths. Member legionaries and centurions, known as *syndexioi*, were 'united by the handshake,' a secret shibboleth, or distinguishing custom known only to initiated postulants."

"And of course," Michael added, "early Christians believed, as they do today, that their religion was the one true faith, and there was only the one God, and all other believers, along with infidels, were doomed until they were converted, and their souls saved from eternal damnation. Christianity faced various competition from other faiths and beliefs—most notably Mithraism, with its not insignificant membership of Roman soldiers—

and believed the only way to win that ongoing war was to eliminate the cult from the Roman Empire entirely."

"And that's where Emperor Constantine came in," Aaron said, picking up on Michael's narrative. "It was around 312 CE when he became the first emperor of Rome to convert to Christianity, and with his backing, followers of Christ were emboldened to persecute followers of rival religions throughout the empire, and in time, Mithraism began to dissipate until it was largely extinguished by the fourth century.

"But," Aaron's lupine-gray eyes took on a conspiratorial look, "legend has it that the Mithraists had secured a truly massive fortune, possibly taken from the Essenes...spoils of war that Roman soldiers had confiscated during their often brutal but lucrative campaigns against other nations. They built thousands of secret underground *mithraea*, temples where initiates met, dined, held formal meetings, and carried out other ritualistic ceremonies called *mithraskana*. You can still find and visit many of these temples today; in fact, there's even one beneath the Basilica of San Clemente, close to the Coliseum here in Rome.

"Each mithraeum featured the same symbolic work of art set against the front wall: a scene of the god Mithras slaying a bull in what's called a 'tauroctony.' Every mithraeum had its own tauroctony, meaningful artwork believed to have had mystical relationships with the stars and constellations. And rumors abound that Mithraism in some form is still alive in small pockets around the world, though I rather doubt it since I've yet to find proof of that."

Hana was surprised she had never heard of this cult before. "And you say it was a legitimately significant *rival* to Christianity?"

"That's the power of the Church for you," Michael admitted. "Constantine and those after him, especially the body of successive popes, worked hard to ensure that only Christianity would be remembered, and recognized as the one, true faith. Of course, by that time, Judaism had already been well established. In fact, the vast majority of early Christians were Jews who converted.

"But Aaron is right about that legendary treasure, and given what Simon told me, we may have clues to its location. Wouldn't that be something? Personally, I'm more interested in the Mithraists' part in all this, and I can't wait to see that silver scroll."

"Mind if I tag along?" Aaron asked eagerly. "I've got nothing going on until next week when classes start, and I'd love to see that scroll, too, not to mention an inspirational trip to the Holy Land."

Michael thought for a moment. "Sure, I don't see why not. It'll be more fun sharing the experience."

Hana picked up her wine glass, sat back in her chair, and looked at them both with slight disdain. "Well, I'm certainly not staying behind if adventure is afoot. Mind a third wheel?"

Michael laughed. "You, dear friend, are always welcome. I'll be asking Karl to join us, too, since I promised him a trip to the Holy Land when next I go. So, that makes an even foursome. But we'll be flying coach, so…"

"I'll try not to suffer too much," she said wryly as the waiters brought their meals to the table.

His rusty white Vespa's old two-stroke engine protesting loudly, Jamal Qureshi crazily steered through the crowded streets of Tel Aviv to the home of Dr. Khalid Zadani in Lev Ha'ir, the heart of the old city.

Zadani, one of Israel's preeminent archeologists, was famous for having helped discover the partially mummified, 1,900-year-old remains of a child in Israel's Cave of Horror deep in the Judean Desert.

Carved into the cliffs towering from the south over the Nahal Hever wadi, the "Cave of Horror" earned its nickname after the skeletons of forty men, women and children were discovered inside—remains of Jewish refugees from the Bar Kokhba Revolt, the last of three major Jewish–Roman wars from 132 to 136 CE.

Given his newfound fame, Zadani could take his pick of assignments with the Israel Antiquities Authority. Having some 30,000 Israeli antiquities sites at his disposal—the vast majority of which had yet to be excavated—his primary area of interest was ancient scrolls. It was very nearly an addiction, his fondness for scrolls...the feel, the smell of old parchments and papyri...the sacred words preserved through two millennia...the meticulous penmanship of scribes who had dedicated their lives to their exacting work. For Khalid Zadani, the seduction was complete and all-consuming.

So much so that, secretly, he even held back certain of his finds, keeping them for himself—a serious breach of ethics in his profession, but as he viewed it, a justifiable personal reward for his years of dedication to the IAA's mission. It wasn't as if he were selling them on the black market. No, he was holding them for posterity. When he died, they would all go to Israeli museums, anyway. But until then, they were his alone to appreciate.

When his sister's son Jamal had called him and told him of the possible discovery of a *silver scroll!*...Well, he just had to learn more—but not on the phone. He would meet the boy here, for he did not trust the government's passion for eavesdropping. Israeli spyware was widely acknowledged as being the best in the world, and he never took such imprudent risks. He installed a state-of-the-art security system and even routinely had his home swept for bugs. After all, one couldn't be too careful in his rarefied world of handling such treasures.

Hearing a knock at the door, Zadani put down the newspaper he was reading and got up.

"*As-salaam 'alaykum,* Uncle. It is very good to see you," Jamal leaned forward to rub his nose against his uncle's in the traditional Arab greeting of trust.

"*Wa 'alaykum as-salaam,* Jamal. *Marhaba,*" Zadani replied, welcoming him into his home.

"Let us speak in my office," Zadani said, leading the boy down a wide hallway and into a spacious room with a large mahogany desk, gleaming computer equipment, a row of black filing cabinets and two comfortable stuffed chairs. Light poured in from tall windows overlooking a lush garden, but Zadani pulled the drapes closed, plunging the room into darkness. He turned on a nearby lamp as they both took seats, then he lit a cigarette. A billow of blue smoke curled in the dim light of the lamp as he exhaled and began speaking.

"So, tell me what you have heard, Nephew. Do not leave out any details, no matter how small."

"Well, a few of us were at the Jasmine Lounge taking hookah when one of the others, a boy named Azim Hourani, told us about some silver scroll he and a friend found in one cave south of Qumran…" Jamal conveyed every detail of the story, and that Azim had already drunk enough Dancing Camels to sufficiently loosen his tongue.

"And where is this scroll now?"

"An antiquities dealer named Ishak Ramzi has it. He has a shop in the *Shuk HaPishPeshim*, but I expect he would have moved it to his home rather than leave it there. Too many lurking thieves in the market, as you know, Uncle. His shop assistant, Faisal, told me he lives in the village of Neve Tzedek."

Zadani took another drag off his cigarette, stubbed it out in an abalone shell ashtray, then brought his hands up, letting his chin rest on his laced fingers, his mind far off as he stared absently at his teenaged nephew.

"Thank you for this information, Jamal. It is interesting, but probably not something I would choose to be involved with at present. I appreciate your telling me, though, and be sure to keep your eyes open for other such opportunities, yes?"

"Of course, Uncle," the boy said, rising. "I will

always tell you of such things, especially where scrolls are concerned."

After they kissed each other's cheeks in farewell, Zadani saw his nephew out. Closing the door, he leaned back against it, his mind now racing.

Alhamdulillah! A silver scroll?! And this Ramzi fellow lives in Neve Tzedek, does he? Well...our friend Abu must soon pay him a visit, then.

CHAPTER
EIGHT

Deep beneath the fabled ruins of Rome's Circus Maximus lies one of the city's largest and most obscure ancient mithraeums. Rediscovered during Italy's fascist years in the 1930s, the second-century temple was among the largest such meeting places for Roman soldiers and fellow Mithraists in the whole of the Empire.

Supported by several tall, fluted marble columns topped with Ionic capitals accented with acanthus fronds, the massive arched ceiling extended some twenty-four meters long and ten meters wide. The room comprised two chambers—a large meeting hall featuring recently restored mosaics, and a smaller chamber with a tunnel running beneath the main hall and into another chamber with a staircase that led to the only door.

At the moment, that door was being guarded by a strapping young soldier in camo fatigues, unarmed save for his formidable size and intimidating demeanor. As each member approached the entrance to the mithraeum —all of them male—the guard held out his hand, expecting the member to initiate the secret shibboleth to gain entry.

As the member gripped the guard's hand, he pressed his thumb firmly in the space between the first and second knuckle joints of the guard's first two fingers, a subtle technique the guard returned to the member's hand. While doing this, both men held each other's gaze while the visiting member would blink twice. The guard then responded accordingly with two blinks, after which the member could pass.

To onlookers, it appeared to be a normal handshake between two men. But if anyone failed in this cryptic pattern, he was politely asked to turn around and leave. Only *syndexioi* were permitted entry.

Proceeding down the ancient, whitewashed steps of burned limestone and clay, the member would make his way through the tunnel, into the small chamber and on through to the large meeting hall, joining not only his fellow initiates already gathered there—nearly all of them Roman soldiers—but also their leader, or *"pater,"* former Italian Army Colonel Niccolò Scarpa.

An imposing man in his sixties, Niccolò Scarpa had been head of the Italian Army's Intelligence Division—*Il Reparto Informazioni e Sicurezza*—for some ten years before retiring to become Commandant of the Vatican's Pontifical Swiss Guard, the post he now held. And though he was Catholic, as is required of every Swiss Guard, Scarpa had a passion for ancient military traditions, and had been a lifelong devotee of the ancient Order of Mithras—not so much for the Mithras deity itself but for the secret knowledge passed down to its discreet followers over two millennia, and for safe-guarding the brotherhood supporting those who went to war on behalf of their constituent nations.

Those who even knew about the little-known sect assumed it had been dormant since the fourth century, when the forces of Christianity ensured its eradication by killing off nearly all members and destroying their temples—at least those that could be found, since all of them were built secretly underground.

But many followers did survive, and though they maintained strict silence about their existence—even developing a new secret shibboleth to distinguish devotees from hoi polloi—on through the centuries they persevered. While hardly on par with such other wider societies as Freemasons, Rosicrucians, or even Zoroastrians, Mithraists had built themselves into one of the most tightly bound minority sects in the world, expanding to such other countries as Italy, France, Germany, Turkey, Egypt and Israel.

But Rome served as its global headquarters, and Colonel Niccolò Scarpa as its leader. Since he had been a young man, when his own father inducted him into the Order, Scarpa had dedicated his life to further building the ancient cult of Mithras. And even at this later stage of his life, he felt he was just getting started.

But he needed resources to fund that growth—financial resources that were scarce, given that its membership was composed of soldiers earning minimal stipends for service to their respective countries. No, Scarpa needed a sizable infusion of cash to see his cherished dream come true. His soldiers deserved that.

And as it happened, the *pater* of his Israeli mithraeum beneath the Western Wall in Jerusalem had phoned him a few days earlier with the opportunity he was so desperately seeking—one involving the discovery of a certain silver scroll in the Judean Desert.

SOUTH OF LOVE Field in Dallas, Texas, lies the more exclusive Dallas Executive Airport in the city's Redbird neighborhood, serving private aircraft owned or leased by the wealthiest of discerning travelers.

On the tarmac outside the upscale FBO offices and hangars of Ambassador Jet Center, a gleaming new Gulfstream G650LE was being serviced and fueled for its fourteen-hour transatlantic flight to Tel Aviv within the hour.

Both the pilot and co-pilot were doing the pre-flight walk-around inspection when a white stretch limousine slowly pulled up to the aircraft and came to a gentle stop at the end of a red carpet laid down for its owner's arrival. The chauffeur stepped out and opened both back doors for his employers: Pastor Gabriel Darwin, dressed in an all-white bespoke couture suit with white patent leather shoes; his petite wife Sue Ann, who wore her favorite little black dress with Jimmy Choo spiked heels; and their teenaged daughter, Tabitha, who—with the generous help of spandex shapewear—restrained her ample derrière into a pair of short, cut-off jeans with a white crop top shirt knotted above her protuberant belly.

Both pilots stopped what they were doing and stared at the tragic young thing, stunned that anyone would try to pull off *that* look. As they were also life partners, one leaned toward the other and whispered, "No way our daughter is *ever* dressing like *that*."

The Darwins boarded the aircraft as the chauffeur transferred most of the family's excessive luggage to the jet's cargo hold, while those marked for carry-on were stowed inside the main cabin. During preflight preparations, Tabitha snapped at the flight attendant to bring her a soda and a cheese plate—*Now!*—then settled into a wide leather seat in the cabin's rear section, plugged in her AirPods, and listened to hip-hop while scrolling through her social media feeds. Accustomed to her daddy's private jets since she was born, she couldn't care less about his newest one.

Gabriel Darwin lowered himself into one of the cabin's front seats, sighed happily as he took in the splendors of his new Gulfstream and that new plane smell, then took out his cell phone to call his assistant.

"Hey, Gloria. Any calls I should know about before we take off?" he asked.

"Well, Pastor, I have *too* many to bother you with now," she drawled on, "but there *is* one from Mr. Shapiro—your agent in Tel Aviv?—that you might want to follow up on. He said it was *very* important and that you'd want to know about it *right* away. Well, *I* told him—"

"Good Lord, Gloria. I pray for patience, but I'm just not getting it fast enough. Please, give me his number. I'll call him now."

She passed on the details which he wrote in the little black book he always carried, then, without saying goodbye, he ended the call. He then punched in the number for his antiquities agent in Tel Aviv, who answered promptly.

"Hey there, Remi. What've y'all got for me?" He listened intently for a while as the agent relayed his efforts to locate the most desirable artifacts for the Biblical Hall Museum. And in that regard, Remi Shapiro may have scored big.

Remi began to explain about the boys and their find when Darwin interrupted him. "Hold on, boy. I've told you I don't need to know details of origination. Plausible deniability and all that, right?" The extensive inventory in his personally funded Biblical Hall Museum displayed artifacts with provenances either best not mentioned or wholly fabricated. Either way worked for Darwin. "Just where might we find this so-called silver scroll now?" he asked eagerly. A few more moments passed as he listened. "Well, shit, Remi! Do whatever it takes to get hold of that thing! Yes, I most definitely want it!...Alright, I'll see you first thing in the morning. Yeah, we're staying at the Hilton, the one on the beach... But I want some good news then, ya hear? Okay, that's settled. We'll see you then."

CHAPTER
NINE

T he shared *sherut* taxi, a minivan accommodating up to ten passengers, departed Ben Gurion Airport northwest up Highway 1 bound for the Hotel Indigo in Tel Aviv, where Hana— ever the team's self-appointed travel coordinator—had booked room reservations for the four of them. Since Simon Ginzberg had also booked the night there, delaying his planned trip to Jerusalem for a day, it made more sense for everyone.

Hana's cousin, Karl Dengler, had never been to Israel before, and he took in the sights eagerly, his head swiveling constantly as he snapped photos of various monuments, synagogues, and quaint clusters of Orthodox Hassidim they passed as the taxi entered the city's diamond exchange district.

After checking in and dropping their bags off in their rooms, Michael called Simon and arranged for them to meet in the lobby. The old man was sitting in the lounge when the group approached him.

"Miss Sinclair!" Simon said, as he pushed himself up to greet everyone. "It is so good to see you again. It has been far too long." He gave her a gentle hug. "And who else have you brought with you, Michael?"

"Simon Ginzberg, this is Dr. Aaron Pearce, an old friend from Loyola. And surely you remember Sergeant Karl Dengler of the Swiss Guard?"

"Yes, of course. Hello again, Karl. And it is very good to meet any friend of Michael's, Dr. Pearce." He shook hands with both men.

"It's Aaron, Simon, and the pleasure's all mine. Michael has told me wonderful things about you."

"Ah, take all of it with a speck of salt. Our friend Michael here is a marvelous storyteller." He winked at the priest with a wide smile. Then, looking around the lounge, he spied a more private sitting area in the corner and gestured for everyone to move there.

As the five took seats, Simon quietly explained, "So... I happen to have gotten a call from an old friend here in Tel Aviv as our ship—I was on a Mediterranean cruise with my daughter—pulled into Ashdod port south of here. We were going to go straight to Jerusalem, but my friend, Ishak Ramzi, called to ask for my help with a particular silver scroll he came across. He is a licensed antiquities dealer here, you see, so I imagine he does come across fairly extraordinary objects from time to time.

"Now, I do not know the provenance of this particular artifact, nor have I asked as to its legitimacy. The

Israel Antiquities Authority has quite thorough regulations about such things, but all that is irrelevant as far as I am concerned. I was only asked to help translate and interpret it. And I must say, it is a most remarkable item.

"Unfortunately, the silver had tarnished such that it required our cleaning then rending it into twelve strips, or panels if you will, in order to read it properly, a procedure which came out fine—though, I must admit, my heart was in my throat as the metalsmith worked his blade. The scroll possesses some of the most fascinating historical content I have come across in my long experience with such things. I took photographs of the panels using my phone, along with my translations, to share with you. I do hope they come out alright."

"Michael said it mentions the *Mithraists*," Aaron blurted, eager to jump ahead. "If so, that's nothing short of incredible!"

Simon smiled at him patiently. "Yes, it does indeed mention the Mithras cult, and the suffering it was experiencing from Christians working to crush Mithraism. The scribe who had engraved the scroll had laid out a disturbing scene of crisis amongst the Mithraic tribe, as if they were preparing to leave their mithraeums for fear of being attacked.

"But the Mithraists also had another problem. Apparently, they had gained a vast treasure from the Essenes and other cultures which had been plundered by the group's members, Roman soldiers known as *syndexioi*. In order to protect their treasure from Christian forces, they spread it around Jerusalem in the most arcane of places. Here, I made some notes. It makes no sense today, as I'm sure you'll agree..." Simon reached into his pocket and withdrew a sheet of paper, then began reading it to the others.

"'Thirty talents of silver can be found under the pillar on the northern side of the big cistern in Acel Dama. When you go sixty cubits into the canal that comes from the reservoir of Solomon, you will find ninety-five talents of gold. Dig down four cubits in the middle of the two boulders in the Valley of Achor, and you will find two pots full of silver coins. At the mouth of the underground cavity in Aslah sit two hundred talents of gold. Seventy talents of silver are located in the eastern tunnel which is to the north of Kohlit. Dig for only one cubit into the memorial mound of stones in the valley of Jericho to find twelve talents of silver. On the north side of Jacob's Well are buried eleven bars of gold, three cubits down.'

"And here's another..." he said, turning the page over.

"'Fifty talents lie under the stairs in the salt pit. Sixty-five bars of gold lie on the third terrace in the cave of the old Washer's House. Eighty talents of silver are enclosed in wooden vessels that are in the cistern of a burial chamber in Kepah's courtyard. Seventeen cubits from the front of the eastern gates lies a cistern. Thirteen talents lie in the canal of the cistern. Five silver bars are located at the sharp edge of the rock which is under the eastern wall in the cistern. The cistern's entrance is under the large paving stone threshold. Dig down three cubits in the northern corner of the pool that is east of Kohlit. There will be twenty-two talents of silver coins.'

"Now, a 'talent' was an ancient measure of weight, which would be equivalent to about thirty-three kilograms, or seventy-three Imperial pounds. I made some very rough calculations from everything I'd read, and I admit I was wholly flabbergasted at the total amount described here, which comes to something in the range of over one hundred fifty tonnes of gold and silver." He paused and looked up at the others, blinking through his thick spectacle lenses.

Hana couldn't bear the suspense. "How much would that be worth today, Simon?" she asked in a hushed tone.

"Based on today's market values, I put it at just shy of three billion U.S. dollars," the old man whispered as he leaned back in his chair, "making it the largest known buried treasure in world history."

CHAPTER

TEN

"*Three billion dollars?!*" Karl repeated in awe.

"*Hey, hey...*" Michael quietly cautioned his friend as he glanced around the lobby. "Keep it down, Karl. We don't want to attract any undue attention."

"Sorry," the young guard murmured, "but I can't believe what I'm hearing."

"I agree," Aaron admitted. "Even way back then, that would have been as massive a fortune as it is today, relatively speaking. Simon, were you able to date the scroll?"

"No, but given that the fear of Christian persecution was described as being so potent at the time, I would probably put it in the late third or early fourth century, about the time Mithraism as a whole had been largely extinguished.

Hana looked puzzled. "I'd known nothing of the Mithraists before this, but I had heard of the Essenes which, by all accounts, were a peaceful and reclusive sect living in poverty. So having that much treasure makes no sense to me."

"Yes, that is a bit of a historical mystery," the old scholar continued, "but there are several theories about their treasure's origins.

"For example, some scholars believe that, if the treasure did exist, it came from Jerusalem's First Temple period—1200–586 BCE—from the temple built by King Solomon himself on the spot where God is said to have created Adam. That temple was razed to the ground by the Babylonians in 586 BCE and the treasure stolen or hidden away at that time. And if so, then that likely means this may also be part of the fabled treasure of King Solomon, rumored to contain such legendary relics as the Ark of the Covenant and epic amounts of gold and silver plundered from the Egyptians during the Exodus.

"But most believe it came from the Second Temple—516 BCE to 70 CE—during which time it was hidden by the Jews in the course of the Roman military blockade of Jerusalem during the First Jewish Revolt in 70 CE, when the Romans destroyed the Temple and plundered the city.

"Either way, how it made its way to the hands of the Essenes is yet another mystery."

Simon paused, smiling at the team's reaction to the colorful history he had laid out for them. "It's a lot to take in, isn't it?" he concluded.

Michael nodded. "It is amazing, yes, all of it. So, now what happens to the scroll? Can *we* see it?"

GARY MCAVOY

"Yes, I told Ishak that your coming all this way would merit some time with the artifact, and that perhaps you might offer suggestions as to what its disposition should be. Let's go visit him now, shall we? He's waiting for us."

"You bet!" Aaron said gleefully, overjoyed at his good fortune. "Mikey, you do live a charmed life!"

"*Mikey?*" asked Hana with an arch of her brow. "Cute, but it doesn't really fit you."

"And let's leave it at that, shall we?" Michael groaned.

KARL DROVE their rental car as the GPS navigation system guided them south down Highway 2, then through various city streets to Neve Tzedek and Ishak Ramzi's house. Karl had suggested they stop at various touristy places along the way, but Simon was anxious to get to Jerusalem to join Rachel and his family.

Arriving at their destination, Karl pulled the car up into the wide circular driveway and stopped in front of the spacious home. As everyone got out, Hana remarked on how gorgeous the garden was. She stood next to a large tropical-looking plant some three meters high with massive, umbrella-shaped leaves, each spanning a meter across with an extremely coarse texture and deep venation.

"Look at these plants...they're practically prehistoric, and as large as an elephant's ear!"

"That is the glorious *Gunnera manicata*, or Brazilian

66

giant rhubarb," Aaron said. "They're my favorite, but they require a *lot* of water."

"Are you into plants, Aaron?" she asked.

"It's kind of my therapy, spending time in the garden at home when I'm not working. I'll have to figure out how to do that now that I'm living in Rome. Once you're hooked on nature, there's no going back."

As the group wandered up onto the porch, Simon noticed the front door had been left ajar. He rang the doorbell.

"Ishak?" he called out in his raspy voice. "We're here." He knocked on the door. No response.

Simon pushed the door open further and everyone stepped inside the bright and airy atrium foyer.

"Ishak?" he called again, then turned to the others. "It is a big house. Maybe he's in the artifact room."

"He has an entire room for artifacts?" Michael ventured. "Impressive."

"It's actually a hidden room. Quite ingenious. Let's see if he's in there."

Leading the way toward the middle of the house and into the library, Simon knocked on the hidden bookshelf door, expecting Ishak to open it. But again, still no response.

Reaching beneath the mantle of the fireplace as Ishak had done, Simon found and pressed the hidden button. The secret door popped ajar, and he pulled it open.

He gasped and stepped back. The body of his friend, Ishak Ramzi, lay sprawled on the floor, his throat slashed from ear to ear. A thick, red patch of blood had pooled beneath his head and spread across the hardwood floor. His vacant eyes stared at the ceiling.

Hana came up behind Simon and gasped when she saw the body, her hand covering her mouth. Michael made the sign of the cross and uttered a silent prayer. Aaron stared in disbelief. Karl pushed his way through, knelt down and instinctively felt for signs of a pulse, though it was clear no one could have survived such a fatal wound.

Tears stung Simon's eyes. "Who could do such a terrible thing?" he asked no one in particular. Michael took hold of his friend's shoulders and led him to one of the nearby stools in the room.

"Sit down, Simon. Would you like some water?"

"I…I think so, yes."

"I'll get it," Hana offered, leaving the room to look for the kitchen.

"Touch nothing, Hana," Aaron cautioned. "That goes for everyone. Simon? Do you think this might have anything to do with that scroll? Where is it?"

The old man looked up at the table on which the silver strips had been laid out.

"It's gone! It was right there," he said, pointing to the large vacant space on the wide table.

"Well, that explains it, then," Aaron mused. "Obviously, someone else knew about it. We need to call the police, Michael."

Michael looked at Karl, a decorated Swiss guard, and their closest thing to law enforcement at the moment. Karl was inspecting the layout of the room. On the ceiling in one corner he spotted the inverse black dome of a security camera. Glancing at the worktable, he found a pair of cotton conservation gloves and slid them on his hands.

"Simon, any chance you might know where the base station is for this security system?" Karl asked as he started looking through the cabinets in the room that covered most of the wall spaces.

"No, he mentioned nothing about that to me. I only noticed many of the cameras throughout the house."

"Yes, I saw two outside as we came in, one on the porch and another monitoring the driveway. The base has to be here somewhere..." Karl spotted what looked like a wall panel but could be a door set flush against the wall, one with no handle and with nothing impeding access to it. He pushed against the wall at its seam, which yielded slightly before popping ajar, much like the secret door to the room itself.

He pulled it open. "Just as I suspected..." he muttered to himself. Inside were several pieces of equipment, including the home's modem and Wi-Fi router and two digital video recorders, with a large monitor set against the inside back wall. The monitor display was split into several windows, each cycling through various camera feeds throughout the house, revealing both internal and external views. After a few moments, one window displayed the room they were in now, showing himself peering into the closet and the others standing around the room, as well as Ishak's body lying on the floor.

"Simon, when was the last time you spoke with your friend here?" Karl asked.

"Well," the old man thought, "that would have to be around ten o'clock last night, after I'd checked in at the hotel and called Ishak to let him know where I'd be."

Pressing a few buttons, Karl selected only the artifact room's video feed, then positioned the playback to start at ten o'clock the previous night, fast-forwarding the replay until he saw Ishak enter the room and sit at the table with what were probably strips of the silver scroll spread out before him. He sped up the replay until suddenly he saw another man walk cautiously through the door wearing a small backpack. Setting it to play at normal speed, Karl watched as Ishak, surprised and angry at the intrusion, stood to take action. But he had no chance to act, for instantly the intruder reached up with his right arm and swung it across the Arab's throat, the flashing glint of steel from an apparent blade evident beneath the bright light above.

The others had gathered around Karl by now and watched silently as Ishak grabbed for his throat, reached for the man, then fell to the floor, struggling for his final breaths. In a matter of moments, he fell still, his vacant eyes wide open in shock.

The intruder wiped the blade on Ishak's shirt and tucked it inside his own pocket, then turned and looked around the room. As he did so, Karl paused the replay and zoomed in on the man's face. It was a face he wouldn't forget.

The man then gathered the silver strips from the table and carefully placed them inside his backpack. He looked around the room again, grabbed the other parchment scrolls he found, then made for the door back out to the library.

Karl stopped playback, then switched the monitor to retrieve the feed for the driveway camera. Fast-forwarding to the approximate time of the murder, shortly before midnight, he watched until he saw the man emerge from the front door. A black Land Rover had pulled up in the driveway. The man quickly jumped in and the vehicle exited at the other end of the circular drive.

Karl backed up the replay until he got a proper angle to read the white license plate on the rear of the SUV, then zoomed in closer to read the black numbers: CD19-348-22.

Gotcha.

CHAPTER
ELEVEN

"We've got to call the police," Hana said with concern. "Obviously, we've been recorded now, so just leaving isn't an option."

Karl had no such inclination. "I have a better idea. This is no common robbery; we need something more than the local law. Remember Yossi Geffen, that Shayetet 13 unit leader from Israel Defense Forces who helped us fight off those neo-Nazis in Argentina and retrieve that Magdalene veil? He's with Mossad now and said to call whenever we might need him—and now seems like the perfect time. Mossad headquarters is right here in Tel Aviv, so he's probably close by, anyway. I have his number. I'll try him now."

"That's a great idea, Karl," Michael said as the Swiss Guard left the room to make the call in the quiet of the library.

"*Neo-Nazis? Mossad?*" Aaron asked, his eyebrows

arching with interest. "I see now what Hana meant by the adventures you're prone to get into."

"You have no idea. This job isn't always just prayers and parchments."

Karl had reached Yossi, as everyone heard him talking familiarly with the Israeli on the phone. A few moments later, he returned to the room.

"Yossi's on his way now," Karl confirmed. "He said to stay where we are and not to touch anything. After he gets here, he will handle getting the police involved. Boy, this could have gone a whole different way. I can't imagine the hassles we would have had. Any explanation for why we were here would involve the scrolls, which would instantly be considered ill-gotten theft of an antiquity which should have been reported immediately."

"We're not out of the woods yet," Hana cautioned. "Remember what they say about looking gift horses in the mouth?"

WHILE THE OTHERS sat in the library talking quietly, Karl and Michael waited in the atrium foyer for their old comrade to arrive, not wishing to be observed by neighbors if they stood outside.

Fifteen minutes later, a rugged Toyota Tundra pulled up in the drive and stopped at the front door. Two people got out of the truck: a tall, muscular man in his late thirties with a buzz cut, doubtless a warrior by his bearing; and an attractive young woman with her dark hair in a pert ponytail, who also looked like she could handle herself, walking with a self-assurance only military training could produce. Michael and Karl went out to greet them.

"Hey, guys," Yossi Geffen said with an engaging smile as he walked around the truck. Reaching Karl first, he held out his arm and gave the young soldier a firm handshake, then did the same with Michael. "Good to see you both again, but not under these circumstances, no? I'd like you to meet my new bride, Sarah. My love, this is Karl Dengler and Father Michael Dominic, both from the Vatican." As they exchanged brief greetings, Yossi started for the front door, not one to waste a moment's time.

Karl leapt around him and led the way back to the library, then began introducing everyone to the new arrivals. Sarah instantly moved directly to Hana first, introducing herself as they all made their way toward the murder scene.

"You must be Hana Sinclair," she said with a thick Hebrew accent, making direct eye contact and pumping her hand firmly. "I'm Sarah Geffen. Yossi has told me a great deal about you and your adventures in Argentina. It is a pleasure to finally meet you."

"You too, Sarah," Hana replied, sizing up her new acquaintance. "And yes, Yossi was immensely helpful in freeing us from those awful neo-Nazis. I imagine he's told you the details?"

"Well, under normal circumstances he could not, but as I am also Mossad, we do share operational specifics, yes."

"You're Mossad as well?!"

"What, you don't think girls can be assassins, too?" Sarah smiled cunningly, but Hana perceived a quiet strength in the woman, a sure confidence in her demeanor. *This is not someone to be taken lightly,* Hana considered. And she had no doubt at all that Sarah had killed before.

"How did you two meet?"

"At a joint operations meeting in a top-secret under-ground military bunker in Tel Aviv. I've been with Mossad as a senior agent for some ten years now, long before Yossi moved over from Shayetet 13 to join the agency. And when we met, he couldn't keep his eyes off me. I indulged him for a while, playing hard to get... you know. Though I was holding out for someone with loads of money, I settled for a hot spy instead." She smiled and held up a hand boasting a modest diamond ring.

Hana couldn't tell if she was joking or serious, but assumed the remark was in jest. "We're going to be good friends," Hana said to the Mossad agent.

Yossi had moved into the artifact room and was standing over Ishak Ramzi's body, taking in the scene with a seasoned eye. Michael related to him everything that had occurred up to then: Simon's first contact with the antiquities dealer, visiting his home, the timing of their last discussion, the silver scroll...anything that might be useful for Yossi's consideration of events.

Karl replayed the security video for him and handed him the slip of paper on which he had written the license plate number of the Land Rover. After watching the video, Yossi pulled out his phone, an unusual model Karl had never seen before.

"What kind of phone is that?" he asked.

Yossi answered absently as he continued searching for the license plate on a special Mossad database online. "It's an IntactPhone, developed here in Israel. The strongest security you can find in any such device, with encrypted communications, protection from eavesdropping, malware, data breaches, you name it. It's completely unhackable. Standard equipment for all Mossad agents these days."

"How do *I* get one?!" Karl asked enthusiastically.

"You can't, really. The State of Israel must approve every purchase from the manufacturer to ensure the technology doesn't end up in hostile hands." He looked down at the young soldier, who was easily a head shorter than he was. "But as a Swiss Guard in the Vatican, you might qualify. Prices start at several thousand U.S. dollars, though…"

"Well, so much for that idea," Karl muttered dejectedly.

Yossi frowned, the center of his forehead creasing as he gazed at the phone's display. "I'm afraid I have some bad news, Karl. This is a diplomatic license plate. It was white, yes? With black letters?"

"Yes, that's right."

"Pity. That will make it nearly impossible to bring the perpetrator to justice. Diplomatic Corps employees have full immunity from prosecution for any crimes committed in Israel; in fact, any country where diplomatic immunity is recognized, not only Israel. But we can certainly follow-up with this person ourselves, see if we can apply a little personal pressure to get that silver scroll back. The IAA may help, too."

"But what good will that do if the law isn't behind us?" Michael said, overhearing the conversation.

"I said 'nearly' impossible," Yossi said with a deadpan smile. "Accidents happen here every day. People should really be more careful crossing the street, for example…

"I'll have this guy's photo run through our facial recognition system and see what comes up. Meanwhile, I'll call a friend of mine who's chief of police here, Maya Kaplan, and explain the situation to her. You'll likely be held briefly for interviews, of course, but they won't take you in, I assure you."

Simon groaned. "Will I be able to leave for Jerusalem soon to meet my daughter and family?"

"I'll make sure they speak with you first, Simon. It won't take too much time."

It wasn't long before several police vehicles, a CSI unit and a coroner's van pulled up in front of Ishak Ramzi's house. Nosy neighbors had already started gathering up and down the block, kibitzing in small clusters.

Commander Maya Kaplan, a sturdy woman in her forties with a no-nonsense disposition, took control of the scene.

"Shalom, Yossi. What have you got for me?" Kaplan

asked brusquely as she entered the house with several officers in her wake.

"An unusual case, Maya, one with an ancient silver scroll at the center of it. From what I'm told—by Dr. Simon Ginzberg, a professor from Rome on holiday here…" Yossi gave Kaplan the full story as he knew it, concluding with the results of his agency's facial recognition scan. "I've already taken a copy of the video coverage; here's the flash drive for your files."

Then, referring to his notebook, he read, "The perp is a military attaché at the Egyptian Embassy here by the name of Abu Tariq, with several priors noted, all minor stuff. We have him on security video clearly committing the crime and stealing the silver scroll, and his vehicle and plates are easily identifiable as well. Not sure he knew he was being recorded, but he's a cocky *ben zona*. Or else his immunity assured him it didn't matter. Either way, he needs to be dealt with. Expelled from the country at the very least.

"But before you head in that direction," Yossi lowered his voice and leaned in closer to Kaplan, "I'd like to see if I can persuade him to turn over the scroll to us. I'm sure the IAA would love to see that course of action before it ends up in a diplomatic pouch bound for Cairo, don't you think?"

"Yes, I'm inclined to agree," the commander said, reaching up to push her hair back over an ear. "Take a couple days and see what influence Mossad might have over this Tariq character. But he will be expelled, regardless. I'll notify the Ministry of Foreign Affairs in a few days; they won't put up with homicide by a diplomat.

Will that give you enough time?" She looked up expectantly at the former Shayetet 13 assassin, only imagining what was in store for poor Abu Tariq.

"More than enough," Yossi said, a grim smile curving his lips.

CHAPTER

TWELVE

At a thousand dollars per night, the Plaza Executive Sea View Suite at the Hilton Tel Aviv afforded its current guests a sweeping view of the Mediterranean and breakfast in the room, all generously paid for by the good flock of the Church of Supreme Divinity back in Dallas.

Pastor Gabriel Darwin and his wife, Sue Ann, were up early, clad in white robes and slippers as they sat at a smoked-glass table on the balcony overlooking the beach at Hilton Bay, taking in the serene, lapping waves below. While reading *The New York Times* International edition, they enjoyed Turkish coffee and Shakshuka, an Israeli dish of poached eggs in a spicy tomato sauce served with feta cheese, with sides of toasted challah bread and hummus, and a thick, tangy, strained yogurt called Labneh spiked with olive oil. There was also salad, an Israeli morning staple, with tomatoes, cucumbers, herbs, and olive oil.

Teenaged Tabitha would have none of it, forsaking breakfast with her parents for a lie on the beach, trolling for young Israeli boys. To her delight, the beach was already packed with them, and few if any girls, so at least competition wasn't a factor. But she noticed that not one boy was paying attention to her.

Had she known that Hilton Beach was *the* place to go for gay beachgoers in Tel Aviv, she might have understood.

PASTOR DARWIN'S phone rang a special tune for certain contacts, and the melody playing now, *Raise a Hallelujah*, informed him the call was from his antiquities acquisition agent, Remi Shapiro. Leaving the balcony, Darwin got up to fetch the phone in the suite's living room.

"Yes, Remi, what is it?"

"Boss, we have a problem," Shapiro said, his voice low and anxious. "The dealer who had the silver scroll is dead. My source with Israeli Police said it was an Egyptian diplomat who took the scroll after murdering the guy in his home. I think we're screwed."

"We ain't leavin' Israel without that scroll, Remi. Do whatever it takes to make sure *you* get it and no one else does. And I mean *whatever* it takes. You follow?"

"Yessir, I follow. I'll figure something out."

Frustrated, Darwin ended the call, then returned to the balcony.

"Goddammit, Sue Ann. The good Lord must love stupid people, He made so many of 'em. And why do folks here eat *salad* for breakfast? Makes no damn sense."

ABU TARIQ ENTERED his private office at the Egyptian Embassy in Tel Aviv, closed the door and locked it. Removing the twelve silver scroll strips from his backpack, he laid them out on the small conference table in the corner by the window and stared at them, glinting in the morning sunlight.

He knew his contractor would be pleased. But now he wondered if his fee shouldn't be higher than previously arranged. After all, this was the long-sought silver scroll, and he took a great risk in acquiring it, not to mention committing such a crime as murder here, of all places. Israeli authorities took a harsh view of such things—especially by diplomats, where they had little recourse for prosecution unless their home country waives immunity, which wasn't likely from Egypt. If he were to be identified—and in his haste he later cursed himself for not having checked for security cameras—he would certainly be expelled from the country, deemed persona non grata, and never be allowed back.

Well, if that were the case, all the more reason his fee should be higher. Besides, he reasoned, he'd been here long enough as it was. He yearned to be back in Cairo anyway, among his own people.

But first, he had to get paid and deliver the prize to his master. He picked up his personal cell phone and dialed a number.

"Zadani," the calm voice answered.

"*As-salaam 'alaykum*, Khalid. This is Abu."

"*Wa 'alaykum as-salaam*, Abu. It is good to hear from you. I assume things went well?"

"I did run into some trouble, as the dealer proved to be resistant to my visit, not surprisingly. I am afraid certain measures had to be taken, and sadly, Ramzi is no longer with us. This was not something I had expected, so I think we need to discuss an adjustment of compensation for the extraordinary risks I had to take."

There was a strained pause on the line. Then, "Did you retrieve the scroll?"

"Of course. It is with me right now, here in the embassy, along with several parchments."

Another pause. "I am not opposed to such an adjustment, Abu. What did you have in mind?"

"Well, considering this is undoubtedly the rare silver scroll mentioned in the Khirbet Qumran copper as being its copy, which scholars tell us contains even *more* details of additional treasure than its copper counterpart… Plus, considering the scroll has already been neatly cut into twelve panels—presumably for easier translation, such as was done for the Khirbet scroll, as you may recall—I would say…oh, an even one million U.S. dollars should cover it."

Yet another pause, this one longer. Tariq could feel the tension, the brewing animosity on the line. He knew he was pushing hard—that was *twice* the previously agreed amount—but if Zadani wanted the long-sought silver scroll others had been trying to find for over two millennia, then he would have to pay.

"Alright. I will agree to your terms in this matter, but I do so reluctantly. I expect you to abide by your word on future assignments, Abu."

"Noted. So then, when and where shall we meet?" Tariq asked, letting the rebuke pass.

"Do you know the restaurant Claro on HaArba'a Street in the Sarona district?"

"Of course. A good choice. All the spies eat there."

"See you at one o'clock. Bring everything with you." Zadani hung up.

INSIDE THE SECURE MOSSAD SCIF—AN impenetrable Sensitive Compartmented Information Facility—Yossi Geffen removed his headset and turned off the recording device as Sarah entered the room.

"So, Abu Tariq is meeting someone named Khalid Zadani at Claro Bistro at one," he said. "Isn't Zadani the archeologist from Cairo? I recall his name associated with that gruesome find in the Cave of Horror. If a name sticks out to me, it likely means he's been on a hot sheet at some point."

Yossi turned to a computer on the conference table and searched through a Mossad database for the name. "Yes, here he is. Khalid Nasir Zadani. Born in Giza, currently lives in both Cairo and Tel Aviv. Has a permanent residency visa for Israel. No priors; seems clean." He glanced at his watch. "They're meeting in an hour. Feeling hungry, my love?"

• • •

CLARO—A chic, rustic and airy two-story brick restaurant nestled at the foot of three soaring black skyscrapers between Mossad headquarters and the Israel Defense Forces complex—specialized in fresh Mediterranean cuisine and discreet tables for conducting guarded conversations; for indeed, Israel's secret agents and the country's top cyber security experts were often found dining at Claro day and night.

Khalid Zadani had arrived early, choosing a shady table beneath the dense canopy of a weeping fig tree on the outside patio. Under the table, gripped between his legs, sat a hefty black leather attaché case containing ten thousand one-hundred-dollar bills in U.S. currency.

"Pomegranate juice for now, thanks, until my friend arrives," he told the server, who went inside to fetch the drink. As he looked up, he saw Abu Tariq approaching from the nearby intersection. A few moments later Tariq sat down at the table, nodding to Zadani and setting his backpack beneath the table between his own legs. As he did so, he bent down and visually inspected the underside of the table for electronic bugs, finding none.

"Are we having lunch?" he asked Zadani as he looked around for familiar faces.

"No time, I'm afraid. Order something to drink if you want to keep the waiter happy and we'll conduct our business and be off. But please reassure me...you *do* have full diplomatic immunity, yes? Which means you do not even have to answer questions should the authorities get involved?"

"That's right. I doubt anyone saw me, though, as it was shortly after midnight and the neighborhood was pitch dark." He didn't think it would be useful at the moment to mention his failure to check for security cameras.

"Good. I cannot afford my name being associated with this sort of thing. I have a reputation to uphold, you realize, which was why I agreed to your unwelcome extortion."

Again, Tariq warily glanced around the patio before speaking. "Now, now, Khalid. It is only business. And what you are getting in exchange is worth far more than that, as you of all people should know. I'm sure the rumors are true and the scroll does mention '*treasure*,' in which case—"

"*If* the rumors are true, you mean. And yes, the scroll itself is rare enough. I have no further qualms. Here comes the waiter. Let's tell him we cannot stay..."

Zadani paid for his drink, made their excuses, and before they rose from the table, furtively exchanged the attaché case for the backpack.

As Tariq took hold of the attaché case, he reached into his pocket, produced a yellow tag clearly marked "Diplomatic Pouch," and strapped it around the case's handle, making it officially untouchable by anyone, including law enforcement authorities.

The two men left the patio and walked off in separate directions, each of them eager to peer inside his respective bags.

. . .

SEPARATED by the floor-to-ceiling glass wall from inside Claro, Yossi and Sarah Geffen watched from a distant table as the two men switched bags and left the patio.

"That was smart of Tariq to strap a diplomatic tag on the attaché case," Sarah noted, then smiled at her husband, "though that hasn't stopped me before."

Yossi looked at her curiously. "I'm more interested in seeing what Zadani has in that backpack," he said. "But we'll let this play out, see what he does with it. Let's keep an eye on him."

CHAPTER

THIRTEEN

The train carrying Michael and his friends from Tel Aviv sped through lush, medieval farmlands and thick fields of olive trees on its way to Jerusalem, passing through the Ayalon Valley, then slowing down through the Judean Hills with its twisting and turning track between deep valleys and tall gorges. Although there was much to attract everyone's attention en route, the brief journey took just over half an hour.

After their traumatic experience finding Ishak Ramzi's body, Michael suggested they all spend a few days in Jerusalem to unwind, following Simon's lead. Both Aaron and Karl were keen to see the ancient city and its sacred memorials, and Hana wanted to look up an old friend from college if time permitted.

Earlier, as they were departing Tel Aviv, Hana called the King David Hotel in Jerusalem to make their reservations. Michael and Aaron offered to share a room while Hana and Karl each had their own.

• • •

JERUSALEM'S YITZHAK Navon Station is one of the deepest underground train stations in the world, with its platforms extending 260 feet below street level. Consequently, Michael's bathophobia—his persistent fear of depths due to almost drowning once—made him anxious to get topside quickly. Everyone crowding into the elevator taking them to street level didn't help matters, and just as his panic hormones were about to kick in, the elevator doors slid open and a fresh breeze swept into the car. Taking a deep breath and offering up a silent prayer, he coaxed himself into a safe mental space. Crisis averted, with no one the wiser.

Simon said his goodbyes as he got into a taxi to meet up with Rachel and the rest of his family, and the others hailed a cab heading to midtown and their hotel.

Built in the 1920s, the stately pink quartz façade of the King David Hotel welcomed the team as they made their way into the grand old lobby. After checking in, they found their rooms on the top floor offered spectacular views of the Western Wall, Dome of the Rock, Temple Mount, and Church of the Holy Sepulchre, four of the most important sites in the ancient city.

Before he left, Simon had shared to Michael's iPhone the images he had taken of the silver scroll and his translations of it, and while Aaron was unloading his backpack into the dresser, Michael sat in their room perusing the documents.

"I wish I'd had a chance to see this scroll in person,"

he said, disappointed. "It's not very often one gets a chance like that. We were so close, too."

"Well," Aaron said, trying to cheer up his friend, "maybe Yossi will retrieve it. One look at that guy and you know he means business. I don't think he'll give up easily."

"One can only hope. Hey, let's catch up with Karl and Hana and see if they want to play tourist a bit before dinner."

"You bet! I'm definitely up for that. How about we start with the Wailing Wall?"

"Sure. Men are required to wear yarmulkes while on the plaza, but they provide complimentary paper kippahs at the gate. And Hana will need a scarf, but knowing her, she likely travels with one, anyway."

PASSING through the sixteenth-century Dung Gate, Michael, Hana, Aaron and Karl went through the stringent security checkpoint for entry into the Western Wall Plaza. Though she was properly attired, including a headscarf, one guard pulled Hana aside.

"Miss, you must use the women's side of the Wall. You are not permitted to accompany the men. Please, proceed this way." He pointed toward a smaller section, away from where all the men were heading. Hana glanced back at Michael, gave him what he knew was an audible sigh, then followed the other women to their separate section of the Wall.

"Let's meet back here in twenty minutes," Michael shouted to her. Without turning, she simply raised her hand in submissive acknowledgment and kept walking.

Neither Karl nor Aaron had been here before, so Michael, who had, led them to the tunnel entrance leading to the Wall. Eager to get there himself, Aaron went ahead through the tunnel, not waiting for the others.

Moments before he and Michael entered, however, Karl literally ran into someone he knew coming out of an obscured door by the tunnel entrance—someone so completely unexpected that he suddenly felt disoriented —for standing before him looking quizzically into his own eyes was his Swiss Guard commandant from the Vatican, Colonel Niccolò Scarpa.

"Co...Colonel Scarpa! What are *you* doing here, sir?!" he asked incredulously.

Scarpa was just as surprised to run into one of his troops here in Jerusalem.

"I could ask you the same thing, Sergeant Dengler," he said, an oddly defensive tone in his voice. "What are *you* doing away from the Vatican?"

"I, uh, took some accumulated holiday time, sir," Karl said, fumbling to regain his balance. "All cleared with the office, of course."

Scarpa had by now broken out in a light sweat, for he did not expect to be seen by anyone he knew while in Israel. Not that he had to explain himself to an underling. But he did see one potential problem to this unanticipated encounter: his young sergeant was with one of the Holy Father's closest advisors.

"Oh, and uh...Father Dominic! You are here too?" he

blurted nervously to the priest. "What a pleasant surprise," he pretended.

Michael was equally taken aback. "Colonel Scarpa! What a small world," he marveled, shaking the man's hand.

"Yes, isn't it?" Scarpa replied.

"His Holiness won't believe this!" Michael laughed good-naturedly.

Scarpa's face suddenly tightened. "Perhaps it is best we do not impose on the Holy Father for such a trivial encounter, Father... Well, I've got to be going. It was good seeing you both." And with that, the colonel abruptly turned and walked away.

Watching him recede, Karl turned to Michael. "That was the craziest out-of-body experience I've ever had," he exaggerated. "Wonder what he's doing here? And apparently by himself."

"Now that you mention it, it does seem odd, doesn't it? Him being alone, I mean, and here at the Wailing Wall, of all places." Michael turned as well to watch the commandant weave through the crowd of people, then disappear. "And I wonder what's behind that door he came out of..."

As they approached the nondescript door, Michael turned the handle, but it was locked, with a combination keypad mounted next to it. Shrugging it off, they continued on to the tunnel entrance to pray at the Wall.

AN ACKNOWLEDGED expert in Mishnaic Hebrew, among other ancient languages, Khalid Zadani had finished translating the silver scroll and sat back in an over-stuffed leather armchair, staggered by what he had read. He lit a cigarette and reached for a bottle of Lebanese Arak, a potent anise-flavored liquor that not only went well with his Turkish tobacco, but helped balance his growing elation.

There is far more here than I could have imagined! he exulted, his mind reeling at the possibility of finding the legendary treasures of King Solomon and the Essenes. *But I need a map of ancient Jerusalem to determine such locations…*

As it happened, he knew of such a map; the earliest one in existence, dating from the sixth century CE. But it was in Jordan, in the city of Madaba—the oldest surviving original cartographic depiction of the Holy Land extant, with detailed emphasis on Jerusalem—laid down as a floor mosaic in the early Byzantine Church of Saint George.

Zadani viewed the mosaic from the church's website, but the detail was insufficient for the kind of analysis his work required.

So he would leave first thing in the morning. Meanwhile, out of convenience and as a precaution, he took photos of both the silver scroll and the parchments, the latter of which he would translate sometime later. The silver scroll was the priority now.

~

THANKS to his paid source on the Israeli Police force in Tel Aviv, Remi Shapiro's only lead was to someone named Abu Tariq, a military attaché with the Egyptian Embassy. The source also informed him that Tariq had diplomatic immunity from prosecution, so the authorities couldn't touch him.

But Shapiro had no such qualms. He had gotten Tariq's address—a luxury apartment overlooking the Mediterranean in Herzliya Pituach, Tel Aviv's most affluent neighborhood—and was now, under cover of darkness, sitting in a rental car outside the building on Galei Tchelet Street, mentally laying out his course of action.

Reaching into the glove compartment, he pulled out the Glock 19 his source had given him, taken from the evidence room from a prior crime. Gun control policies in Israel were exceedingly strict, and if he were caught without a permit, he would most certainly end up in jail.

And an Israeli jail is not where he wanted to be.

Regardless, he had a job to do. Exiting the vehicle, he tucked the Glock in the small of his back, made sure he had his lock-picking tools in his breast pocket, and made for the entrance to the Ocean Beach Apartments.

Getting past the outside security gate was a simple matter, and once inside the building, he took the stairs to the third floor. Walking up the carpeted hall to apartment 312, he could hear the crashing waves of the ocean through an open window at the end of the hallway. Undoubtedly, one needed abundant resources to live on this, the most expensive street in all of Israel.

He pressed his head against the door of 312 and

could hear the distant sound of a TV, but no other talk-ing. Hopefully Tariq was alone.

Quietly thrusting a tension wrench into the bottom of the keyhole, Shapiro applied slight pressure, then inserted a pick at the top. Giving it a modest torque, he scrubbed the pick back and forth until all the pins were set. Then he gently turned the door handle and removed the Glock from his back belt.

Entering the apartment, he slipped inside the foyer, then closed the door behind him, making sure it was locked. The sound of the TV was coming from a room down the hall to his left. His pistol raised slightly, he peeked around every corner, ensuring each room was clear, making steady progress toward the sound of the television.

Finally, he reached what appeared to be the master bedroom. He could see the large, flat-screen TV mounted on one wall, so the bed was obviously directly opposite. He entered the room, his Glock calmly extended.

Laying on the bed, fast asleep, was a fit man in his forties, his glasses askew on the bridge of his nose as his head lay limply on a pillow. Shapiro walked over to the TV and shut it off, then stood by the side of the bed, held the Glock against Tariq's forehead, and nudged his shoulder with his other hand.

Tariq awakened and slowly opened his eyes, which flew open wider when he saw a hand holding a pistol to his head.

"Ma le'azazel!" he cursed in Hebrew. "Who are *you?* What do you want?"

"I understand you have a particular object my employer has need of. A scroll. One made of silver. Just show me where it is, and I'll be on my way. And no one will get hurt."

Tariq was apprehensive. He could probably take the guy, but not with a gun at point-blank range.

"I do not have it anymore," he said flatly. "I already sold it."

"You're lying." Shapiro pressed the pistol harder against the man's cheek.

"No, I am telling you the truth. Look around, you will not find it. I swear to you, I sold it to a man named Khalid Zadani. I do not know where he lives, but he is a famous archeologist here in Israel. You should easily be able to find him."

Shapiro paused, admiring the man's cool. *Damn…he is telling the truth.*

"This is your lucky day," he said to Tariq. "Since you're obviously involved in some shifty business, it's unlikely you'll tell anyone about my visit. Right?"

"I think you've got the measure of it, yes. You can just go, and we'll leave it at that."

Shapiro backed out of the room, then walked back down the hall, secured the Glock back inside his belt, and left the apartment.

So, now I need to find this Khalid Zadani fellow. Pastor Darwin won't be happy without that silver scroll. What a hassle.

FOURTEEN

T el Aviv's Savidor Station was bustling with commotion on all three platforms as passengers were boarding or disembarking from the six trains currently parked on either side of the platforms. The electric thrum of the mighty locomotives created a subtle but constant vibration throughout the station.

It was the early morning rush hour and Khalid Zadani—having no luggage for the two-hour trip, since all he needed was the scroll transcription in the leather-bound journal he carried—boarded the train bound for Madaba, Jordan, and the old Church of Saint George.

As he picked out his seat toward the front of the car and settled himself in for the journey, Yossi and Sarah Geffen took positions at the back of the car, flipping through magazines as they blended in with the other passengers.

Remi Shapiro, however, took the seat directly behind

Zadani, in case the Arab made a phone call he could listen in on. His head kept swiveling behind him, checking to see if he recognized anyone else on the train —or if anyone might recognize him.

Since Zadani's home office was listed on his website, it had been relatively simple for Shapiro to follow the archeologist from his home that morning, having no idea he'd end up on a train to Jordan. Good thing his visas were all in order, as an Israeli citizen who traveled frequently.

But once Sarah noticed him, she couldn't take her eyes off Shapiro, certain she recognized him.

"Yossi," she whispered, "see that man sitting right behind Zadani? I'm sure I know him from somewhere, but I can't place him."

Yossi looked up from the magazine and saw the object of his wife's interest as the man's head turned back again. "You're right. That's, uh…Remigius Shapiro, the artifacts agent, isn't it?"

"Yes, that's it! I knew I'd seen him before. He was involved in that joint Israeli-Egyptian operation a few months ago…the one where a dozen parchment manuscripts went missing from the National Library while in transit from the Dar el-Kotob Library in Cairo. Don't you think it's coincidental that he's on this train—and sitting mere inches behind our rabbit, who's also a manuscript buff?"

"You know I don't believe in coincidences," Yossi murmured, laying the magazine in his lap while thinking through this fresh development.

"Neither do I, *motek,*" she said endearingly. "Which means he probably knows about the silver scroll, too."

"This is crazy. How many people might know about this by now?"

"Word travels fast in the underground manuscripts market, and there are always leaks. The temptation is too great. Especially if, as Simon said, treasure is involved. So, now we have two people to keep tabs on, with the possibility of more to come."

SOME THIRTY KILOMETERS southwest of Amman, Jordan's capital, lies the ancient Bronze Age city of Madaba. Mentioned several times in the Bible, the city is now widely recognized for its spectacular Byzantine and Umayyad mosaics, most notable among them the oldest known map of the Holy Land, and particularly Byzantine Jerusalem.

Laid down piece by piece in the sixth century on the timeworn floor of what is today the Greek Orthodox Basilica of Saint George, the Madaba Map features some two million colored stone tiles vividly depicting villages and towns in Palestine and the Nile Delta, including hills and valleys, buildings and bodies of water, roads, bridges, town borders and other more granular features. Scholars have used the map to better understand the physical layout of historical Jerusalem before its destruction and the start of rebuilding in 70 CE.

And to scholars' surprise, later excavations of the Jewish Quarter of Jerusalem in 1967 revealed two prominent landmarks—the Cardo Maximus and the Nea Church—to be in the exact locations depicted on the map, as well as the 2010 discovery of a road running through the center of Jerusalem consequent to further excavations. Serving as confirmation of the map's accuracy, both discoveries proved to be of priceless value to archeologists.

As HE ENTERED THE CHURCH, Khalid Zadani was moved by its sumptuous interior, with elegant wood and marble colonnades and colorful mosaics on virtually every wall and column. Though a Muslim, as an archeologist, he could appreciate the Christians' devotional architecture, much as any faith invests in their temples and places of worship.

But his mind was fastened on one object—the expansive map of old Jerusalem depicted on the floor. As he approached the cordoned-off area protecting the floor mosaic, he pulled up the transcription of the silver scroll from the images on his phone and got to work. Previously, he had made notes of certain towns and other places mentioned in the scroll, hopeful that the map would offer something comparable.

Focused as he was on the task at hand, Zadani failed to notice that he was being followed and observed by three people posing as ambling tourists amongst the many visitors in the church that day.

Over the next half hour, his head bobbed up and down, checking his notes for scroll references to specific locations, then seeking to find mention of those on the map. He was not hopeful since, after all, the map was made some two hundred years *after* the scroll had been written, so it was possible that none of the references would be shown. On the other hand, not much had really changed over that period. There had been no technology, no industrial advantages enjoyed by more modern developments of civilization. Geographic features in the earliest centuries did not evolve rapidly, which he viewed as favorable to his pursuit. But he also knew that distances on the map were unlikely to be completely accurate, and scale had to be an issue since no aerial views were possible then.

He wasn't having much luck until he hit upon a point on the map reading "Jacob's Well," a reference matching something he'd read on the silver scroll: "*On the north side of Jacob's Well are buried eleven bars of gold, three cubits down*," his notes read.

Zadani's pulse quickened. Finally, something matched! Then, some distance across the map, he saw the name "Acel Dama," matching yet another reference from the scroll: "*Thirty talents of silver can be found under the pillar on the northern side of the big cistern in Acel Dama.*"

It only then occurred to him that, accounting for the common occurrence of spelling variations over time, "Akeldama" was the potter's field in Jerusalem that was bought with the bribe money the Apostle Judas Iscariot had been paid for betraying Christ. *Thirty pieces of silver!*

Filled with remorse over his betrayal, Judas had returned his payment to the chief priests at the Temple. But as it was against the law to put this into the treasury, since it was considered blood money, the priests used the funds to buy the potter's field. And much later, a portion of the treasure was buried there.

Zadani's heart was racing. Taking out his phone, he snapped several closeup photos of that section of the map, then took images of the rest of the mosaic from different angles while he was at it.

Sarah Geffen, who was standing closest to Zadani, discreetly observed his avid interest in the Jerusalem section of the map and, relying on her peripheral vision, watched as he bent over the red-chained cordon to peer more closely at particular spots in the most historic area, the Old City. Given his keen interest, he was surely on to something, but it was impossible for her to make out the specific details on which he was focused.

Just then, he looked up at her, holding Sarah's eyes directly. She returned the look only briefly, as any other person might, then casually returned to playing the unremarkable tourist. But she did see Zadani hold his eyes on her for several more moments before returning to his task.

After another twenty minutes of comparing his notes to the map, Zadani was apparently finished. He pocketed his phone and headed for the exit with an air of restless determination.

Sarah and Yossi exchanged glances from across the room and—after watching Remi Shapiro also head toward the exit following the archeologist—joined up and followed both men out into the bright sunlight of Madaba.

CHAPTER
FIFTEEN

The entrance to Jerusalem's upscale restaurant Mona was reminiscent of a lush desert oasis, with enormous, thirty-meter-tall Judean date palms framing the entry.

After a long day taking in the sites of the ancient city, Hana, Michael, Karl and Aaron were famished, ready to enjoy some of Israel's finest modern cuisine. Sarah had called Hana saying she and Yossi had arrived in Jerusalem, with much to tell them.

Hana invited the couple to join them at Mona for dinner, and as it didn't appear that Zadani was leaving his room for any nighttime excavations, Sarah accepted the invitation. They would meet at the restaurant.

"Table for six, please," Hana informed the maître d'. "Two friends will join us soon. And might we get something out on the garden patio?"

They were led through the dining room to a stone-walled garden in the back where several intimate tables were nestled amid a panoply of tropical trees and aromatic herb bushes beneath the open sky.

"Dinner is on me tonight," Aaron announced, motioning to the server for the wine list. "I've had the best time so far and it's the least I can do." Glancing at the list briefly, he ordered two bottles of pinot noir and a bottle of chardonnay.

As everyone was reading their menus—the food being a fusion of Italian and French fare, all locally sourced—Sarah and Yossi walked up to the table and took their seats, greeting everyone.

"So...a lot has happened in the past two days since Ishak Ramzi's murder," Sarah told them quietly. "We know who the perpetrator is: an Egyptian diplomat named Abu Tariq. As such, he's untouchable from a law enforcement standpoint, but he did have the silver scroll until he presumably sold it to a prominent archeologist named Khalid Zadani.

"We followed Zadani on a train to Madaba, Jordan, early this morning, where he apparently consulted the notes he had taken from the silver scroll and compared them to a map mosaic of ancient Jerusalem on the floor of an old church there. Yossi and I think he plans to excavate parts of the Old City tomorrow to find the rumored treasure of Solomon. That's the only thing that makes sense. But we'll be watching him from a distance."

"Oh, and on a curious note," Yossi added, "someone else was following Zadani, too—a man we recognized from a previous mission, someone with a keen interest in ancient artifacts, especially manuscripts. We witnessed the man follow Zadani to a hotel, where both checked in separately. We also arranged an open-ended room reservation for ourselves, dependent on whatever Zadani is up to. That silver scroll is certainly getting a lot of attention. We phoned in our report to Commander Maya Kaplan of Tel Aviv Police. Maybe it will help her case."

"Well," Michael cautioned, "good luck finding that treasure. I don't know about that map, but from what Simon told me, those archaic references would be pointless today."

"I'm not so sure about that, Mikey," Aaron said. "Having Simon's translated notes, I'm thinking we should head over to Jordan ourselves and have a look at this Madaba Map. We'll never get another chance to do something like this! And who knows what we might find?" His eyes were alight with the passion of a true academic.

Sarah turned to him. "From a historical perspective alone, I think you'd love it," she said. "It really is quite beautiful."

Aaron mouthed *Thank you!* to her and the table suddenly went silent as the server returned with three bottles of wine, opened one red and the white, then filled glasses as each person signaled his preference.

He then took their orders: a mélange of crab bisque, tuna tartare and oysters, polenta with mushroom ragout and asparagus, yellowtail crudo with grapes and spring onions, beef fillet with sweetbreads and purple cabbage, and red tuna sashimi with chili.

"*L'chayim*," Sarah said, raising her glass in a toast as the others joined in. "To life!"

They all tipped their glasses, each mind swirling with the possibilities of these recent events.

"Where is this Zadani guy staying?" Aaron asked.

"At the King David," Sarah replied. "Same place as we are, where we can keep an eye on him. It's also the hotel closest to the Old Quarter of East Jerusalem."

"We're at the King David, too!" Aaron exclaimed. "I assume this other guy is staying there as well? What was his name, again?"

"I didn't say," Yossi said warily. "But it's Shapiro. Why do you ask?"

"Hmm," Aaron muttered. "Oh, no reason, just curious. Like you said, many people seem to want that scroll pretty badly."

Sarah and Yossi exchanged quick, furtive glances. Then she said, "Hana, shall we go powder our noses before dinner comes?"

"Do girls even say that anymore?!" Karl asked, chuckling.

"Women," Sarah corrected him. "And I did, just now. Didn't you hear me?" She smiled assertively as she got up, joining Hana for a trip to the ladies room.

"How well do you know Aaron, Hana?"

Surprised at the question, Hana replied, "Not well,

really. I only met him a few days ago. But Michael has known him since college. They're pretty good friends, from what I can tell. Why?"

"Just a feeling, nothing more. As you might imagine, Yossi and I live in a suspicious world. We're conditioned to think that way, unfortunately. It comes with the job."

"Well, he's got a PhD in classical studies and recently landed a position as professor at a Loyola campus in Rome starting next week. I can't imagine him having a double life, if that's what you're thinking."

"No, you're right. Aaron seems like a good guy, I'm sure it's nothing. Let's rejoin the others. I didn't bring powder anyway..." They laughed as they made their way back to the table.

IT WAS SHORTLY before midnight when Niccolò Scarpa's cell phone vibrated on the nightstand. Still awake as he lay in bed, he reached for it. "Yes?"

"Sorry if I woke you, Colonel," the voice said. "But I have two names for you: Khalid Zadani and someone named Shapiro, both staying at the King David Hotel. Each of them appears to have a separate interest in the silver scroll's treasure and likely are going after it tomorrow."

"Thank you," said the colonel. "We still want the scroll itself, too."

"Yes, I'm working on that."

"Good. I'll be in touch, then."

BOTH TAMIR PINSKY and Azim Hourani learned of Ishak Ramzi's death three days after he was murdered. Since Muslims are buried within twenty-four hours of passing, they were unable to attend the funeral.

But though they were sad about their friend's passing, they were more upset at having lost out on their rightful commission for finding the silver scroll and parchments. After Ishak's body had been removed from the house and his family left to stay with relatives, the boys broke through the police crime scene tape and gained entry into the home to see if their treasures were still there. Having been in the dealer's secret room before while conducting previous transactions, they now searched it and discovered the artifacts had gone missing.

At Ishak's request several months earlier, Tamir had been the one who installed the cloud-based digital video security system, that being his day job with a local security services firm when he wasn't plundering caves. So, it was instinctive for him to look at the prior days' monitoring and see if any clues surfaced as to the disposition of the scrolls.

In horror, the two boys watched the replay of their friend's throat being slashed by an unknown assailant, then the attacker taking the cut scroll panels and parchments, and then sometime later, a large group of people discovering the body and getting the police involved.

Rewinding the digital playback, Tamir zoomed in on the face of Abu Tariq. He would not forget this man, but he printed out a copy of the best closeup video frame to take with him.

He would do whatever it took to find him, recover the scrolls, and avenge the death of his friend Ishak Ramzi.

CHAPTER
SIXTEEN

The Western Wall, often called the Wailing Wall by many who pray there, is one of the most revered and controversial holy sites in Israel, dating from the second and first centuries BCE. It is believed by Jews to be the actual western wall of the Second Temple, which was destroyed by the Romans in 70 CE during the Siege of Jerusalem.

Twenty meters tall and some fifty meters long, it is built of thick, corroded limestone and stands next to a narrow courtyard where the faithful gather to pray. It is sacred to both Jews and Muslims, wherein lies much of its contentious history, a control and ownership dispute that goes back generations. It is especially revered by the Jewish people who consider it a place of devotion and pilgrimage, with visitors often slipping scraps of paper containing written prayers into the wall's multitude of holes and fissures.

Khalid Zadani did not need to enter the Wall's courtyard for this mission, however, which meant he wouldn't have to deal with Israeli security. No, his objective lay south of the Wall, in a rocky, stone-walled, labyrinthine section of ancient ruins called the Old City, excavated areas of which were still largely intact from biblical times. Sand-colored stones of every shape and size, stacked in deep, rugged mounds, formed shapes of walls and foundations. Steps appeared out of nowhere, leading to doorways long since demolished.

It was evening, just getting dark, and before leaving the hotel, he had tucked a small folding shovel into his backpack, expecting to dig at some point. No tourists were around at that hour, since most were more interested in other adjacent night-lit sites: the Dome of the Rock, Temple Mount, and Church of the Holy Sepulchre.

As he walked around the Old City's Muslim Quarter, he came across an ancient *hammam*, or bathhouse, connected to a warren of bygone cisterns beneath the tunnels to the Western Wall. Such bathhouses were originally used by Muslim pilgrims wishing to engage in ritual cleansing before prayers at the nearby Al-Aqsa Mosque.

And an old dry well was next to it.

Was this it? The landmark called "Jacob's Well?" He took out his phone and checked the map image for where he was standing, trying to make out adjacent markers or monuments on the tiny phone display. He noted the old stone steps down to the former cisterns, the same as on the map. *This has got to be it!* he thought.

With a cubit being eighteen inches, three cubits puts it at about a meter and a half deep.

Pulling out the shovel from his backpack, Zadani took off his jacket and quietly began digging on the north side of the well—as described on his notes—his head bobbing up to glance behind him from time to time, making sure nobody was approaching. If he were to be caught by the authorities, punishment would be swift and severe. He was taking a great risk, but the potential payoff was too seductive not to try.

The first hole yielded nothing. He kept digging.

He heard a group of young women laughing and chatting in Arabic as they walked near to where he was standing in the shadows. He backed up even deeper into the dark recesses of the *hammam*, waiting for them to pass.

When silence returned, he resumed shoveling. This time, about a meter down, his blade struck something hard. It was probably just another rock, but he was excited nonetheless.

Shining his flashlight into the hole, what he saw made him gasp out loud.

The light was shining on something long and golden. Tossing the shovel aside, he began digging fiercely with his hands, pushing away dirt and roots and enlarging the hole, until he could clearly make out several buried bars of gold, their protective wrappings of cloth and straw deteriorating in the soil.

Pulling one out of the hole and wiping it clean with his shirttail, he could make out crudely engraved assayers marks on one side. These were Roman ingots, probably from around the early fourth century.

What a discovery! he marveled with joy. *Such treasures buried here for two thousand years and only found by me! And with the silver scroll confirming locations, that means so much more was yet to be found!*

Dropping the find inside his backpack and returning his attention to the hole, he dug down for other bars he could see in the light of his torch. The supply was seemingly endless. By the time he was done, there were indeed eleven bars, as accurately predicted on the silver scroll. Zadani was already well off, but now he was rich —not to mention having the silver scroll itself and the other parchment scrolls he'd gotten from Abu Tariq.

But he had one problem. Everything would have to be moved on the black market, for there was no way the Israel Antiquities Authority would allow him to keep them.

Of course, he would keep the silver scroll for his own collection. But he would have to give this whole question of disposition further thought.

Suddenly, he heard footsteps, more than one person's, coming down the nearby stone staircase. He receded back into the shadows…

NOT ONLY WAS darkness a challenge for watching Zadani's movements, but Yossi was in such a position where actually observing him do whatever it was he might be doing was near impossible. So—knowing where Zadani was but unable to monitor him without having line of sight—he waited for him to emerge from the pit near the old well, which had no other way out.

Curiously, he had not seen Remi Shapiro anywhere. He fully expected to be watching for both men. And that concerned him.

But he did notice two other men he had seen more than once ambling back and forth in the area. Both had strong builds and the disciplined bearing of soldiers— and they were now descending the old stone steps into the well area where he presumed Zadani had gone. Yossi stood up straighter, curious as to what might be happening.

Minutes later, he had his answer.

He watched as three men came out of the enclosed well area, the two soldiers walking beside and either supporting or restraining Zadani in the middle, his backpack slung over the shoulder of the larger of the men. By all appearances, the bag was filled with something very heavy from Yossi's perspective—certainly much more than what Zadani had gone down there with. The soldier kept having to adjust the weight balance of the backpack as he and his partner firmly guided their apparent prisoner to a dark-green panel van parked not far up the street. Once they had shoved him in the back of the van, both men got in and the vehicle pulled away, driving toward the Christian Quarter of old Jerusalem.

EARLIER, Remi Shapiro had decided not to follow Khalid Zadani that night in favor of seeing what he could find in the archeologist's hotel room at the King David instead. If nothing was found, he could then lie in wait for the unsuspecting Zadani to arrive with any spoils he may have unearthed.

Using his trusty lock-picking tools, he made quick work of entering the room. Once inside, he began his search. He found nothing in the closets—no clothing anywhere, for that matter—which meant he likely didn't plan to stay in Jerusalem long. Opening the drawers of a dresser, he was more optimistic, finding maps and papers strewn about, along with a curious leather pouch about a foot long with a drawstring. He untied the knot and pulled open the fastener.

At first, Shapiro didn't know what he was looking at. There were twelve pieces of slightly curved silver panels stacked inside, each with what appeared to be ancient glyphs engraved on one side. *Could this be the silver scroll? But why is it cut into pieces?* he worried. If this was what all the fuss was about, then his boss would be very happy indeed. He hoped so, anyway. Pastor Darwin was a fickle man, and he may look at this as a ruined artifact. *A likely case of 'Don't kill the messenger!'*

He found the other parchment scrolls, too. These were in fine condition, and he was pleased that his intuition paid off today. *Praise be! The pastor will be over the moon.* Tucking the small parchment manuscripts inside his own backpack so as not to rub or tear against the silver panels in the pouch, he made for the door.

As he opened it, a fist suddenly thrust through the

doorway and slammed him hard in the face. Shapiro fell backward, down onto the carpeted floor, unable to yet make out his attacker. He reached up to his nose, which felt broken. The pain was crippling! Blood flowed down his cheeks and onto his jacket, and he felt dizzy. Then the door closed behind the intruder.

"I see you beat me to the prize," Sarah Geffen said, her Glock 19 poised expertly in front of her. "I'll take that, thank you." She reached down to pick up the leather pouch, confident Shapiro was sufficiently immobilized.

"Who are you?!" the injured man cried out nasally as his hand tried to stanch the flow of blood. "And where the hell did you come from?"

Sarah reached into her pocket and withdrew her badge. He blinked at it through the pain, his mouth opening in shock. "That's right, Remi. Mossad. You made a big mistake. The Israel Antiquities Authority will be in touch with you soon, and I wouldn't say your chances for escaping prosecution are all that great. If I were you, I'd name names, as in, who's paying you to find these artifacts?"

Shapiro was stricken with fear. *Mossad? How does Mossad know about me?... About any of this?!* "I have nothing to hide!" he cried, confessing with pitiful ease. "I was hired by Pastor Gabriel Darwin, the American televangelist. He's the one who wants the silver scroll. Hey, I really need a doctor here—"

"I assume that's what's in the bag? The scroll?"

"I think so. It's cut into pieces, so I'm not sure whether that's it."

Sarah opened the bag to check its contents. Sure enough, she noted, Remi was telling the truth. In the pouch was the silver scroll in the condition described by Simon. To ensure that she could locate Shapiro later should he make a run for it, she discreetly pinned a tiny tracker in an obscured gap beneath the top flap of his black canvas backpack resting on a nearby chair.

"Okay, Remi. The IAA will contact you soon, but in the meantime, I'm taking this pouch into custody." Still holding her gun on him with one hand, she motioned for him to get up. Then she pushed him with the other hand toward the bathroom. "Go get yourself cleaned up but don't plan on going anywhere. You should call the front desk for a doctor, but from the look of it, it's only a minor nose fracture. It could have been much worse."

After the Mossad agent left, Shapiro went into the bathroom and cleaned up as much as he could of the blood. *What have I gotten myself into here? Darwin didn't say this would be dangerous.*

But at least she didn't take the parchments, for what good those are.

CHAPTER
SEVENTEEN

Roughly ten rocky meters beneath Jerusalem's Western Wall lies one of the earliest Mithras temples of the Roman Empire. Constructed under the aegis of Roman Emperor Commodus in the late second century, the mithraeum's broadly arched limestone ceiling was supported by sturdy round marble columns for a good thirty-meter distance underground. Now lit by electricity, its flickering, torch-like bulbs were reminiscent of those ancient days' actual fire torches, and a revered tauroctony at the head of the room still shone as brightly as the day it was painted two millennia earlier.

With knowledge of its secret existence having been passed down from father to son over generations, the Western Wall mithraeum was known only among the cult's initiates. Not even local authorities were aware of it, unless they were secretly Mithraists as well. There would be no more excavations anywhere near the Wall, so its location was safe from being discovered by anyone, its doorway virtually hidden from view by anyone walking the tunnels. And Colonel Niccolò Scarpa intended to keep it that way.

Entrance was gained only by two doors: the oldest one which now happened to be inside the Israeli security checkpoint at the Dung Gate—which was rarely used by any member, for obvious reasons of potential discovery—and another, the primary entrance and exit, located inside one of the tunnels running beneath the Western Wall in all directions. That door was accessible from within a small, inconspicuous house in the Old City owned by Scarpa, to which only a select few had the key—including one of the two soldiers who had dragged Khalid Zadani in an hour earlier, having found him digging near an ancient well in an excavated part of the Old City.

With his hands and feet bound, Zadani was now sitting in a wooden chair in the old mithraeum, having finally awakened from the heavy sedative effects of the benzodiazepine Rohypnol administered during his capture and transport to the mithraeum.

"We have been watching you with fascination for some time, Dr. Zadani," Colonel Scarpa said as he sat in front of his involuntary guest. "I wanted to personally thank you for finding these exquisite bars of Roman gold, and for so generously donating them to our cause."

"What cause? And why am I here?" Zadani pleaded groggily. "Who are you people?"

"That does not matter. I do apologize for our rude

behavior in getting you here, but have no fear. You will be free to go once you turn over the silver scroll to us. That is all I ask."

"Silver scroll? I don't know what you're talking about. I have no such scroll."

"Come now, Khalid. As I said, we've been watching you. We certainly know that you received the scroll, and perhaps something more, from Abu Tariq at the Claro Restaurant three days ago. And I must assume that, based on your translation of its contents, that is how you came upon this ancient gold. So, if you wish to leave here intact, just answer the question: where do you keep the scroll?"

Zadani weighed his options, of which admittedly few were at hand. He looked around at his surroundings. Obviously, they had brought him to some sort of subterranean room. The arched limestone ceiling was unusual, yet somehow familiar. Then he saw the unmistakable tauroctony painted on the front wall and instantly knew where he was.

"This is a *mithraeum!*" the archeologist said in wonder. "I did not realize these still existed in Israel. How did you find this place?"

"All in good time, Doctor," Scarpa murmured as a soldier approached him and whispered in his ear. Listening with interest, his bushy gray eyebrows furrowing on hearing the words spoken, the colonel moved away from Zadani to speak with his lieutenant. After a few moments, he returned to his captive.

"Well, it appears you may be correct, my friend," Scarpa said wryly, "in that you do *not* have the silver scroll. My people have just searched your hotel room, and it was nowhere to be found."

Zadani was stunned. *"What do you mean? It's gone?!"* he cried, then checked himself, mentally cursing his slip.

"Ah, so now you admit you had it. Well, too bad for both of us, then. But on the upside, you are now free to go. My men will escort you back to Jerusalem. It is doubtful our paths will cross again, Khalid. But as others will surely come looking for that scroll—as it appears someone else already has—if I were you, I'd leave the city and not return. Besides, we have your most generous translations of the contents, from which we might ferret out other locations of the treasure."

Scarpa turned and disappeared inside another room of the mithraeum while the same two soldiers who had initially apprehended Zadani administered another small dose of Rohypnol. Fifteen minutes later, he slipped into unconsciousness. They cut his bindings, then took him by the arms and dragged him to the exit leading to the tunnels. As they did, one man placed a burlap bag over their captive's head in case he awakened. They then carried him through the tunnel, through the nondescript house in the Old City, and back into their panel van.

Several minutes later, they pulled the vehicle to the side of a dark alley near the King David Hotel, removed the burlap bag from over Zadani's head and laid his unconscious body against a fence. They opened a bottle of whiskey, poured a little over his clothing, put some in his mouth, then set the bottle between his legs, got back in the van and left the scene.

Azim Hourani and his best friend, Tamir Pinsky, walked into the Tel Aviv Police Headquarters in Jaffa and asked to see Officer Jesse Loeb, someone they had encountered previously when they had been caught on one caving expedition. They had been able to talk their way out of it then, but wisely stayed in touch with Loeb, since having an inside man was never a bad idea for young men who sometimes found themselves on the other side of the law. And the young officer had taken a shine to the boys, feeling he was helping them stay on the straight and narrow.

Loeb, who had just returned from a two-martini lunch and was in a chatty mood, seemed happy to see the boys and invited them into his private office.

"Azim...Tamir!" he gushed. "How are you both doing? Good, I hope?"

"Yes, very good, Officer Loeb. Thank you for asking."

"So, what brings you here today?"

"We have a favor to ask," Azim said, turning to Tamir, who produced the photo image of the man who murdered Ishak Ramzi in his home, though they did not reveal that detail. "Can you please run this through your facial recognition system and tell us who it is? This man was driving a car that scraped Tamir's as he was making a turn and the dash cam caught it. We just want to talk to him and maybe handle this without going through the insurance company. Nobody wants their rates any higher than they are, right?" He laughed as he handed over the photo.

Loeb chuckled with him. "Yeah, I know what you mean. Sure, that won't be a problem. It will only take a few minutes. Our system is pretty fast, and I'll isolate the search to Tel Aviv." Getting up, he inserted the printed facial image into the system scanner, then pressed a few buttons on the keyboard. Mere seconds later, a positive match came up on the system display, revealing the man's frontal image plus personal details in his file.

Loeb instantly recognized the name as the one he had given to Remi Shapiro in relation to the Ramzi murder case. Tamir sat forward, eagerly taking in as many details as he could from the information revealed on the screen: home and work addresses, phone number, relevant personal details.

"That's interesting," Loeb noted. "I happen to know of this man. His name is Abu Tariq. He's a diplomat, a military attaché for the Egyptian Embassy here. Good luck getting anything out of him, though. Those diplomats can literally get away with murder and don't seem to give a damn about mundane things like insurance claims."

"Well, we can always try," Azim said. "Maybe appealing to his better angels will help. Thank you so much, Officer Loeb. We owe you one."

CHAPTER
EIGHTEEN

E arly the next morning—Michael having agreed with Aaron's suggestion that they all visit Jordan to view the Madaba Map—the team got on the train and made their way east to the ancient city in less than two hours.

Entering the Church of Saint George, Michael dipped his fingers into the font of holy water just inside the church doors, making the sign of the cross as he walked toward the altar.

While Greek Orthodox don't bless themselves in such ways as Catholics do, the Eastern rite provides holy water for anyone to use or even take with them. Michael had read that this church wasn't built until the end of the nineteenth century, but when excavators discovered the incredibly artistic mosaic map of old Jerusalem—only a quarter of which had survived from its original fabrication over two thousand years earlier —it opened up new doors of research for scholars worldwide, making the church one of the most popular tourist spots in Jordan.

Aaron, Karl and Hana gathered around the red chain-link cordon and were instantly enraptured by the sixth-century map on the floor, while Michael was initially more interested in the Byzantine architecture of the church itself and in how the Orthodox rite celebrated their divine mysteries. He observed the subtle differences between a Roman Catholic sanctuary and this one's abundant iconography found in all directions. He sat in one of the many individual, high-backed, wooden pew chairs and prayed for a few moments.

As so often happens during prayer and meditation, thoughts naturally drift to and merge with other thoughts. Even for a disciplined priest, Michael found his meditation turning to his current quest, and what it might mean in the greater scheme of things. Treasure was of little interest to him, but there were greater rewards ahead; he felt it. Maybe his desires in piecing together this current puzzle were more an indication of piecing together his own life, like his future in the priesthood, or his relationship with Hana. Where it was all heading, he hadn't a clue. But for now, at this moment in this church, he was at peace.

Moments later, he got up, joined the others, and turned his full attention to the map.

Opening his iPhone, he pulled up images of Simon's translated notes of the silver scroll, then began piecing together identifiable landmarks and named places. The others had each taken a section of the map, transferring it wirelessly using AirDrop to study on their own phones. With two million stone tiles, there was much literal ground to cover.

Aaron was keen on finding established patterns on both the map and the scroll notes, assuming no one else would have this kind of intimate opportunity to perform such historical matchmaking. He had to make the most of it.

As he gazed at the extraordinary mosaic stonework, making out town names and other ancient points of reference, he came across the words "Acel Dama," and something recognizable sparked in his mind.

"Hey, Michael...does 'Acel Dama' sound familiar to you in any way? I know it from somewhere, but it's eluding me."

Michael came up next to him, peering at the map. Aaron pointed down at the two words appearing on the floor mosaic. Aaron could almost hear his friend's mental gears turning as he considered the phrase.

"Yes, now you mention it..." the priest nodded, speaking slowly. "It's not spelled the same, but Scripture tells us Judas Iscariot died in a town called 'Akeldama' in the Hinnom Valley. That's what it was famous for, anyway, that and the abominable, fiery sacrifices of the children of apostate Jews to a pagan god called Moloch. It's described in Second Chronicles, as I recall.

"Judas had been paid thirty pieces of silver for betraying Jesus, and when he tried in remorse to give the silver to the temple priests as atonement, they harshly refused it as 'blood money,' which couldn't go into the temple's treasury. Instead, they used it to buy a potter's field in which to bury foreigners and those not of the Jewish faith."

"Yes, that's it!" enthused Aaron quietly, now remembering the biblical passage himself. "And since then, it's been called the 'Field of Blood.' I *knew* it was familiar. And look here…" On his phone he pointed to Simon's notes which Michael had shared with him earlier. "It shows here on the scroll that, '*Thirty talents of silver can be found under the pillar on the northern side of the big cistern in Acel Dama.*' Now look on the map—there's the cistern, east of the Monastery of St. Onuphrius at Akeldama. I think we've found something here!"

Michael was growing excited, too. "Yes, I remember now. In Aramaic the name had various spellings, *Aceldama* and *Hakeldama* among them. I think you've hit on something here, Dr. Pearce!"

"Think we should take a brief side trip to the Hinnom Valley?" Aaron probed eagerly.

"Well, as long as we'll be in Jerusalem, why not? Let's keep looking for anything else here while we're at it."

"What's all the excitement going on over here?" Hana whispered, joining them after observing their animated behavior from across the room. Michael filled her in.

"You've got to be kidding!" she murmured rhetorically. "I smell another adventure in the air. Wait till Karl hears about this…" She casually walked over to her cousin and whispered in his ear.

With everyone now feeling renewed energy in their quest, they spent another hour trying to forge further connections with the map and the notes from the silver scroll, but little more came of it.

As they walked back to the nearby train station to return to Jerusalem, Michael's phone rang. It was Sarah.

"We've got some news here, Michael," she stated matter-of-factly. "Are you sitting down?"

"Walking, with no place to sit. But I promise I won't fall. What have you got?"

"Well, as Yossi was surveilling Khalid Zadani late last night, he observed two military types apprehend him and toss him into a panel van. They were also carrying something visibly quite heavy in a backpack, one they did not have before meeting up with Zadani, so it must be his. Though it's only intuition, Yossi suspects it might be some of the treasure. Oh, and I have the silver scroll now, too," she said impassively, as if it were no big deal.

Michael stopped in his tracks. The others did as well, noticing the shocked look on his face.

"Good grief, Sarah, you buried the lede!" Michael exclaimed, nearly shouting with exuberance. "You should have started with that!"

She went on to tell him of her encounter with Remi Shapiro, and of his relationship to a televangelist named Darwin who's in contention for all the scrolls.

"We are well aware of this Darwin character, Michael. He has an unsavory reputation at the IAA, and most museums here won't even let him visit their galleries, afraid he might poach their exhibited artifacts from wealthy lenders. I should say I'm surprised he's heard about these scrolls by now, but I'm not. He has moles everywhere in the antiquities market."

"Yes, it's surprising how fast word is spreading about these things," Michael exclaimed.

"Well, the ancient artifacts world here is small, and rife with rumors," Sarah replied. "And when something like this is in the wind, everyone hears about it. It's like chum in the water attracting sharks."

"So, *you* have the silver scroll now! But what about the parchments?"

"Parchments? What parchments?" Sarah asked, a mix of concern and interest in her voice.

"Four parchments were discovered with the silver scroll. Simon has seen them all and took photographs of them. But who knows what they reveal? It would be good to have them, regardless."

"All I found on Remi was the silver scroll," she said. "I wonder where they could be?"

CHAPTER
NINETEEN

As the train back to Jerusalem slowed through the winding twists and turns of the Judean Hills, Michael and Hana, sitting together, stared out the window, taking in the desolate yet historically romantic landscape. The locomotive lazily made sharp right turns followed by sharp left turns, back and forth, motions giving them a feeling that the train was navigating an intricate maze through tangled shrubs and thorny bushes as it made its way through deep wadis and across the desert terrain. Long-abandoned railway stations of crumbling old limestone reinforced the notion that they were far removed from civilization, akin to what it must have felt like to pilgrims of those early centuries traveling on foot to the Holy City.

"It's breathtaking, isn't it? Looking out over the land Jesus once walked," Michael asked Hana in a sleepy whisper. She looked up at him, the toing and froing of the train making her drowsy.

"It is, yes. I'm so glad you let me come with you. I wouldn't have missed this for the world. Such history all around us, and yet another grand crusade with my favorite traveling companion."

"Surely we're more than just that by now…" Michael murmured with a smile, also taken in by the rocking motions of their journey. After all, they had known each other going on four years now, and through all the shared adventures each had saved the other's life, and more. And all in spite of the obvious limitations placed on him as a priest—boundaries which had been tested many times.

"Of course, we are," Hana replied softly, her hand reflexively reaching for his arm in assurance. "I've never had a relationship quite like what we have, Michael. And I doubt I'll have another like it, which makes it that much more…uncommon."

"Uncommon it is," he conceded, "and I wouldn't trade it for anything. Or you." As their eyes met, something subtly amorous passed between them. Without warning, Hana's eyes betrayed her sudden desire. Sensing it, Michael returned her gaze with restrained longing, instantly feeling impious in the act. It lasted the barest of moments, but both were aware of what had transpired.

So much for 'just being friends,' Michael thought, recalling their last real discussion on the matter. *What am I doing?!*

He sat up a little taller in his seat and cleared his throat. She gave his arm a last squeeze, then pulled hers back, hesitantly, letting it rest on her lap.

"What time is it?" she asked, brushing her hair back with her hand.

Michael glanced at his watch, now wide awake. "Two o'clock. We should be in the city in a half hour. Got plans for dinner?"

Hana laughed, breaking the tension. "Let me check my calendar…uh, nope. All free. Were we planning to go to the monastery today, or…?"

"Yeah, there's still time to do it justice. Then we'll find a wonderful restaurant and end the day properly."

"Sounds good to me," Hana said, a touch of wistfulness in her voice.

A KILOMETER SOUTH of Jerusalem's Western Wall lies the ancient stone Monastery of St. Onuphrius, now home to a small community of Greek Orthodox nuns. Oral tradition has it that most of the apostles hid there, in an earlier, since-destroyed structure, following the Roman apprehension of Jesus at nearby Gethsemane.

As Mithraism gave way to Christianity in the late third and early fourth century, Brother Onuphrius emerged as one of the prominent Desert Monks who lived in the Roman province of Upper Egypt, and with other hermits and wise men of the time, he had a major influence on the development of Christianity as he spread the gospel in the desert. Much like other ascetic monks, Onuphrius was notable for his long, luxuriant beard extending the entire length of his body, which—

apart from a loincloth composed of leaves and grasses—served as his only "garment."

Perched on a hillside overlooking Jerusalem, in the old potter's field of Akeldama called the "Field of Blood," the monastery still stands over a honeycomb of underground tombs and burial caves filled with thousands of bones of early pilgrims who came to visit the Holy City, but never survived to return to their homes. The routine loss of life was so great that crusaders known as the Knights Hospitallers built an underground charnel house there to store the remains of over fifty patients who died every day in the Old City's Knights of St. John Hospital.

As THEY MADE their way to St. Onuphrius Monastery by taxi, Michael, Hana, Aaron and Karl reviewed their collective notes and maps describing the location of the supposed treasure buried near the nunnery.

"'Thirty talents of silver can be found under the pillar on the northern side of the big cistern in Acel Dama,'" Aaron again read aloud. "Do you think they'll really let us dig on their property?"

Everyone looked at Michael for an answer. "Well, I don't know!" he said in mock defense. "But surely, we can ask. The worst that can happen is they say *no*." Having driven the steep, winding dirt road up the hill through the monastery gate, the taxi discharged its passengers, then sped off, leaving a plume of dust in its wake. Looking up, the team took in the many buildings terraced upward on the hills, their pale brown façades blending into the arid desert landscape surrounded by tall green cypresses and fat, gnarled olive trees.

Approaching what appeared to be the main entrance, Hana knocked on the faded oak door. A few moments later, she knocked again.

"They likely don't get many visitors," she said.

Suddenly, they heard an inside latch being unfastened, and the door opened a crack. Standing in the narrow opening was a pretty young nun in a cornflower blue habit, her matching blue eyes peaceful but wary. Michael stepped forward, speaking to her in Hebrew.

"Good afternoon, Sister. My name is Father Michael Dominic. We have come from Rome to visit Jerusalem and, among other things, see some of the religious sites your city offers. Obviously, you live here on sacred land with a rich history, and we were hoping to just walk around your property for a while, taking in the experience of Akeldama. Might we have your permission to do so?"

The young nun's wariness turned to a more welcoming demeanor as she opened the door wider, and a soft smile appeared on her face.

"I speak English if that makes it more convenient for you, Father," she said. "Our Mother Superior is not here at the moment, and she is the one from whom you would seek permission." She glanced behind her furtively, "but as she is unavailable, I see no problem with your visiting our grounds. I cannot permit you inside, if that is acceptable."

"Of course, I completely understand. And thank you! We won't be long. We only want to walk around, get a spiritual feeling for the place." He felt slightly disingenuous in the ruse, but it wasn't entirely a false statement. As a religious historian, he wanted the mystical experience as well.

"Enjoy your time here, then, Father." As she was about to close the door, Aaron spoke up.

"Excuse me, Sister, but have you seen an old cistern on your land here?"

"Yes," she replied without hesitation, "it's about a hundred meters east of where you now stand." She pointed in that direction, smiled, then closed the door, refastening the inside latch.

Smiling eagerly, Aaron turned and led the group across the drive and through the chaparral to the area of the cistern. Several moments later—while they all tried to appear as though they were casually taking in the rest of the scenery and didn't have any particular agenda to locate the cistern—they found the now-dry water tank composed of original Herodian period stones covered with thick brush and desert grasses. Carved deep into the bedrock and lined with plaster on the inside, this reservoir, like many throughout the ancient kingdom of Israel, once provided clean water to support early desert-dwelling communities.

"So, what now?" Karl asked, ambling around the brush. "Isn't there supposed to be a big pillar on the northern side? I see nothing."

"Well, that's what the scroll said," Michael noted. "But let's face it, after two thousand years, things have obviously changed. And who knows, the treasure may have already been dug up and pillaged."

As the four walked around the cistern looking for remnants of a pillar, they heard the approach of motor vehicles, more than one, coming from lower down the hill they had come up in the taxi.

"Think the Mother Superior travels in a motorcade?" Hana asked wryly.

They watched as two white Land Rovers appeared in the driveway, circled around, and came to a stop. Several brawny men, military types, emerged from each vehicle and gathered around one man who appeared to be in charge. All at once, they turned and looked directly at Michael and the others.

Karl cursed under his breath. "It's Colonel Scarpa again! What's *he* doing here?"

CHAPTER

TWENTY

"Come, Papa, we must pack up our things and head to the airport soon," Rachel Ginzberg shouted to her father from another room in their family's guesthouse.

"Yes, yes, I'll be along soon, my dear," the old man replied from the dining table as he bent over digital images of the pale-yellow parchments that had captured his attention that morning.

Earlier, Rachel and her family had gone out to take in some sights of the Old City while Simon stayed back at the house. Having quiet time on his hands, he turned to the images he'd taken of the old parchments that had accompanied the silver scroll, something he hadn't done before that moment. Intrigued by their provenance, he had intended to review them earlier, but family obligations had occupied him. Now that he was alone, he fell into his comfortable pattern of transliteration and discovery.

As he continued scratching out his renderings from Aramaic to English on a notepad, the fascination of life in those earlier times captivated him, as it always did. And here he was, learning much more about the lives of the Essenes on documents which few others yet even knew existed! He considered his good fortune at having the opportunity appear to him quite by providence and was eager to reveal his findings in a paper he planned to publish on the discoveries once he returned to Rome.

But as he continued transcribing the second of four parchments, the words he was writing began to take on new meaning as he realized what he was actually reading. His earlier slower, studied pace picked up as new translated words now fell onto the notepad—important words, words painting an incredible picture.

This just can't be! Could these things really be true?!

How could they not? he answered himself cogently. He already knew part of the story he was reading. Scholars had struggled for years with this! Yet here it was, proof of what had previously only been conjecture, now laid down in the clean, uniform glyphs of those long-ago scribes in the caves of Wadi Murabba'at near Qumran, cousins of the famed Dead Sea Scrolls themselves. And if carbon dating and other analysis confirmed its apparent provenance, this plain parchment would be *far* more valuable than even the silver scroll itself.

Simon sat back, his aching neck longing for relief. Stretching his head from side to side, he both marveled at and struggled over the explosive images that lay before him on simple parchment pages the color of wheat. He set down his pencil and considered what to do. His travel arrangements with Rachel prevented him from staying in Jerusalem to further explore this incredible turn of events himself.

But of course, he knew someone who could.

He must tell Michael Dominic.

"PASTOR *DARWIN?*" Gloria drawled on, emphasizing the end of most every statement as if it were a question, "I was *finally* able to get you and your family that private VIP tour of the Temple Mount? The three-thousand-dollar fee has been paid on your church account, but you need to show up promptly at one o'clock tomorrow, and the girls have to wear long skirts or pantsuits to cover up their legs, though they don't need a scarf. And you cain't bring a Bible or anything. You cain't even *pray* in the Temple Mount, for Pete's sake! It's against the *rules?* So, your tickets will be waiting at the box office or whatever they call it...you know, wherever you get your tickets? Your private tour guide is a gentleman named Levi Samuel. Now there's a good Christian name for you, right out of the Bible!"

Seven thousand miles away Gabriel Darwin listened absently, admiring his freshly manicured nails as his secretary droned on. "Thank you, Gloria, I appreciate the effort. Now, have you heard from Remi yet? He hasn't called me in a day or two and I need to hear from him. For some reason, I cain't get through to his cell phone from here."

"Well, no, I haven't," she replied, now worried. "Do you think he got himself into some sorta trouble? Ya know, I've *heard* these stories—"

"No, I doubt he's in any trouble. Though it's possible. Anyway, keep tryin' to reach him, will ya? Tell him I'm waitin' and he can reach me day or night. And while you're at it, tell him to send me photographic images of those parchments so I can see 'em."

"Will do, Pastor. Y'all have a pleasant visit to the Temple Mount now, hear? Maybe you could bring me back one of those cute little snow globes?"

Darwin ended the call.

AT THAT VERY MOMENT, Remi Shapiro was sitting in the chic Gatsby Cocktail Room near Zion Square sucking down his second Red Snapper—a Bloody Mary laced with double gin rather than vodka—as he drowned his sorrows for having lost the silver scroll to a Mossad agent. Well, at least he still had the parchment scrolls. He was lucky he wasn't in jail again, though. He'd done enough time in the joint for one life.

Maybe Pastor Darwin would be happy with just the parchments, he considered. Not that anything important was likely to be on them. Parchments were practically a dime a dozen on the black market.

The phone in his pocket rang. Taking it out, he saw it was the pastor's secretary.

"Hi, Gloria," he answered glumly.

"Hey, Remi. Listen, Pastor Darwin is trying to

contact you but isn't getting through. Maybe something to do with you both being in Israel? Anyhoo, first, he wants you to email him photos of the parchments you have. Second, he really needs to see you, and I know they'll all be at the Temple Mount tomorrow at one o'clock. So, meet him there, yeah? Good, I'll let him know. Bye now."

"But—" he managed, but she had already hung up, not giving Shapiro a chance to say a thing. She'd rolled over him nonstop.

Just like everyone rolled over him, he thought gloomily. The drinks were having a morose effect on his attitude. *I don't have the spine for this. I should sell these parchments myself and be done with it.*

CHAPTER

TWENTY-ONE

Michael smiled at the sight of Colonel Scarpa standing by the Land Rovers. Sneaking about to uncover ancient treasure, even with the best of intentions, could have unwanted consequences, but as head of the Swiss Guard, the colonel was highly regarded by the pope himself. Here could be the ally they might need.

However, Karl couldn't believe the odds of encountering his commander yet again in Jerusalem, first at the Wailing Wall in the Old City. And now, of all places, at this ancient monastery tucked away in the hills above the city. The Swiss guardsman, now dubious about the coincidence, suspected something more than met the eye.

As he approached the colonel's entourage from a distance, it initially appeared as if Niccolò Scarpa was getting back in his SUV, ducking his head down as if not wanting to be recognized. Then—in apparent resignation of his plight, knowing he *must* have been seen by his young sergeant—he slowly reemerged from the vehicle, then made his way to the group, with several of his lieutenants following him.

"Colonel Scarpa! This is either incredibly serendipitous or…well, I don't know what else to say," Karl said as amiably as he could.

"Yes, interesting to see you again too, Dengler," the red-faced commandant managed. "What are *you* doing way out here?"

"In all candor, sir, and with no disrespect, I might ask you the same thing."

Both men were silent as they held each other's gaze, their respective teams standing behind them, aware of what was visibly an awkward moment.

"Okay, look," Scarpa began, accepting the situation. "The truth is, I've come across information that an important document, a silver scroll, has recently been discovered here in Israel, and it may contain knowledge of a long-lost treasure connected to, or even belonging to, an organization of which I have been a member for a very long time. In fact, I am currently its leader. I'm afraid I cannot go into more detail about it with you, Sergeant, but in effect, it is important that we find this treasure, for many reasons."

"Well, as it happens, Colonel, *we* are looking for the same treasure!" He waved a hand to his companions, who were now approaching as well. "Which at least accounts for us having bumped into each other twice now."

"You're aware of the Mithraists' treasure?!" Scarpa asked with amazement.

"*Mithraists?* We understood it to be King Solomon's treasure. But how do you even know about *them?*" Karl exclaimed, now thoroughly befuddled.

Hearing the cult's name mentioned, Aaron quickly stepped forward.

"Colonel Scarpa, I'm Dr. Aaron Pearce, a friend of Father Dominic's from Loyola University. I couldn't help but overhear you say that you were the leader of an organization whose name you preferred not to mention. But, given these circumstances, I must conclude that you speak for the legendary Mithraists. Am I correct?" Aaron knew he was taking an enormous leap posing such a question, since he had assumed Mithraism to be long dead. But there *were* those rumors…

Scarpa looked up at the scholar with mild shock, carefully evaluating his response. He reached out his arm.

"Very good to meet you, Dr. Pearce," he said somewhat reluctantly as they shook hands. "I had not intended to reveal my personal identity—well, beyond my relationship with Sergeant Dengler and the Pontifical Swiss Guard, that is—but your astute assumption is correct. I do have the honor of being the *Pater* of a 'new' global Mithraist movement. Since you appear to know about it, though, it's important to note that this incarnation does not at all challenge Christianity, as in past manifestations. No, our goals are much more firmly aligned with broad support for soldiers in our constituent member countries, regardless of faith or creed. We provide a special form of camaraderie for members of our mithraea; though similar to its ancient roots, a secret—some might even call it sacred—brotherhood is involved. You might equate it to the Freemasons, for example, with its attendant rites and rituals, and with no improprieties."

Aaron was jubilant at hearing this, and his enthusiasm showed. "I have so many questions for you," he said admiringly.

Scarpa was taken aback by both the man's knowledge and his unbridled interest. "Well, I'm afraid those will have to wait for now since, given our mutual aim here, I have rather pressing questions of my own. Tell me, have you found anything yet? And how did *you* come across knowledge of the treasure we both seek?"

Before answering, Michael carefully considered how much he should share with Scarpa. He knew the pope trusted the man implicitly, and that was a hard feat for anyone in the Vatican to have achieved. So, he saw no reason to hold out on Scarpa; indeed, the more he knew, the more likely he might be of help in Michael's team's own endeavors.

"Colonel, if I may?" the priest said, stepping up next to Aaron. "That's a rather long story..." He told Scarpa about Dr. Simon Ginzberg's involvement through a colleague in Tel Aviv, of their getting Simon's translations of the silver scroll, about the murder of the antiquities dealer Ishak Ramzi and their visit to the Madaba Map in Jordan, of their Mossad colleagues ultimately gaining the scroll itself, and through Yossi and Sarah, what little they knew about the capture of someone named Khalid Zadani and the obscure involvements of people named Remi Shapiro and Pastor Gabriel Darwin.

"However it happened, it seems too many people already know about these scrolls, and a wider hunt, born out by the sighting of armed men then kidnapping Zadani, appears to be on for this long-lost treasure," he finished.

"Well, as for Zadani," Scarpa said, "that was my team who picked him up as he was excavating one location mentioned in the scroll. We managed to acquire several gold bars from him—gold which rightfully belongs to the Mithraists, since it was our group who buried it two thousand years ago. And that largesse will help fund our global activities to support underpaid soldiers whose families need our help. There is no personal gain for us in this endeavor. Our only goal is to serve our constituent members. And we have far more than you might imagine, Father Dominic. But you spoke of this 'Madaba Map.' Can you tell me more about it?"

Michael explained the details of their visit to the sixth-century mosaic in the Church of Saint George and offered to share his images of both the map and Simon's translations, if that would help their cause.

"We aren't in this for the treasure itself, frankly," Michael admitted. "It was a fascinating historical exercise for all of us, but to be honest, your charitable mission makes far more sense, assuming you're prepared to deal with the Israeli authorities. That, of course, is entirely your decision."

"Yes, thank you. I'll attend to that as needed. And I appreciate your generosity in sharing this valuable information. I'm truly grateful." Then, turning to Karl, Scarpa added, "And Sergeant Dengler, I would certainly encourage you to become a member of our Rome mithraeum, if you'd like. Membership is by invitation only, and you must adhere to certain secrecy requirements. But you're the type of candidate we want—and I'm sure your colleague Lukas Bischoff would qualify as well." He smiled knowingly at the young soldier.

Karl was stunned to hear Lukas's name mentioned by their commandant. *Did he know about their relationship?!* he wondered apprehensively.

Sensing an awkward moment for her cousin, Hana came forward and introduced herself to Scarpa, adding, "So, Colonel... shouldn't we all be looking for the silver bars we came here for? I assume that's why you're here?"

"Yes, of course," he said, clearing his throat. "Have you found the cistern yet?"

"We have," Aaron confirmed, "but the pillar is missing, and we were just about to dig when you showed up."

Moments later, the whining engine of an old blue and white Volkswagen Minibus struggled its way up the long dirt drive and parked in front of the entrance to the monastery. Two nuns stepped out, one with a grim look on her face as she stared harshly at the congregation of trespassers.

"Ten to one, that's the Mother Superior," Hana suggested, "and she doesn't look very welcoming." The two women approached them, lifting the hems of their habits so as not to get them caught on the thorny bushes and tall weeds littering the grounds. She addressed them in Hebrew.

"May I ask what you are doing on our property?" she inquired sternly.

Michael stepped forward, his arms raised in submission, replying in her language.

"Reverend Mother, I am Father Michael Dominic, from the Vatican. My friends and I were admiring your beautiful monastery. I was explaining to them some of its remarkable history. We had no intention of intruding, but we did get permission from one of your sisters earlier. We were just about to leave, actually."

The steely nun was in no mood to receive uninvited guests.

"Now that you've had your visit, Father, you may go. Good day," she snapped, then abruptly swung around, lifted the hem of her habit, and joined her companion returning to the nunnery.

"Well, she told you!" Hana chuckled. "Reminds me of my days in high school. Makes me shudder thinking about the nuns back then." She rubbed her hands together, massaging her knuckles at the memory.

"Yes, well, I think we'd better be on our way," Michael murmured, chastened by the bad-tempered woman.

"But...but there's still treasure to be had!" Aaron protested.

"We can always come back under cover of darkness," Karl suggested. "Like the kind of mission I was trained for." He glanced at his commander.

"That's not a bad idea, Sergeant," Colonel Scarpa

agreed. "Once they're tucked in for the night, I'll give you a couple of my men to help. Given that Khalid Zadani kindly 'gave' us the eleven bars of gold he found in the Old City, there's a good chance the silver bars mentioned in the scroll might very well be within easy reach of where we now stand."

The group looked around at each other, the excitement of the hunt clear on their collective faces. Suddenly a loud humming was heard from someone's phone. Everyone checked their pockets to see if it was theirs, at which point Michael pronounced, "It's mine." He answered it.

"Michael, this is Simon!" the old man said feverishly. "Are you in a place where you can speak freely?"

"Sure, Simon, go ahead." The priest instinctively moved away from the others and lowered his voice. His old friend was excited about something.

"Michael, I finally found some time this morning to read and translate two of those parchments that were found with the silver scroll. You have something most incredible here. But since I'm about to head back to Rome, there's nothing I can do about it. For that matter, there's really nothing *to* be done! It's just...remarkable!"

"What is it, Simon?"

"Most of these parchments were written by the Essenes in the early first century. They go into some detail confirming early biblical passages and so forth. One, in fact, specifies its author as Saul of Tarsus—who we also know as Paul the Apostle from Tarsus, who became St. Paul! And what he wrote made my hair stand on end."

"And that is?"

"Michael, it reads, *'Y'shua bar Yosef, Miriam, Mariamene e Mara of Magdala, Yose, and Yehuda bar Yeshua, were all entombed together here in Jerusalem.'*"

Stone cold silence bridged the gap as both men waited for the other to say something.

"Are you still there, Michael?"

"I am, Simon, yes. I'm trying to process the implications of what you just said."

"Well, I can assure you, it's perfectly clear to me: St. Paul himself asserts that Jesus, Mary Magdalene, and their son Judah, along with Jesus' mother, Mary, and his brother, Joseph, were all buried together in one tomb in Jerusalem!"

CHAPTER
TWENTY-TWO

"This is unbelievable, Simon," Michael said. "This changes *everything!* Do you think this somehow relates to Jerusalem's famed Talpiot tomb? The one proclaiming Jesus' family was buried there in several ossuaries?"

"It would indeed if what I've read here supports theories put forth by many scholars. Of course, that whole matter has been quite controversial for some years. But this document by St. Paul himself would surely confirm the assertion that, yes, that would be the 'Jesus Family Tomb.'"

Many progressive scholars believed the East Talpiot neighborhood of Jerusalem was the final resting place for Jesus of Nazareth, his mother Mary, his wife Mary Magdalene, his son Judah, his brother Joseph, and perhaps other relatives. But just as many scholars did not believe it. So far the only "proof" was mainly on epigraphs inscribed on the sides of six of ten ossuaries, or bone boxes, discovered in 1980. Those epigraphs neatly named the deceased as Jesus and his family. However, all the names inscribed on the ossuaries were very common for the period. So, some saw this as merely a coincidence. Others saw the exact names of Jesus' family being all together in what was clearly a family tomb, as all the proof they needed. Now, here was substantiation from St. Paul himself!

Simon continued, his voice displaying the awe of the implications. "But this affirms that it was not just where his family was buried, but Jesus himself! Who has those parchments now, Michael?"

For the moment, Michael couldn't allow himself to consider the possible humanity of Jesus and the fallibility of the Resurrection. He had dealt with such doubts before, like when the Magdalene veil had been discovered in a previous adventure that had shaken his faith. He'd dealt with those personal doubts then; but now...Pope Ignatius's very legacy could be shaken if...

"Michael?"

"Oh, yes, well, Sarah took the silver scroll from someone named Remi Shapiro, who's an agent for an American televangelist, or so she told me. That seems odd, frankly; but she mentioned nothing about the parchments. I wonder if Shapiro still has those."

"A televangelist, you say?" The old scholar sounded simultaneously skeptical and curious. "Tell me, what was his name?"

"Sarah said his name was Gabriel Darwin."

Simon paused briefly as he considered this, then sighed. "Michael, Darwin is a notorious and very wealthy collector of biblical antiquities. He has some sort of museum in Texas featuring thousands of manuscripts, pottery, ossuaries and other biblical artifacts, much of which has sketchy provenance or illicit acquisition issues. And he has a reputation for throwing money at problems that stand in the way of his getting such items. If he's involved in any way with these parchments, he cannot be trusted to do the right thing. He's been a thorn in the side of the IAA for years.

"And despite its supposed treasure locations, that silver scroll is *nothing* compared to the content of at least this one of these manuscripts. I'll translate the others when I return to Rome and will let you know if I find anything else substantive. Meanwhile, you *must* find those originals, Michael. This one manuscript alone is historically monumental. They should all be turned over to Israeli authorities at once, of course, and *not* sold on the black market." Simon was agitated over such an important discovery, fearful the parchments might end up in the wrong hands or vanish into some private collection.

"I'll speak with Sarah and Yossi and let you know what comes of it," Michael said. "Their resources are much more robust than ours."

"Yes, I imagine Mossad has far more inventive ways of handling such matters. Alright, I will leave it with you, then. We'll speak again soon, my young friend. Shalom for now."

WALKING through the Western Wall Plaza near the Old City, the hot afternoon sun beating down on them, Gabriel, Sue Ann and Tabitha Darwin pushed their way through the crowd of tourists heading toward the Mughrabi Gate, the only entrance to the Temple Mount complex allowed for use by non-Muslims. Hundreds of people of varying nationalities were lined up to visit the holy site, fanning themselves with hats or brochures to fend off the oppressive heat. Though admission is free to everyone, Pastor Darwin had insisted on the exclusivity of a private tour, as much to avoid waiting in line as to enjoy the benefits of his wealth and privilege.

"We're supposed to meet our guide at some kinda ticket booth, Sue Ann, so be on the lookout for one," Darwin huffed. "The guy's name is Levi Something… something biblical, Gloria said… Samson, I think. Yeah, Levi Samson, that's it. I sure hope it's air conditioned inside. It's hotter than a stolen tamale out here."

Approaching a small building with a sign reading "Tickets," they spotted a thin, dark-skinned man holding a cardboard placard with the name "DARWIN" printed on it in black capital letters.

The pastor approached him. "You must be our tour guide. Levi, is it?"

"Yes, Mister Darwin! Levi Samuel, at your service," the man said in heavily accented English, smiling widely. Darwin noted he was missing a couple of teeth, but otherwise seemed pleasant enough.

"Can we go inside now, Daddy?" Tabitha whined. "I'm hot."

"You bet, darlin'. Lead the way, Levi. We're right behind you."

A voice not far away was heard shouting, *"Pastor Darwin! Pastor...?"*

Darwin turned around to see Remi Shapiro weaving his way through the mass of people crowding the plaza.

"Remi? What the hell you doin' here, boy?" Darwin shouted back, causing heads to turn. "Where've you been? I been tryin' to reach you for days."

Finally catching up to them, Remi was breathing heavily, sweat coursing down his face, his shirt soaked with perspiration.

"Whew, it's hotter here than hell's waiting room."

"That it is, my boy. Hey, what happened to your nose there? Well, anyway, we're about to go in and see the temple. Come on, join us. We can talk inside, where it's cooler."

Despite Remi's confused look on hearing this, Levi led them to the entry gate, where he presented his special access pass to a guard holding an Uzi submachine gun, then said to his guests, "The men must wear the kippah when visiting the temple site. Please, take one." He presented a stack of paper kippahs for the two men.

"I ain't wearin' no beanie!" Darwin declared. "I'm a Christian, not a Jew. What's this all about, Levi?"

"It is a show of respect, sir, and is compulsory for all men before entering the Temple Mount. You must wear it, or you cannot enter. But do not worry, they are provided free of charge."

Darwin sighed, then unfolded the white paper

yarmulke and placed it on his head. "Forgodsake, I look like a damn fool wearin' this thing. Get yourself one of these, Remi. I ain't doin' it alone."

Shapiro, a Jew himself, reached into his pocket and withdrew his own embroidered yarmulke. "I came prepared, boss."

Darwin looked at him skeptically, then drawled, "Alrighty, let's get this show on the road."

As Levi led them through the special gate to the plaza of the Temple Mount—past all the other tourists waiting in line owing to his clients' VIP tickets—he began describing its history. "In Hebrew, we call the Temple Mount *Har Habayit*, and it is traditionally believed to be where Abraham sacrificed his son Isaac to show his true devotion to God. The first temple was built by King Solomon but was destroyed in 586 BCE by the Babylonians. In the sixth century BCE a second temple was built, and stood on this spot for six hundred years before the Roman Siege of Jerusalem in 70 CE..." He continued explaining the history of the temples when Darwin suddenly interrupted him. "Well, where's the dang temple, Levi? I need to get my family outta this heat."

The guide was perplexed, looking at Darwin with confusion. "But sir, this *is* the holy site where the temples stood. They have both been destroyed. There is no 'inside.'"

"Well, what about this gigantic building here with the golden dome on top?"

"Oh, that is the Dome of the Rock, sir, an Islamic

shrine. Only Muslims are permitted entry to the Al-Aqsa Mosque."

Darwin rolled his eyes. "You mean we came all this way for nothin'?"

Levi looked at the man blankly, uncertain how to respond.

"Pastor," Remi began, trying to placate his boss, "what he says is true. No one other than a Muslim may enter the mosque. But, here we are at one of the holiest sites in the world, the famous Wailing Wall." He pointed to the western wall of the plaza, where a crush of people —including Orthodox Hassidim dressed all in black with long beards, curly *payes* side locks swinging from beneath their black Borsalinos as they rocked back and forth—were praying next to the Wall. "See, you can even write prayers on little slips of paper and fold them into the cracks of the Wall. It is a time-honored tradition."

"*Daddy!* It's too hot out here!" cried Tabitha.

Darwin groaned. "Levi, is there a snack bar or something around here where we can cool off for a bit?"

"Well, yes, the Holy Café is not far from here. Would you like me to take you there instead?"

"Yeah, that'd be a good idea."

As they turned to leave the Temple Mount plaza heading for the café, Remi was working his way up to telling the boss about losing the silver scroll when Darwin beat him to it.

"By the way, Remi. Where's that silver scroll? Did you bring it with you?"

"Uh, well, Pastor, I've been meaning to speak with

you about that," Shapiro began. "You see, I had it safe and sound in my hands when suddenly this female Mossad agent busts into my hotel room and punches me in the face." He pointed up toward his bruised nose as though it weren't already apparent. "And she pointed a gun at me, demanding that I give it to her. I had no choice, Pastor. She would have killed me! You can't imagine what those Mossad agents are like!"

Darwin was furious. "You got pistol-whipped by a *girl?!* Forgodsake, Remi. That's the whole reason we came here! You *need* to get it back. That was *my* property. Don't you have any contacts with the Israeli government?"

"Pastor, Mossad is practically an entire government in itself… They pretty much do what they want. No, I'm afraid the scroll is gone. But…" He briefly struggled with whether he should tell Darwin about the parchments or keep them for himself—then gave in. He could always get parchments if he wanted, but keeping a free-spending whale like Darwin as a client, that he couldn't chance losing. That church of his was a gold mine.

"'*But*' what, Remi?"

"Oh, right. I meant to say that…well, the silver scroll came with four parchments the Mossad agent didn't get. Those were found in the same cave, too."

"Those all came out of a *cave?* I don't recall you mentioning that." Darwin was accustomed to his archeological discoveries being usually 'unearthed' out of someone else's collection. "So, that means no one has ever even seen them yet, yeah? Well, Remi, that's a horse of a different color! Let's see those parchments."

"I have them back at the hotel, Pastor. I'll get them to you before you leave. When *are* you leaving, by the way?"

"We got another couple o' days yet. Sue Ann and I are preachin' at one of our Jewel Ark Chapels here in Jerusalem tomorrow night, over in what they call the Christian Quarter. Why don't you meet us there? Bring the parchment scrolls then, too. I can't wait to see 'em. In fact, just email me copies of 'em right now, so I can have my guy back in Dallas look at 'em."

Shapiro did as he was told, selecting the four parchment images from his phone and emailing them to his boss. *Well, the decision's been made for me, then. They're all his now. Hopefully that placates him enough since there is no way that I can get that silver scroll back.*

CHAPTER
TWENTY-THREE

Night had fallen over Jerusalem, and from the hills of Akeldama Karl, along with Jake and Saul, the two men Scarpa had sent with him, looked down over the Old City, the golden Dome of the Rock above the Al-Aqsa Mosque glowing brightly in the distance.

Colonel Scarpa had impressed upon them the urgency of acting sooner than later, since it was now apparent that more people had become aware of the silver scroll's content in recent days. The clock was ticking if others were also in on the chase.

The monastery gate had been closed for the evening, and they had easily worked their way around it through the surrounding unfenced brush land, heading for the cistern and the prospect of finding a literal ton of silver —or at least as much as they could carry down to their Land Rover parked at the bottom of the dirt drive. *If* they found any silver at all.

They each had brought shovels and reinforced duffel bags, hoping since the map had been right once so far, it could be right again.

Reaching the cistern, Karl snapped on a dim red torchlight so they could work without drawing much attention to themselves. The area was far enough away from the nunnery that they weren't too concerned about being discovered.

"The scroll said *'Thirty talents of silver can be found under the pillar on the northern side of the big cistern,'* so that's where we start. Obviously, the pillar is gone now, so we'll start digging to the north, right about here." Karl shone the torch on the designated spot, its scarlet beam exposing red clay and volcanic basalt beneath the dry chaparral.

Jake and Saul began digging while Karl held the torch, keeping an eye out for wandering nuns.

Twenty minutes had passed, finding nothing more than earth and stone. Karl handed the torch to Saul as he joined Jake to continue digging a farther bit north and wider, since the instructions weren't very specific.

"See how red the soil is here?" Saul noted gravely as he sat aiming the light on it. "They say it is because of all the human blood spilled here. In fact, Akeldama literally means 'field of blood.' In the Bible, Matthew says it is Jesus' blood, while Luke claims it to be Judas' blood, for he died on this very spot. This is sacred ground we are tampering with."

Jake was more pragmatic than philosophical. "Well, hopefully soon it will be a field of silver." He reached up to wipe away the sweat from his brow.

At that moment a bright spotlight flickered on from the roof of the monastery, flooding the surrounding landscape with light. The three men instantly fell to the ground, ducking behind bushes. Saul snapped off the red torchlight. Then the front door opened.

A nun emerged from the entrance, someone Karl recognized from earlier—the Mother Superior. And she had a dog with her on a leash, its bushy white tail curled forward over its back as it wandered around, seeking the perfect place to relieve itself.

As they lay in the bush, some ninety meters from the door, Saul barely whispered, "That's a Canaan dog. The Bedouins used them to guard their herds and camps. Do not move or make any sound." As if they needed to be told.

The nun lit a cigarette, waiting for the dog to do its thing, then turned and glanced in the cistern's direction. Karl was praying hard that they would not be discovered.

Moments later, they watched as the dog suddenly stood poised, likely alert to their presence. They heard a growl, then a bark. The dog was staring in their direction! It barked again, then again. The nun, apparently accustomed to false alarms—stray polecats, night birds, sand cats and such—admonished it in Hebrew, stubbed out her cigarette in a pot on the porch, then pulled the dog back inside and closed the door. A moment later, the floodlight was extinguished.

"Whew. That was close." Karl exhaled. "Jake, your turn to hold the torch."

Saul joined Karl in continuing to dig. Another hour

passed, the digging getting deeper and wider north of the cistern, when suddenly Saul's light shone on something unusually shiny in the hole.

"Wait!" he whispered excitedly. "There! Something under that rock. What is that?"

Seeing the object, Karl bent down, pulled out the covering rock, and wiped away some of the excess dirt. The torch's light shone on something shiny, buried deeper. Karl dug his shovel beneath it, rocking it back and forth to loosen it. Reaching down, he pulled out one oblong piece of something heavy. Saul shone the light on it.

It was pure silver!

Karl looked up into the faces of both men, smiling. *"Eureka!"* he whispered jubilantly. "That's what Archimedes said when he discovered how to determine the purity of gold—and this is as good a moment!" He let the bar bounce in his hands a few times, taking the measure of its weight. "I'd say this is easily five kilos. Look, there's more!" Handing the bar to Jake, he shoved his spade into the earth again. Now two more bars poked out from the red clay.

"The colonel is going to be thrilled," Saul said. "Let's keep digging and load up as much as we can in the duffels, then fill the hole back in and cover it with brush. If that scroll is correct and nearly a thousand kilos of silver might be buried here, it's not going anywhere any time soon. We can always come back later."

∿

Pastor Gabriel Darwin's "guy" in Dallas was Dr. Leon Becker, curator of the Biblical Hall Museum and a respected scholar in Hebrew manuscripts and period artifacts of the Roman Empire. Having received the images of the parchments the pastor had sent him, he printed them out then went about the translation process, not knowing much more about the scrolls than what lay before him. Becker, like Darwin, usually preferred to not know the origins of the artifacts that the good Pastor "procured" for the museum.

As he began reading the first of the parchments, morning coffee in hand, it was clear he was dealing with original manuscripts of the Essenes, which fueled his interest in them significantly as being among the oldest documents he had yet dealt with and the closest in relation to actual scriptural events and people of the early biblical era. Within two hours, Dr. Becker had read through three of the four parchments and his enthusiasm could hardly be contained.

Then he came to the fourth parchment, and his mind reeled.

No, this cannot be! No…! Am I truly reading a letter in the hand of St. Paul himself?! This is…inconceivable! The content is simply extraordinary…

With shaking hands, he lay the papers down on his desk. He glanced at the clock on his office wall. Just past ten. Which made it just past six in the evening in Jerusalem. The boss's event started at seven-thirty, but he might be able to reach him beforehand and give him the good news.

Pastor Darwin was going to be one lucky man.

CHAPTER
TWENTY-FOUR

K halid Zadani was despondent. After he had
been captured, kidnapped really, by an
apparent band of Mithraists—*Mithraists?! In
this day and age?*—he had returned to his hotel room,
grateful to still be alive, only to discover that, in his
absence, he had indeed been robbed. The silver scroll
and the parchments were now missing. Add to that all
the gold he had discovered that had been taken from
him by Scarpa, and his frustration was complete.

Who even knew he'd had the scrolls? He had told no
one, though he wouldn't put it past that scoundrel Abu
Tariq to somehow manage a reacquisition ploy. Dealing
in ancient antiquities was an often-unscrupulous business, the underbelly of the rare arts market, and he had
dealt with an entire cast of shady characters throughout
his career. He would have gotten out of it altogether if it
weren't so lucrative, so easy to manipulate eager buyers
who wanted their own treasured piece of holy history.

Speaking of which, he had yet to translate those four small parchments that had accompanied the silver scroll. He assumed they were unlikely to contain anything of significance, since the vast majority that had been found were penned by scribes whose job it was to duplicate other writings, the equivalent of modern-day copier machines. Many times, the more interesting notations were found in marginalia—little doodles, ciphers or symbols meaningful only to each scribe which appeared in the outside margins of a manuscript.

But as Zadani now continued reading one particular parchment scroll, enlarged on his iPad display, he had no interest whatsoever in marginalia, or even the silver scroll at this point. No, his interest was now consumed by what he was translating from Aramaic—by the words, *"Y'shua bar Yosef, Miriam, Mariamene e Mara of Magdala, Yose, and Yehuda bar Yeshua, were all entombed together here in Jerusalem."*

He read it once, then reread it carefully, letter by letter, making sure his transliteration was absolutely correct. Then he discovered its author.

Praise be Allah! Zadani was dumbstruck. Of all the historically important manuscripts he had ever dealt with—and those were many—*nothing* had come close to reaching this level of global historical impact. That silver scroll required much more work by comparison. And that this shocker came from St. Paul himself... Well, you couldn't have a stronger provenance documenting Jesus' history—for Paul of Tarsus, a later apostle, was conceivably *there* at the time!

Zadani was certainly very familiar with the excavated and since resealed "Jesus Family Tomb" in the East Talpiot neighborhood of Jerusalem, the controversial spot many progressive scholars believed was the final resting place for Jesus and his family.

But this...*this* affirming parchment—as close to a first-hand experience as one could get from the early-first century—changed everything, Zadani reasoned. It undermined the very basis of Christianity: that Jesus was taken up to heaven in body and spirit in Resurrection. He swallowed back the implications on millions of the faithful. And the impact on the powerful—and wealthy—Catholic Church who might want this proof buried. And be willing to pay extreme amounts to hide it.

First, however, he had to find the original. To retrieve it from whoever had it now. Who was that, though, and how would he find out?

Wait...

Security cameras! He opened the door to his room and glanced down the hall. At each end, the telltale inverted black dome of a hotel security camera clung to the ceiling.

Grabbing his wallet and room key, he made his way down to the concierge, who referred him to the security office down the hall. Only one person occupied the security desk, a dour young man clearly bored with his job.

"What can I help you with, sir?" he asked without interest. Zadani had already prepared his cover story.

"Yes, I am a guest here in 614, and someone broke into my room within the past two days and stole some very important documents from me. I am an archeologist working on behalf of the Israeli government, and those documents are part of an official state inquiry. The people we are investigating may have taken the papers to suppress evidence.

"I need to see your video coverage for the past forty-eight hours, please." He had palmed a two-hundred-shekel note and slid it over the edge of the countertop, his fingers splayed, revealing the denomination. "This is for your time, and I won't mention the matter of a security breach at your hotel."

After discreetly pocketing the cash, the young guard's mood shifted quickly to one of interest and accommodation as he pulled up the archived video feed for the days and room location in question. A few minutes later, they both watched as one man approached the door to 614. Then, apparently using lock-picking tools, he entered the room and closed the door. Zadani got a clear look at his face but did not recognize him.

Several minutes later, they saw a woman with her hair in a ponytail approach and stand by the door, her ear against it now, listening. Suddenly, her posture changed to one of a standing brace, her left foot behind the right. Then the door opened and, in a flash, her right arm lunged forward, visibly delivering a facial attack on whoever opened the door. Zadani was about to dismiss her, too, as unrecognizable, when he suddenly looked at her again, closely this time.

It was the ponytail. He was certain he had seen this woman before. But...where?

Madaba! The Church of Saint George in Madaba! That was it. Their eyes had met briefly as he was surveying the map mosaic. Who could fail to notice such an attractive woman?

First in Jordan, now a hundred kilometers away in Jerusalem? This was no coincidence. He was being followed. But why?

Zadani and the guard continued watching the video until they saw the woman leave the room, the leather pouch containing the silver scroll gripped firmly in her hand.

But he knew the parchment scrolls were too large for the leather pouch alone—so where were they? The video revealed a few minutes later the same man leaving Zadani's room, with a hand to his nose, wearing the same backpack he'd worn when entering. The man who broke into his room must still have them, he reasoned. But who was *he?*

Zadani did not appreciate being robbed or taken advantage of. He must get those parchments back at any cost.

"Tell me," he said to the security guard, "have you seen that man since then?"

There was a pause. "I'm, uh, not sure, sir...giving out that kind of information could get me in a lot of trouble..." He glanced up at the archeologist with a bland, expectant look on his face. Zadani sighed, then reached into his wallet, produced another two-hundred-shekel note, and tossed it on the desk. "Feeling less troubled now?" he scowled at the young man, who suddenly became quite chatty.

"That man is a registered guest in the hotel. He's been here for several days." The guard's fingers flew over the computer keyboard. A few moments later, he announced, "Mr. Remigius Shapiro, from Tel Aviv. He's in room 714, right above yours, in fact. For what it's worth, he's still checked in. Looks like he'll be with us for a few more days."

"Excellent. Thank you very much," said Zadani, a grim smile pursing his lips as he walked away.

So, it was not Abu Tariq after all. Which means his services could once again prove useful.

Having returned to his room, Zadani called the Egyptian military attaché—a more refined title for the discreet undercover spy that he was, a ruse typical of every country's diplomatic corps.

"Abu? Khalid Zadani here. Are you available over the next few days? Good. Here's what I need you to do…"

Listening in on their conversation at Mossad headquarters, Yossi Geffen was intrigued. Zadani's elaborate plan would likely succeed, he considered—unless it suffered an interruption. He picked up the phone and called Sarah.

"Shalom, my love. Do you have a moment? Good, then listen to this…" He replayed the recorded conversation between Zadani and Abu Tariq for her benefit, then spoke again. "I'm tied up here on another project for a while, but I think you should follow up on this and obstruct Zadani's plan to gain the parchments. Those

belong to Israel, and the IAA should handle their disposition. But if they make it across the Egyptian border, we
may never recover them. Perhaps take Hana with you,
and the Swiss Guard. Both could help with diversions if
you need them. And Karl can certainly handle himself if
it came to that."

CHAPTER

TWENTY-FIVE

"Check *this* out!" Karl said proudly, as he handed a tiny, oblong bar of silver to Hana as Michael and Aaron looked on, captivated. "We found loads of these north of the cistern, mostly much larger ones, as the scroll predicted. We could only carry so much out, though, so we took what we could in three duffels, then covered up the site with brush. The colonel can go back later if he wants, but I've given what help I could for now. He gave me this small bar as a token of his gratitude."

"So, there *was* silver on the grounds of Akeldama," Michael said, admiring the extraordinary find. "Given time, manpower and patience, this collective treasure— if indeed it is valued in the three-billion-dollar range— could make Colonel Scarpa and his Mithraists exceedingly wealthy. Assuming he can negotiate any jurisdictional and legal issues. Then I can only hope that it is earmarked as he stated, for the soldiers."

"You don't think he's being entirely honest?" Hana asked.

"Well, not necessarily. It's just that money in such staggering amounts can seduce people into rethinking their priorities, that's all. And by all rights, they really should turn this treasure over to the Israel Antiquities Authority. The law is clear on that. Unfortunately, unlike other countries, the Israeli government does not offer any kind of reward—only freedom from the punishment of going to prison if the finder fails to report their discovery and turns over what they found to the IAA. It's hardly motivation for treasure hunters to be honest and forthcoming, understandably, thus the lucrative black-market activity."

"Well, what should I do with this?" Karl asked apprehensively. "If I do report it, there are obviously going to be many questions about where it was found, and so forth. I can't expose my commandant like that!"

"Well, Karl, that's for you to consider," Michael advised. "Let's see what the next few days hold for us before deciding—but for now, let's keep quiet about that silver. Don't even tell Yossi and Sarah.

"But more importantly," the priest added, "I've been meaning to tell you what Simon told me about the parchments. He translated at least two of the four, and one of them is profoundly consequential—and I mean, greater than all the treasure combined, at least given its historical significance and far-reaching impact.

"The parchment was written by the Apostle St. Paul of Tarsus himself. It was penned in Aramaic, and clearly states that Jesus and Mary Magdalene, and their son

Judah, along with Jesus' mother, Mary, and his brother, Joseph, were all buried together in the same tomb in Jerusalem."

"*What?!*" Aaron exclaimed, leaping up from his chair. "That's insane! *St. Paul himself?!* And it appears genuine? You're absolutely sure?"

"Well, I have not seen the parchment in person myself, but I do have photographic images of them all on my phone, and Simon—who surely has the authority and credibility to evaluate such things—is certain it's legitimate. We were so focused on the gripping impact of the silver scroll's treasure hunt that no one had given any attention to the accompanying parchments. That is until Simon found a little free time before leaving Jerusalem to review and translate two of the manuscripts. And he was as shocked as you are. It certainly appears authentic, and its provenance is impeccable. And there is no doubt as to its being priceless.

"Moreover," Michael continued, "this would definitively confirm the legitimacy of what has been referred to as the Jesus Family Tomb in Jerusalem's East Talpiot neighborhood. Ten ossuaries were found entombed together in one burial chamber, six of them inscribed with Hebrew epigraphs for the names of Jesus, son of Joseph, Mary, Miriam—which was attributed to Mary Magdalene—Judah, Joseph, and Matthew. And of course, this significantly conflicts with the Resurrection, no small matter when it comes to the foundational beliefs of Christians worldwide. I *must* speak with the Holy Father about this."

"Where are the parchments now, Michael?" Hana asked.

"The agent for that American televangelist, Remi Shapiro, apparently has them. I assume he's still in Jerusalem, but I'm going to ask Sarah if she can track him down again, since she was so effective at getting the silver scroll from him a few days ago. There's no way a document so historically distinguished and enormously important should end up in the hands of some private collector."

"Hmm. Curious timing," Hana noted. "I read in *The Jerusalem Post* this morning that Pastor Gabriel Darwin, the televangelist you referred to, has a big event scheduled at some place called the Jewel Ark Chapel in the Christian Quarter tonight. Maybe we should check it out?"

"Good idea," Michael said. "It's likely this Remi fellow might be around then. And Sarah would surely recognize him. I'll call her now."

GABRIEL DARWIN SLID into the back seat of the black Mercedes-Maybach S-Class limousine, joining his wife and daughter, when his cell phone rang. He reached inside his jacket pocket and plucked it out.

"Hyyellow," he answered jauntily, winking and smiling at Sue Ann. Darwin was always happy and charged up just before a preaching event, and he was thrilled to have an Israeli Christian audience that evening.

"Pastor? It's Dr. Becker, at the museum."

"Hey, Leon. How're they hangin'?"

As usual, the urbane curator ignored Darwin's often crude remarks. "Pastor, you'll be quite taken by what I've discovered in these parchments you have. They are indescribably valuable. Priceless, in fact. Or at least one of them is, written by St. Paul himself! Pastor, this is the biggest archeological find since the Dead Sea Scrolls themselves!"

"Well, how about that!" Darwin beamed. "I cannot *wait* to see 'em myself. Remi's bringin' 'em by the Jewel Ark Chapel tonight. And did I hear you say '*priceless*,' Leon? I do like the sound of that. Tomorrow I want you to tell me more about what St. Paul had to say in it. In the meantime, you find a nice place of prominence in Biblical Hall for these now, y'hear? I'll be bringin' 'em back with me in a couple more days. Gotta go now. Buh bye." He tapped the red end call button.

As the limo pulled away from the Hilton Tel Aviv for the hour-long ride to Jerusalem, Pastor Darwin sat back in his plush leather seat, filled with a sense of righteousness. All things were going his way, the way it should be. He was a man in charge of his own destiny.

It's good to be the king, he thought, recalling a line from a movie. Then he chuckled at the memory of it.

TWENTY-SIX

T ucked inside the walled Old City of Jerusalem, surrounded by the larger Muslim Quarter, Armenian Quarter and Jewish Quarter, lies the tiny Christian Quarter, the hemmed-in home of some seven thousand Christians. One consolation of living in the smallest quarter is adjacency to its fourth-century Church of the Holy Sepulchre, which many believe to be the holiest place in all of Christendom. On this sacred ground visitors will find the two holiest sites known to Christians: the place where Jesus was believed to have been crucified, called Calvary or Golgotha, and the empty tomb where Jesus is believed by Christians to have been buried and from which he resurrected.

Not far west of this revered landmark, through the narrow, twisted streets and alleyways, sits the Darwin Ministries' Jewel Ark Chapel, one of hundreds of world-wide satellites of the grand Diamond Ark Cathedral in Dallas. The chapel—much like its mother church, built in the shape of an ark—can accommodate up to a thousand congregants, and Sundays found it packed with standing-room-only crowds, from both the quarter and traveling in from other areas, to see and hear the prerecorded satellite feed from Dallas. Pastor Darwin's unique formula of evangelical worship rituals, passionate choir performances, and fiery sermonizing regularly drew in a loyal attendance, and the congregation was growing steadily every month.

Darwin's scheduled personal appearance had been advertised well in advance in *The Jerusalem Post* and smaller local bulletins, and a large audience was expected. As the bells in the nearby twelfth-century Crusader tower of the Church of the Holy Sepulchre struck seven o'clock—a half hour before the start of the event—people were already pouring into the chapel. Pastor Darwin's limousine threaded its way through throngs of street crowds until it finally pulled up to the stage entrance door. Given the ancient narrow streets paved with centuries-old stones and surrounded by high brick walls, the sight of a stretch limousine was such a reverse anachronism that the mostly poor local residents gawked at it as if they had never seen one before. And many hadn't. But most Jews likely wouldn't understand the Christian prosperity ministry, either.

As the Darwins were being escorted out of the limo and into the backstage door, Sarah, Hana and Karl were still in line, soon to enter the Jewel Ark Chapel, when they noticed how out of place the limo was.

"I'll bet *that's* not something locals here see every day," Karl said dismissively.

Hana was also taken aback. "It takes some nerve to put on such a display of wealth in such a less-privileged area as the Old City."

"No kidding," Sarah added. "But I'll bet Darwin still rakes in donations from overzealous believers who hang on every word hucksters like him preach. And looking at the clothes some of these people coming in are wearing, they are better off than one might imagine. They're probably from the wealthier parts of Jerusalem."

Just then, Karl gasped as he recognized one man entering the building whose photo he had seen before—the man who killed Ishak Ramzi. "There's Abu Tariq! He's going in the door now. See him?"

Hana and Sarah peered over the long line of heads in front of them but failed to see Tariq before he'd slipped inside.

"It's good to know he's here, then, confirming what Yossi overheard," Sarah said with a satisfied confidence. "We've got to stay sharp and get those parchments from Remi Shapiro before Tariq does."

HAVING FOLLOWED Abu Tariq on the train from Tel Aviv to Jerusalem earlier that day, Tamir Pinsky and Azim Hourani were also standing in line for the chapel's main event that night, a mere two meters behind their target. Tamir's fixed-combat bowie knife was strapped to his belt beneath a black windbreaker. His left hand repeatedly reached up to the handle, gripping it anxiously, assuring him it was at hand and ready for action.

His plan was to wait for just the right moment when

the crowd was actively standing and all eyes were on the preacher. That this was a house of God gave Tamir a moment's pause, and his thoughts were edged with guilt at the prospect of killing a man in church. But then he thought back to his friend's lifeless body lying on the floor of that secret room in Tel Aviv, his throat slashed mercilessly, a vision that allayed any concerns he had about the venue he now found himself in. In the meantime—since Abu Tariq had no reason to recognize either Tamir or Azim—they both took seats next to him, to his immediate right, in an aisle of pews toward the left side of the chapel. Tamir was mere inches from him. His knife was even closer.

FOR HIS PART, Tariq had been on the lookout for Remi Shapiro, knowing he was here to hand over the parchments to his boss, Gabriel Darwin. After entering the chapel and surveying the animated crowd, he finally spotted Remi sitting at the far left end of a row on the left side of the chapel, his backpack still slung over his shoulder but resting on the seat space to his left. Tariq took the seat directly behind him, also at the end of the row, giving him easy escape access after he snatched the backpack. In his right jacket pocket was a fully charged stun gun, ready to deliver 50,000 volts from its two protruding metal prongs at the simple press of a trigger. In his left pocket was another device he hoped he wouldn't have to use, but was pleased to have thought of bringing it. Looking at the crowd around him now, he suspected he would most surely need it.

. . .

SARAH, Hana, and Karl finally got in the door moments before the ushers had stopped more people from entering because of overcapacity. Standing on the high balcony floor inside the entrance, all three looked down across the arena, taking measure of the venue. The building was indeed shaped like an ark, an oval stadium with 360-degree seating surrounding a low center stage, with faux ship rib beams designed as aisle stair bannisters separating the long rows of seats. A thousand people weren't really that many faces to scan, and with three pairs of eyes taking sections of the chapel to find Remi Shapiro, it wasn't long before Sarah caught sight of him—sitting on an aisle seat in a row on the left side of the oval stage. A few seats were still available near him, so they quickly made their way through the aisles down to the designated section and took seats two rows behind Remi, also on the aisle.

It was but a few minutes later when all the lights in the arena slowly dimmed to darkness. The only light came from hundreds of flickering votive candles surrounding the podium like stage lights, with a large white wooden cross as the centerpiece on the stage. Vases of red roses and green ferns were clustered in abundance, lending the stage a dignified but funereal appearance. Near-total silence took hold of the arena, with the crowd expecting *something* to happen in the darkness.

And then it did. In dramatic fashion, a bright spotlight suddenly flared on and a pipe organ came to life, quickly rising to a crescendo as an introduction. Standing at the edge of the stage in a circle of light was Pastor Gabriel Darwin, his snow-white suit and patent leather shoes literally ablaze under the bright light, some specialized fabric in the suit giving the appearance of actually shimmering. Large-carat diamond rings on both his hands sparkled flamboyantly beneath the light. It was a truly surreal spectacle, lending itself more toward the miraculous than the mundane. Cheers and a tremendous applause erupted from the adoring crowd as the pastor swayed onto center stage, doing his little dance while the choir belted out a popular evangelical gospel song. The man knew how to choreograph an entrance.

Behind the pastor, his wife Sue Ann and daughter Tabitha walked onto the stage, clapping and singing along as they both sashayed toward a white sofa placed at the foot of the towering cross. They, too, were attired all in white. Even Tabitha was dressed sensibly, playing her part in the family business.

After the choir finished their rousing gospel tune, Darwin—his voice booming through a lavalier microphone on his lapel—greeted the crowd in Hebrew.

"Erev T'ov, Ha'verim Yeka'rim!" he said jovially. *Good evening, my friends!* Though he continued speaking in English, a Hebrew translation of his words appeared on jumbotron displays hanging high at each end of the arena. Everyone was still standing, many with their hands raised in adulation, some overtaken by emotion, many swaying with their eyes closed.

As Darwin went about his sermonizing, Remi

Shapiro stood contentedly, watching the boss do his thing. *He is so good at this! No wonder he can afford the treasures I round up for him...look at this crowd. They're mesmerized.* He reached over and patted the backpack, assuring himself the boss would be very pleased with what he would bring him after tonight's event.

Abu Tariq, watching the back of Remi's head, saw his left hand reach over and rest on the backpack, as if safeguarding it. He also noticed the strap hanging from his left shoulder; fortunately it wasn't slung around his neck, which would make it more difficult to seize and run.

Standing behind Tariq, Karl stared balefully at the back of the man who had so brutally killed Ishak Ramzi. If this wasn't a house of God, he might be tempted to take matters into his own hands, avenging Ishak's death for their mutual friend Simon Ginzberg.

Sarah visualized her own scene: arresting Tariq for murder after the ceremony, while Karl and Hana held Remi for interrogation and retrieval of the parchments.

As Tamir stood next to the man he would kill, his anger grew. He was working up the nerve to make his move, timing it with a rousing from the crowd to mask the bloody action. It would be so simple. Pull the knife out of its sheath, thrust it to his left, then push up and twist. But each time the crowd applauded and cheered, he hesitated. His hand hovered over the knife's handle, ready to grasp it any time now, just waiting for the courage to act.

He turned to Azim on his right. "Be ready to run to our left and out the exit when I make my move."

Azim nodded, a look of nervous trepidation on his face.

Standing right behind Tamir, Sarah clearly overheard what he'd said to Azim. Her instincts were on full alert now, knowing something was about to come down quickly, but not knowing what. She leaned in close to Karl and said, "Be prepared. Something's going on with these two." She nodded toward Tamir and Azim.

Suddenly the organ ramped up in loud tribute to something Darwin said, and as the crowd went wild, Abu Tariq subtly reached into his jacket pocket and withdrew a smoke bomb canister with a wire-pull igni-tion system. Yanking on the pull-ring, he dropped the canister in front of Tamir on his right. Smoke instantly filled the immediate area, making it impossible for anyone to see anything.

But Abu was prepared. His other hand pulled out the stun gun, which he shoved high in front of him. Reaching up to grip Remi's left shoulder, Abu slammed the stun gun against the man's neck. As Remi went down, Abu grabbed the leather strap of the backpack and pulled it toward him, free of Remi's other convulsing shoulder.

Tamir had chosen that moment to act as well. As he reached for his bowie knife, he suddenly found himself in a cloud of smoke, apparently coming from the floor beneath him. Driven by rage and confusion, he thrust the knife to his left, thrashing it wildly, seeking purchase with Abu's body. The knife struck something, but it didn't feel like flesh. In fact, the knife had struck the backpack—a backpack that was pulling away from the knife as Abu left the row and quickly made for the exit, unaware of the blade wielding or the attempt on his life. Tamir continued poking the blade in the smoke-filled air, but his target had vanished.

Sarah acted quickly, grabbing Hana's hand while pushing Karl toward the aisle exit. "Move! There's going to be panic any moment now. You two get out of here. I'll meet you outside."

As Hana and Karl headed up the aisle, Sarah moved down two rows to check on Remi. She found him, his body suffering the spasmodic effects of being tasered. But the backpack was gone.

People were screaming in the smoke's vicinity, then others farther away thinking the room was on fire were now running up the aisles seeking to escape as the smoke spread further out from its source.

Seeing the smoke and the commotion, Pastor Darwin advised the assembly not to panic, but to calmly make for the exits. Naturally, everyone panicked anyway. There was a mad rush for the doors, Sarah now stuck amid the crowd.

Except for Abu Tariq, who—with a black canvas backpack slung over his shoulder—was already out on the dark narrow street walking casually toward the Church of the Holy Sepulchre to find a taxi to take him to a car rental agency. His destination: Saint Catherine's Monastery, near the southern tip of Egypt's Sinai Peninsula.

CHAPTER
TWENTY-SEVEN

Hana, Karl and Sarah finally made it outside and onto the street, coughing from the noxious effects of the zinc-chloride in the smoke, as were many others who had been sitting in their section.

Catching her breath, Sarah sputtered, "I checked on Remi as we left. He was immobilized from being tasered, presumably by Tariq, but his backpack was gone—which likely means Tariq dropped the smoke bomb, then grabbed the parchments and fled during the chaos. If the plan Yossi heard on the phone tap is still in play, he's heading for the Egyptian border, with Cairo being his most likely destination.

"So, depending on where Tariq goes, we'll have to enter Egypt to carry this off. My Mossad ID won't be entirely welcome there, so I'll use my diplomatic passport—yes, we're prepared for everything. And we're setting the two of you up with diplomatic passports as well to avoid any Egyptian delays. It's a quick stop at one of our safe houses near here."

"But shouldn't we be following Tariq now so we don't lose him?" Karl asked.

Sarah smiled confidently. "When I took the silver scroll from Remi, I pinned a tiny tracker to his backpack —the one Tariq now has. My IntactPhone is equipped with the tracking app, so we'll know where he is at all times."

"Brilliant," Hana said, glancing at Sarah with admiration. "So, how long will it take to get our passports?"

"All we need are your photos, and our specialist can have them ready within the hour. Then we head for Egypt."

"I should give Michael a call and update him as to what's been happening."

EARLIER THAT MORNING, Michael and Aaron had looked into the so-called Jesus Family Tomb to which the parchments alluded. They went to visit the Talpiot neighborhood in southern Jerusalem to look for the tomb itself. Although they found the location of the burial chamber —next to a quiet community of newer apartment buildings—it had unfortunately been covered over with a slab of concrete following its earlier discovery and excavation of the ten ossuaries found in the tomb. Michael asked one of the neighbors where the recovered ossuaries had been sent, and was told that the IAA moved them to their warehouse in Bet Shemesh, not far from Jerusalem.

Michael had met the director of the Israel Antiquities Authority, Dr. Byron Rabin, on one of his past trips to Israel, and called for an appointment to see him. Pleased to have a representative from the Vatican visit his agency, he insisted Michael come at once, if that would be convenient. He would make time for such a distinguished guest.

INSIDE THE HIGH fence surrounding the IAA's vast warehouse complex in Bet Shemesh, Michael and Aaron were met by tall rows of sturdy metal outdoor shelving supporting hundreds, if not thousands, of exterior architectural components arranged on wooden pallets.

For his part, Michael was looking forward to conversing with Dr. Rabin and, in time, sharing the explosive revelation with him at the appropriate moment. Aaron, however, had become quite animated in his enthusiasm for seeing Israel's oldest and most valued antiquities. Such an insider's opportunity would never have otherwise been afforded him.

Dr. Rabin met both men as they emerged from their rental car, with Michael making introductions. The three entered the immense building, where Rabin led them downstairs into a climate-controlled underground warehouse featuring row upon row of sturdy metal shelves on which were placed thousands of ossuaries, reliquaries, ceramic vessels, statuary, tools and implements, and various potsherds, all arranged by time periods. The sheer number of objects on display was mind-boggling.

"You see, Father Dominic," Dr. Rabin explained as they were inspecting the contents of the Talpiot tomb, "ten ossuaries were originally discovered during the 1980 excavation of the Talpiot site. But somehow one of them seems to have gone missing in the interim, as our inventory shows only nine now. And as you may have read, there has been some controversy over what's been called the James Ossuary, which could be that missing tenth one. The Aramaic inscription on that ossuary reads '*Ya'akov bar-Yosef akhui diYeshua*,' which translates as 'James, son of Joseph, brother of Jesus.' Which refers, of course, to James the Just, not only Jesus' brother but the leader of the early Christian movement in Jerusalem.

"Suffice to say, we are still left with no positive determination whether the Talpiot tomb was in fact the burial site for the family of Jesus. Four of the ten ossuaries had inscriptions that would surely make up the same names that are given in the Bible: Jesus; his mother, Mary; Mary Magdalene; and Joseph, brother of Jesus. A fifth one was attributed to a Matthew, who is believed to be the husband of one of the women in one of the four unmarked ossuaries. Most surprising, though, was a sixth ossuary inscribed with the name Judah, son of Jesus.

"However, given the population makeup of Jerusalem at the time, scholars and statisticians have calculated that the people in one family tomb having identical names to those in biblical gospel accounts represents an extraordinarily high probability—to the exclusion of mere likelihood—that it is most likely Jesus' family tomb.

"Now," Rabin concluded ruefully, "if all this were true, and it was indeed the bones of Jesus himself in that ossuary—not to mention his having a son—well, then, at the very least that would certainly contradict the foundational Christian belief of the Resurrection, wouldn't it?"

"Spoken like the true Jewish scholar that you are," Michael grinned, fully aware that Jews do not recognize Jesus as the Messiah, and that both the cross and the tomb are beyond their own beliefs and cultural frames of reference.

"You bring up good points, Byron," Michael continued. "But what if I were to tell you that evidence has emerged potentially confirming that your ossuary did in fact contain the bones of Jesus, as confirmed by none other than St. Paul himself?"

Rabin was visibly shocked. He just stared at the priest.

"To be honest, I was skeptical when I first heard about it, too," Michael added. "But then I read the actual parchment—a parchment that was very recently found in a cave in Wadi Murabba'at, along with the famed silver scroll referred to in the Khirbet Qumran copper scroll. Personally, the concept alone has me shaken to my core, but I'm suspending judgment until Vatican and biblical scholars can study the manuscript and interpret it properly. These things take time, and one cannot make snap decisions at such moments of discovery as this."

Rabin was practically speechless, stammering for the

right words. *"Silver scroll?!* The one referred to in the copper scroll? You say this has been *found?* How come this is the first I am hearing of it?!"

"With apologies, Byron, things have been pretty fluid these past few days, with many people jockeying for those parchments, it seems. As for the silver scroll, that's now safely in the hands of Mossad. We've been working with two of its agents, Yossi and Sarah Geffen, who have been of tremendous help. Sarah was the one who retrieved the silver scroll from one of the...well, let's just call them purveyors."

"At least I am assured that Mossad will turn this scroll over to us at the appropriate time," Rabin said, partially mollified. "But tell me more of this St. Paul manuscript you spoke of. This would be very rare indeed, Michael, and perhaps the greatest of all archeological finds to date. He specifically mentions Jesus by name?"

"He definitely described the entire family's names as being buried together in Jerusalem." The priest reached for his phone and pulled up an image of the parchment itself, showing it to Rabin. The older man peered at the small screen, enlarging the Hebrew characters to read it himself.

"This is unspeakably overwhelming! Which compels me to ask, how did all this come to you? We must establish an authoritative chain of provenance."

Michael explained how Simon Ginzberg contacted him about scrolls that a pair of boys from Tel Aviv found in the cave, which they turned over to the antiquities dealer Ishak Ramzi, and his resulting murder by Abu

Tariq, then Sarah's retrieval of the silver scroll and what little else he knew about the path the surviving parchments had since taken. He purposely omitted their trip to Madaba and the mosaic map and the resultant discovery of treasures by Colonel Scarpa, something he felt was Scarpa's responsibility to act on.

As he finished, his phone vibrated in his pocket. Retrieving it, he saw it was Hana, and he instantly felt a warmth flow through him. He'd missed talking with her.

"Hey, how are things with you?" he asked, turning away from the others.

"We're on our way to Egypt, if you can believe that," Hana replied, "and going in as diplomats, no less. Sarah's made, um—'special arrangements'—to make it easier for all three of us to enter the country without delay. We're going after Abu Tariq and the parchments he now has. He's headed to the Sinai Peninsula for reasons we can't yet fathom." She wrapped up the past day's activities for him, including the dramatic events at the Jewel Ark Chapel. Then, "How about you? Keeping busy?"

"Well, we've hardly had the kind of excitement you've enjoyed, but right now we're at the IAA's main warehouse examining the Talpiot ossuaries. I've told the director, Dr. Rabin, about the St. Paul manuscript, and it left him shaken. You *must* get hold of those parchments, Hana. That one document alone could be the most significant manuscript of that period in existence. I wonder how Egypt comes into play here? Think Tariq is trying to sell them?"

"I wish I knew, Michael. Sarah's placed a tracker on him, so as long as he doesn't discover it, we should be able to monitor his location."

As things were speeding up pretty quickly, Michael made a decision. "Look, we'll be done here soon with nothing in particular to do afterward. Why don't Aaron and I fly down and meet you in Cairo? It's only a ninety-minute flight. That is where Yossi said Tariq was heading, isn't it?"

Hana felt a little excitement at the thought of everyone meeting up again—especially Michael—and the exotic adventures awaiting them in the land of the pharaohs.

"Yes!" she exclaimed, then tempered herself. "I mean, yeah, Yossi said Cairo was part of their plan somehow. And it would be a lot more fun with you here, anyway. So sure, let's meet in Cairo!"

CHAPTER
TWENTY-EIGHT

Abu Tariq's pomegranate red Mercedes C-Class sedan sped south along Route 90 from Jerusalem to the Sinai Peninsula, bound for Saint Catherine's Monastery in Egypt. His mission was two-fold: first, to find out why so many people so desperately wanted these parchments. Over the years he had dealt with many antiquities in this unsanctioned black market side pursuit of his, but as he was finding, none had ever elicited the provocative level of interest these had.

For that, he would need to find some form of translation and authentication expertise—and that's where his longtime ally, Brother Masud Sharif, came in. The head librarian for Saint Catherine's Monastery was the ideal resource: highly knowledgeable, impeccably discreet, and morally pliant. If these manuscripts were of significant importance, he could be trusted to keep his mouth shut, though Tariq knew he would also do whatever he could to acquire the objects himself.

And that was his second mission: finding a buyer. If he and Masud could come to some agreeable arrangement, then fine, he might be amenable. It all depended on the appraised value. His instincts, however, led him to consider taking the parchments to Cairo, where there were well-heeled buyers for such merchandise as ancient biblical parchments and papyri, especially those of such rarity that price would be no object. Tariq doubted the simple treasury of Saint Catherine's Monastery could compete with Cairo's oldest and most vibrant marketplace, and the rich Egyptian collectors whose communal ears were always to the ground listening for rumors about the rarest of the rare.

And, of course, there was Khalid Zadani to consider. This was, after all, his mission.

Or was it? After everything he'd gone through to get this far, Abu Tariq had pretty much resolved that he was now on his own. Given the once-in-a-lifetime opportunity he had been blessed with, why share it with anyone at this point? He would be set for life.

Such comforting thoughts swirled around his mind as the Mercedes sped on toward the small UNESCO World Heritage city of Saint Catherine. He would arrive at the monastery in another two hours, where stage one of his operation would begin.

~

BEFORE LEAVING THEIR HOTEL, Hana and Karl had quickly packed an overnight bag, then loaded everything into Sarah's Toyota Tundra. Taking a circuitous route, instinctively cautious about being followed, Sarah drove them to one of Mossad's secret safe houses in north Jerusalem, where she had called ahead to ready their passport-provisioning expert.

On arrival, photographs were taken of Hana and Karl and brief but relevant personal background details were devised in case they faced interrogation while in Egypt. Arrangements were even made with the Israeli Embassy in Cairo to recognize Karl and Hana as having affiliated diplomatic immunity while in the host country, ensuring coordination with all germane parties.

Meanwhile, the tracking beacon on Sarah's Intact-Phone continued showing Abu Tariq moving south along Route 90 on the Sinai Peninsula. Sarah headed the Toyota south on Route 1 out of Jerusalem, her foot heavy on the pedal. They would make Tariq's general location in about five hours.

So far, everything was going according to their hastily made plans.

AT THE FOOT of Egypt's famed Mount Sinai—where, according to the Jewish Torah, the Christian Bible and the Qur'an of Islam, Moses received the Ten Commandments from God—lies the Eastern Orthodox Monastery of Saint Catherine, the oldest continuously inhabited Christian monastery in the world, though it is held

sacred by Jews and Muslims as well. All Abrahamic religions find reverence there.

Built around what was believed to be the legendary
Burning Bush—the presumed spot where Moses was
chosen by God to lead the Israelites out of Egypt and
into Canaan—Saint Catherine's Monastery is completely
encircled by a massive Byzantine fortification ranging
from ten to thirty-five meters tall in places, conforming
to the mountainous terrain surrounding the ancient
complex of hewn limestone and red clay buildings. Built
between 548 and 565 CE, it also houses the oldest
continuously operating library in the world, now over
1,700 years old.

Owing to his eminent position as the Monastery's
current head librarian—following in the historic footsteps of hundreds of his predecessors over the centuries
—Brother Masud Sharif was a recognized authority in

evaluating and authenticating ancient manuscripts. Apart from frequently being called on to perform that scholarly and most sought-after function, Sharif was always looking to gain only the finest materials for his museum's growing collection, which presently exceeded three thousand manuscripts, not to mention priceless books and a vast accumulation of religious icons, mosaics, and other archaic treasures.

To be first in getting some especially desirable artifact—and in this case, snatching it from the competitive grasp of the Israelis—would be a prime motivation for Sharif, whose intense personal pride in his country's prestigious library on the Sinai Peninsula knew no ethical bounds.

ABU TARIQ PULLED the Mercedes up alongside the tourist buses parked outside the monastery walls. People of varying nationalities wandered the rocky grounds and posed in front of Mount Sinai for photographs taken by enterprising young local boys who handled the cameras for one Egyptian pound per tourist—the equivalent of about five cents American. Vendors had erected folding tables and pop-up kiosks to sell all manner of commemorative tchotchkes, and business looked to be brisk as Tariq passed them on his way onto the monastery grounds.

Having been there countless times before, he knew his way to the library where he could usually find the reed-thin Brother Masud poring over some spellbinding papyrus or lecturing tourists on the history of Saint

Catherine's, a task to which he more reluctantly acceded the older he got.

"*Assalaam 'alaikum*,"—*May peace be upon you*—greeted Masud as he shook Tariq's hand.

"*Wa 'alaikum assalaam*," Tariq replied, returning the handshake firmly. *And peace be upon you.* "Good to see you again, old friend. As I mentioned on the phone, I have something with me which I believe you might find extraordinary. At least, that's what I am hoping. But as always, I defer to your expertise in such matters. There seems to be much interest in these parchments, though, by many parties, and I am keen to hear your evaluation of them."

"Then let us see what we have here, shall we?" Masud offered, smiling graciously as he took the portfolio from Tariq. While he gently withdrew and laid out the parchments for review, a young sister from the nearby convent prepared *karkadeh* for them, an Egyptian herbal tea made from boiling dried red hibiscus flowers, which is then chilled, sweetened by cane sugar, and reheated for serving. She set the tea on a side table, away from the manuscripts, which she knew was Masud's customary practice.

After some time reading and translating each of the parchments into a pad of paper, Masud showed no particular reactions—until he got to the last manuscript. As Tariq carefully watched his old friend read it, the monk paled. His hands quivered as he held the parchment up at an angle, peering at it more closely now under the light, as if what he had read couldn't possibly be what he had read.

Without a word, he laid down the document, set down his pen, then turned and—with both hands, to prevent them from trembling and spilling it—picked up his cup of *karkadeh* and took a long draw of the steaming tea.

Gently setting the cup back down, he turned around and looked directly into Tariq's eyes as his own glistened with emotion.

"I have so many questions," was all he could think of saying. "But in the main, it comes down to but one thing: what would it take for me to acquire this extraordinary document?"

"But tell me what it is first, Masud!" Tariq said heatedly under his breath, not wanting to draw the attention of others in the library. "The suspense is killing me!"

The monk explained what the manuscript purported to be and, if it were indeed genuine, its profound implications on history. He further described the background of the Talpiot tomb in Jerusalem and what such a revelation would mean to Christians worldwide.

Abu Tariq pulled out his phone and snapped photographs of each translated page. As he read over the translations for himself, at long last, he finally understood.

And all he could do now was smile like a mad fool.

CHAPTER
TWENTY-NINE

Situated on the Nile River in northern Egypt, Cairo—the long-serving capital of Egyptian civilizations for over six thousand years—was the largest metropolitan area in the Middle East, with a sprawling population of nearly twenty-two million. Nicknamed "the city of a thousand minarets" for its proliferation of Islamic architecture, Cairo's strategic location at the juncture of the Nile Delta and the Nile Valley placed it at the confluence of major trading routes between the Levant and North Africa.

After centuries of ancient settlements having suffered continual sieges and conquests by marauding forces, by the tenth century Cairo was a closed city, meaning no commoners were permitted access to it. It was composed mainly of palaces inhabited by the caliph's family, notable sultans, state officials and other high functionaries associated with operating the Fatimid Caliphate, an empire comprising much of North Africa and the Levant. It wasn't until the twelfth century that merchants and other outsiders were not only permitted entry but became fundamental in establishing Cairo as a prominent economic and trade center in the Middle East.

At the center of the city's early trade network were its fabled bazaars, or souks: enormous open-air markets where mingling locals and traveling merchants could find anything they might wish for. And while many ancient bazaars still abound in Egypt, none of them date as far back as Cairo's Khan el-Khalili, which opened its first souk in 1382.

LONG STRINGS of colorful tapered pennants fluttered overhead in the late afternoon breeze as Abu Tariq wove his way through the labyrinth of alleyways in the Khan el-Khalili bazaar, the scents of exotic perfumes and pungent spices permeating the air. He was on his way to see someone known only as "Saladin"—a man who, he had been told, was the most well-connected antiquities fence in all of Egypt, maybe the entire Middle East. Buyers could be found for any artifact, but finding them was the challenge. For the right fee, Saladin would bring together both buyers and sellers in discreet locations to the satisfaction of all parties.

This particular introduction was made for Tariq by Brother Masud Sharif, who, to the monk's despairing chagrin, was unsuccessful in his own bid to acquire the St. Paul parchment. Had Masud not shown his hand by displaying such a pronounced reaction to reading the manuscript in Tariq's presence, things might have gone differently. But as he himself was so moved by the artifact, there was neither time nor suitable composure for setting up a more cunning acquisition plan. As a result, Tariq knew instantly that he now had something very special indeed, something poor Masud's comparatively meager budget could never accommodate.

But, owing to their longstanding relationship, the monk reluctantly put his friend in touch with Cairo's most venerable intermediary in such illicit matters. Saladin dealt only with the most discreet buyers and the finest objects: such authentic pharaonic artifacts as mummies and sarcophagi; original papyri bearing ancient hieroglyphics; gold, silver, loose gems and figurines raided from Egyptian tombs. If it carried high value but could not be moved through "traditional" commercial means—in other words, if its origins were shady or flat-out illegal—Saladin could manage to work through those issues, including secure and discreet transportation out of Egypt on behalf of the buyer, often through legitimate diplomatic channels. To no one's surprise, everyone had his price.

Tariq was told to meet Saladin at the popular Qahwat El Fishawy coffeehouse at the west end of the market, a very public place known by everyone in Cairo.

∼

FROM THE TOP of the tall, slender minaret of a nearby mosque, the tinny recording of a muezzin's voice solemnly proclaimed the call to prayer across the city as Michael, Hana, Sarah, Karl and Aaron made their way through the dense alleyways of the Khan el-Khalili bazaar.

Michael and Aaron had flown in from Jerusalem a few hours earlier and met up with Hana, Sarah and Karl at the Sofitel Cairo Hotel on El Gezirah Island, where Hana had arranged rooms for everyone. Apart from Sarah, none of them had been to Cairo before, and their collective senses were assaulted by the chaotic atmosphere mixed with perfumed and savory aromas coming from many of the stalls, shops, and cafés.

With the tracking beacon on her IntactPhone guiding them toward Abu Tariq's location, Sarah led the team through the market as she wove between small, crowded shops hawking all manner of bazaar merchandise: lustrous jewelry, stained glass lanterns, brassware, aromatic candles, handmade carpets and sheer fabrics, hookah water pipes...and it seemed every other shop featured colorful mounds of aromatic spices—cinnamon, cloves, sumac, cumin, dried red peppers, saffron, mint, and more. At every turn, all senses were engaged: the goods on display both eye-catching and breathtaking, and the cacophony of sellers bargaining with buyers was both audible and visual theater in itself. Hana was particularly fascinated by the experience, her attention being drawn to her left and to her right and back again. It was a good thing Michael was leading her by the hand since she did not know where they were in the vastness of Cairo's largest open-air market, several blocks long. She trusted that, as long as he held on, she could happily immerse herself in the sensual experiences, as if she were on a magic flying carpet.

As for Sarah, she had one aim: to find Abu Tariq and acquire the parchments.

As they walked through the crowded market, Michael asked her what she would do to Tariq once she found him.

"Well, I can't very well arrest him in his own country for crimes committed in Israel, since Egyptian law prevents extraditing an Egyptian citizen for legal proceedings in a foreign country while that case is under investigation in Egypt—which could be indefinite, assuming one was launched at all.

"Yossi tapped a call between Abu Tariq and Khalid Zadani a couple days ago, and he told me they spoke about the prospect of eventually finding a buyer in Cairo—*if* Tariq were successful in getting the parchments back from Remi Shapiro and they had been provisionally authenticated by some monk at Saint Catherine's Monastery. So now I need to find out where this planned transaction will take place, then somehow attempt to intercept the documents and make haste back to Israel."

And as she observed, the tracking beacon had stopped moving. They would soon be on top of Abu Tariq and the elusive parchments.

CHAPTER
THIRTY

The spacious and noisy Qahwat El Fishawy coffeehouse, whose doors first opened in 1797, was no ordinary café. Sitting at the nexus of Cairo's richest area of Islamic architecture and historical institutions, El Fishawy played host to everyone from Egyptian kings and sultans to writers and artists, and simple peasants who, on a good day, could only afford a nurturing cup of hibiscus tea with a sprig of mint.

Large oil paintings of prominent, long-dead Egyptian intellectuals hung on walls next to ancient mirrors whose gilded, arabesque frames, inlaid with mother-of-pearl, drew the eye away from scattered patches of desilvered mirror-rot.

Back in a far corner, a tiny round table, its cracked marble top barely held together by a battered aluminum rim, sat between the heavyset man named Saladin and Abu Tariq, a man half the size of his companion. Saladin wore a spotless, flowing white *dishdasha* buttoned up to his neck with loose tailored sleeves. His head was wrapped with a red-and-white-checkered *ghutra* held in place with a black corded agal, the kind of headdress worn by most men in Arabian Gulf countries. A heavy black beard and shaggy eyebrows punctuated his ensemble, but his bright blue eyes were his most striking feature, as they beheld the object of their attention with a piercing scrutiny, as if no one could be trusted. Saladin was not a man easily forgotten.

An attentive server in a soiled white kaftan with tight sleeves came by and wordlessly set down a fluted, long-handled copper pot filled with bitter Arabica coffee, along with two glass cups and a bowl of sugar, then left them alone.

"I presume you brought the St. Paul parchment for me to inspect?" Saladin's baritone voice stated more than asked. There was no need to speak discreetly since the babel of other patrons more than masked their conversation. Just the same, Saladin spoke in English rather than Arabic.

"I brought all the parchments, yes. Would you like to see them now?" Tariq glanced at nearby tables to see if anyone was paying attention to them. Sitting at each of the two closest tables were two men in dark suits who frequently looked in their direction. He was just about to mention it when Saladin spoke up.

"Those men work for me," he said matter-of-factly. "Now, show me what you have. We will not be interrupted."

Tariq reached into the backpack he had been holding possessively in his lap and withdrew four parchment pages. Before taking them, Saladin reached into his sleeve, produced a white handkerchief, wiped his hands clean with it, then tucked it back where he found it and accepted the manuscripts. He knew that wearing gloves was not particularly necessary for handling ancient parchments, but took care that his hands were free of the typical particles one picks up.

"You have had the St. Paul manuscript translated, yes?" he asked.

"Yes, of course," Tariq replied, taking out his phone and calling up the translated notes that originated with Simon Ginzberg. He passed the phone to Saladin, who read it with interest over the next several minutes.

"Fascinating," he muttered to himself, then looked up at Tariq. "This could make for some long and very uncomfortable discussions in the Vatican—indeed, for Christians everywhere. And you have had this authenticated as well?"

"Yes, provisionally at least, by Brother Masud Sharif himself, head librarian at Saint Catherine's Monastery in the Sinai. Such things are subject to confirmation and various analytical tests, of course. Sharif desperately wanted to acquire it regardless, but, sadly for him, it was outside his budget."

"Oh?" Saladin leaned forward, his bulk inching the table a bit. "So, you have established a price for this already, have you?"

"Well, no, not really." Tariq was fumbling for the right words while struggling to maintain a confident posture in the bargaining. "I alluded to something in the 'many millions' of U.S. dollars, speculatively, at which point he knew he was out of any potential bidding. But that is where you come in, Sayyid," he offered, using the Arabic honorific for *Master*.

Saladin beamed optimistically. "I can tell you with full certainty that this will make for a very good sale. An extraordinary sale, in fact. Yes, I have one or two people in mind already…" His gaze turned distant as he imagined either the collectors of whom he spoke or the value of his potential commission.

"But you must not tell a soul about this, Abu. My clients require not only complete anonymity, but the right of first publication should they choose to do so. You must agree to these terms before I can take on this consignment. And my fee for handling the transaction is fifteen percent from each party. Take it or leave it. But because you came to me, obviously you are aware of my reputation. I have an impeccable list of prosperous clients around the world who trust me. I offer complete discretion to both parties, and certain desirable services to the buyer, besides managing the sale and escrow of funds and materials.

"So…do we have a deal?" Saladin stretched his hand out across the table as he smiled and held Tariq's eyes with an ominous gaze, as if saying *No* wouldn't be the prudent response.

"Yes, we have a deal!" Tariq replied eagerly, grateful to have this matter out of his hands. "Do you take the manuscripts now, or…?"

"Of course, I must be able to present them to my clients in person. My staff will prepare high-resolution scans and associated materials for confidential review by select clients. I will also need a copy of that preliminary translation to show them. You can email it to this address." He pulled a business card out of his pocket and handed it to Tariq.

As Tariq began emailing the translation file, one of Saladin's men got up and approached the table. In his hand was a slim, black acid-free portfolio, into which Saladin slid the precious parchments. The man then placed that inside an attaché case handcuffed to his wrist, locked it, then remained next to Saladin as the other three men also stood, waiting to leave when the boss was ready. Looking up, Tariq noticed bulges beneath their clothes: obviously, they were wearing shoulder holsters. He felt some assurance that his documents would be quite safe in the interim—but suddenly realized he had no formal documentation staking his claim of ownership to the manuscripts. As if there could even *be* one. This transaction was based completely on trust and Saladin's reputation.

He decided not to mention it. The handshake alone would have to suffice.

FIVE PEOPLE SAT at a slightly larger table several meters away, closer to the entrance of El Fishawy, discreetly watching Abu Tariq converse with a large man wearing a white *dishdasha* with the traditional *ghutra* draped around his head. Michael and the others were savoring hibiscus tea and a variety of nuts and figs as they tried to imagine what was going on there in the back of the café.

"See those two tables on either side of where Tariq is sitting?" Sarah asked the group. "Those four men are armed, and that man is undoubtedly their leader. Whoever he is, he's important."

Then they watched as the large man held and reviewed a parchment—presumably the St. Paul manuscript, Michael expected—then handed several of them to one of the other men who placed them in a box, then a briefcase. Without a word passed among them, the team's collective spirits sagged as they realized their prime objective for being here was now leaving inside a heavily armed protective detail.

"What are we going to do?!" Aaron whispered anxiously. "We can't just sit here!"

"Oh, yes we can, and that's exactly what we're going to do," Sarah cautioned as the five men walked silently past them, leaving Tariq on his own as he finished his coffee. "But I've got an idea. Follow my lead." She got up and walked purposefully toward Tariq, still sitting alone at the back of the café. When she reached the table, she sat down in Saladin's seat. Michael and Aaron took one of the other tables, Hana and Karl the remaining one. All of them turned toward Sarah and Tariq.

With no hesitation, Sarah took out her badge and held it up to his face. "Abu Tariq, my name is Sarah Geffen. I am an agent of Mossad, and we know that you have received certain parchment manuscripts that lawfully belong to the State of Israel."

Tariq was stunned motionless, his coffee cup midway in the air somewhere near his open mouth, as Sarah's stern gaze held his own surprised look. His peripheral vision caught four others taking seats where Saladin's men had been. *Were they all Mossad, too?* he wondered. Not taking any chances, he carefully set down the coffee, looked into Sarah's eyes and asked, "What was that, again?"

CHAPTER
THIRTY-ONE

"You heard me," Sarah said as she pocketed her badge. "I assume that the man who just left is either a buyer or your fence for moving the parchments, right? Who is he?"

Abu Tariq stared at her mutely for a few moments, a sardonic look spreading across his face, then said candidly, "You have no authority here, Agent Geffen. In fact, as a credentialed diplomat for my country, if I informed the local police that an Israeli Mossad agent was here in Cairo questioning Egyptian citizens, they would surely arrest *you* as a spy. Come to think of it, that's not a bad idea..." He started to stand when Karl, sitting closest to Tariq and with his chair turned to him, held out his leg to block his movement, then revealed a SIG Sauer pistol discreetly aimed at him.

"That would be unwise, Mr. Tariq. Please, sit down and answer the signora's questions."

"Ah, the Swiss Guard from the Vatican, I presume,"

Tariq said, sitting back down as he glanced at Karl. "I was told you might be in the country. All right. What harm can a little chat do at this point?" He sat back down, casually crossed his legs, and took another sip of his coffee.

"You are correct, of course. I do not have authority to act here," Sarah said. "But if it came to that, you must know that we can make your life a living hell, wherever you are. So, why not cooperate so we don't waste each other's time?"

Tariq looked down at his coffee cup, his finger absently circling the rim as he considered the subdued but very real threat.

"What is it you wish to know?"

"Who was that man?"

He paused a few moments before answering. "I only know him as 'Saladin.' He is a broker, of sorts, and he is now finding a buyer for the manuscripts I handed over to him. It should be no concern of yours how I got them in the first place."

"We already know you snatched them from Remi Shapiro in the Jewel Ark Chapel when you dropped that smoke bomb. We were standing right behind you at the time."

Tariq's arched eyebrows and wry smile revealed genuine surprise at Sarah's acknowledgment. "Well... you are much better at this than I might have given you credit for. But why didn't you try to intercept them then, in Jerusalem?"

"We tried, but I must admit, your plan was better executed than our readiness."

With his lingering grin, he was obviously pleased to hear this.

"So," he asked her, "I expect our business here is concluded, then?"

Sarah looked at Michael and the others, offering them a chance to weigh in. Karl was the only one who spoke up.

"Was it really necessary to kill Ishak Ramzi in such a savage, cold-blooded way? How can you live with yourself? If circumstances were different right now, I'd take it on myself to avenge his murder."

Tariq looked at Karl blankly, as if a response was hardly needed. "I simply did what needed to be done in the moment."

"Spoken like a true psychopath."

"I think we're done here," Sarah said after a brief pause. Then she stood up. "Be careful our paths do not cross again, Abu. You may not like where the next road takes you."

The others rose as well, following Sarah out of the café and back to their car.

TAMIR PINSKY and Azim Hourani were sitting outside El Fishawy café on a bench in the crowded market alleyway when they saw the man they had been waiting for emerge from the wooden arched doorway of the hookah lounge. Abu Tariq was alone.

He was easy to spot in his orange shirt, white cotton pants, and white fedora, with a green backpack slung over his shoulder, but as they followed him, they kept some distance between them anyway. Tariq seemed to be in no hurry as he ambled down the alley, stopping to look in the shop windows from time to time.

Tamir was anxious to see what was in that backpack. He suspected that's where the silver scroll and parchments were, if the man still had them at all. But he had a plan.

He had his own spacious, zippered backpack, which he held by its handle at his side, one which Azim told him he wanted nothing to do with—mainly because from time to time, ever so slightly, the contents shifted.

As he made his way through the souk alleyway, Abu Tariq's tradecraft intuition was paying off. He sensed more than saw that he was being shadowed, which was confirmed when he stopped to look in an angled shop window and caught the reflection of two young boys a short distance behind him staring at him, apparently waiting for him to do something.

He wouldn't disappoint them.

Coming to a side alley, Tariq turned into it and casually walked the distance to the end of the block, then turned right into another alley. Immediately after turning, he put his back against the stone wall of a building and took out his bowie knife as he waited for the young spies to appear.

He heard the sound of running sneaker footsteps approaching the corner and prepared himself by setting his backpack on the ground next to the wall.

As they neared the end of the alley, the running footsteps abruptly came to a measured halt, then the boys casually turned the corner. Tariq was ready for them.

Reaching out to the closest one as they made the turn, he grabbed the boy's shirt at the chest and yanked his body toward his own, turning him so his back was against his own chest, Tariq's right hand holding the blade of the knife to poor Azim's throat.

"Who are you and why are you following me?" he murmured icily.

Both boys were taken completely by surprise, but Azim was so suddenly terrified that he spontaneously wet himself. Tamir, ever the fast thinker, recovered quickly.

"*Sayyid! Sayyid!*" he pleaded. "We mean you no harm! We…we came to give you something from one of your associates at the embassy. You *are* Abu Tariq, yes?"

Tariq loosened his grip on Azim and lowered the knife. *What harm can two teenagers be, anyway?* he considered. "Yes, that is my name. Who are you? And what is it you have for me?"

Now free, Azim pulled away, moving behind Tamir, but clearly upset by his current state of hygiene.

"Oh, we are only messengers, Sayyid. But here is what we were told to give you…"

Tamir held up the backpack he was carrying, subtly shaking it as he did, then raised it chest high as he approached Tariq and quickly unzipped the opening.

Tariq naturally bent down to look inside. At the same moment the hooded head flare of an angry black desert cobra shot out of the backpack, jaws wide open, sinking its long fangs into the flesh of Tariq's face and hissing loudly as it wrapped its slithering body around the man's neck, instinctively constricting its prey.

Tamir and Azim moved back a safe distance, slack-jawed in rapt amazement as they watched the reptile chew on Tariq's cheek while the man screamed in mortal terror. As the venom quickly worked its way through his body, he fell to the ground, paralysis and respiratory distress kicking in faster than the boys had imagined. Tariq's flush-red face instantly swelled up, and he began vomiting and convulsing as the potent neurotoxins entered his bloodstream.

"Let that be a lesson to you, *ya ibn el sharmouta!*" Tamir spat. He didn't know much Arabic, but *sonofabitch* was one of the curses Azim had taught him, and it suited the moment.

As the provoked cobra continued to do its work on Tariq's face, Tamir reached over and grabbed the diplomat's backpack. Then he and Azim hustled back to their car parked around the block.

Anxiously digging through the backpack, they were discouraged to have found none of the precious manuscripts they had discovered in the desert cave and entrusted to their friend Ishak Ramzi.

But they had taken their revenge on both counts, and that was some consolation.

THIRTY-TWO

"So, what now?" Michael asked Sarah as they left the café. "Don't you think we should try to get those parchments back from Saladin somehow?"

"That's exactly what I think," Sarah replied curtly, her face intent but distant. Michael couldn't help but notice there was something odd in her demeanor.

"Are you alright, Sarah? You seem a little preoccupied."

The Mossad agent looked up at him. "I've, uh, just got a lot on my mind, not least of which is how to get to Saladin. I've got some ideas but need to check in with headquarters. Why don't we find a pleasant restaurant where you guys can have lunch while I make some calls?"

"Fine. I'm sure everyone's as hungry as I am." He turned around to see Hana, Karl and Aaron nodding their heads. "That's the plan, then."

"We passed a place on our way to El Fishawy that I think looked good. It's just up here a bit."

Soon they found themselves back at the Khan el-Khalili restaurant, on the border of the famed bazaar.

"Okay," Sarah said, addressing the group, "you order up some Egyptian cuisine here, and I'll attend to some business and be back to join you later, maybe half an hour."

"Deal," Hana replied. "Should we order something for you?"

"No. I'm not hungry, thanks. I'll catch something later. Shalom." With that, she gave a little wave, turned, and blended into the crowd.

Hana walked up to the restaurant host's podium, waiting for the greeter to return. The smells of frying olive oil, cumin, and the fragrance of other undefinable spices made everyone's stomachs rumble as they waited to be seated. Soon the greeter returned with a big, welcoming smile, then led them to a table for four in the middle of the large airy room. A server appeared, set down a basket of pita chips and a bowl of fresh hummus, then passed out menus to everyone. As this was a touristy restaurant, the meals had color photos and descriptions in English.

A short while later, their food was brought to the table by two servers. As they were digging in and chatting amiably, a young boy approached the table holding a stiff, wrapped package, roughly twelve inches square.

In passable English, he asked, "Father Michael Dominic?" as he looked around the table at the men.

"I'm Father Dominic," Michael said, raising his hand slightly. The boy walked around the table and handed the package to the priest.

"This from lady name Sarah," he said shyly. "She say keep but not open. Oh, and you must wait. She come soon."

"Thank you," Michael said, then reached into his pocket for a few coins and handed them to the boy, who turned and left.

"Well, that seems strange," Hana remarked. "Why wouldn't she have waited until she returned herself?"

"Does seem a little odd," Aaron said, "but these intel spooks have their own ways of doing things, I suppose."

"Whatever," Michael said as he dropped the package into his backpack. "I'm sure we'll know more when she returns." He and the others went back to their meals.

When they finished eating, they ordered strong arabica coffee while waiting for Sarah to return. The next twenty minutes were filled with chatter about Cairo and their observations of the people and customs, the sights and smells of the city, and what they still hoped to visit when they returned to Israel. Aaron, in particular, had a complete list of sights he wanted to check out when they got back to the Holy City.

Hana excused herself to use the restroom, taking her bag with her. In the meantime, while the others were talking, they didn't notice several armed soldiers in camo fatigues enter the restaurant, accompanied by one man dressed more formally, who seemed to be their leader.

Spotting Michael's table and the three men around it talking to each other, he motioned for his soldiers to head in that direction—which they did, surrounding the table as the group suddenly glanced up with questioning looks on their faces.

"May I help you?" Michael asked the man in the dark military suit, who was obviously in charge. Standing up, he set his napkin on the table.

"I am Major Kamal Fareed of the Mukhabarat. Egyptian intelligence. Your papers, please," he stated, holding out his hand.

"I am Father Michael Dominic, from the Vatican. Is there a problem here, Major?"

"I only need to see your papers, Father. So, you are a Catholic priest?"

"Yes, I am." As he spoke, Michael reached into his backpack and produced his passport. Karl and Aaron handed theirs to Michael, who passed them to the officer. Karl didn't think to use the diplomatic passport Sarah had provided him, but was leery of using it anyway.

"What is your business here in Egypt?"

"We are only tourists, here to enjoy your country's history and...hospitality." He emphasized that last word, hoping to imprint their economic value as tourists.

By this point, everyone in the restaurant was silent, gawking at the three men in the center of the room who seemed to be in some trouble.

"We will check your bags now, please," the major said flatly, issuing a brief command in Arabic to his men. The soldiers reached for each person's backpack and rifled through them recklessly.

"What's the meaning of this?!" Michael protested. "We have done nothing wrong. As I said, we are here purely for pleasure." The officer ignored him.

As Hana emerged from the restroom, she first noticed that the usual din of the restaurant had diminished, that it was spookily quiet except for one man somewhere speaking loudly. As she turned the corner and saw the commotion at her table, she held back, watching and listening to what was going on.

One soldier holding Michael's backpack pulled out the wrapped package sent by Sarah. He unceremoniously ripped off the paper, tossed it on the table, then handed the contents to his superior.

It was an ancient parchment in a protective Mylar sleeve, stiffened with a thick sheet of acid-free mat board behind it.

The major took it, peered at it carefully, then took out his cell phone, apparently to look at several images for reference. As he was doing this, Michael looked up, saw Hana against the back wall of the restaurant, and as their eyes met, he discreetly held up his hand for her to stay put.

Satisfied with what he found, the major looked up into Michael's eyes with contempt.

"Father Dominic, you are in illegal possession of a historically important manuscript stolen from the Egyptian National Library a few months ago. I am placing you and your colleagues under arrest for theft of cultural artifacts.

"Take them away," he instructed his men.

CHAPTER

THIRTY-THREE

B efore calling her contact at Egyptian intelligence and setting up Michael and his friends to get them out of the way, Sarah had reached Mossad headquarters and requested contact details of the infamous Cairo antiquities dealer Saladin.

Mossad's global intelligence network on its own was alarmingly extensive but supplemented with sensitive data from its allied partners—notably the United States National Security Agency with its top-secret ECHELON program—it had virtually unlimited powers for the collection and accessing of data on any person of interest anywhere in the world.

One of the NSA's most secretive communications satellites, codenamed PAN, was currently positioned in a geostationary orbit 36,000 kilometers over North Africa, where the speed of the satellite remained in the same relative position matching Earth's rotation. At Sarah's request, Mossad systems engineers could instantly locate Saladin's cell phone and give her his exact present location and home address, and, if she wished, the ability to eavesdrop on any of his calls.

But, she thought, that may not be necessary. At least she knew where to find him.

~

FIELD MARSHALL WALEED MAHMUD, the middle-aged director of the main Cairo branch of the Mukhabarat— Egypt's counterpart to Israel's Mossad—had a problem.

Created decades earlier under special training by the U.S. Central Intelligence Agency, the Mukhabarat survives even today under the specific conditions that Egypt remains loyal to the United States and never stands in opposition to Israel. Though his agency was now the most effective of all intelligence communities in the Arab world, many roundly criticized it as being a "shadow state," essentially controlling Egypt's government leaders and their military policies.

Waleed Mahmud had a great deal of latitude in how he performed his duties, suffering minor oversight by meddling politicians who were hardly predisposed toward intellectual honesty. Except for one: the Minister for Tourism and Antiquities—who also happened to be his wife, Salma.

But, as mandated by the CIA, his close association with Israeli Mossad offered him many opportunities, not least of which was to foster a special relationship with one of its senior agents: an attractive younger woman named Sarah Geffen, whom he had taken as a lover during one particular joint intelligence operation. The affair still continued despite her recent marriage to a fellow Mossad agent.

And that was also the problem, apart from the unfortunate fact that he sometimes confused Sarah's name when making love to his wife Salma, which fortunately —on the flip side of that coin—was not very often.

Mainly it was having to deal with Sarah's increasingly cumbersome requests for special favors, most recently the acquisition of an ancient parchment from his wife's ministry collection for some entrapment scheme Sarah had engineered, which included the apprehension of a few people who held no particular interest for him, anyway. And, of course, he obliged her, as he always did when he heard her voice, imagining her toned, athletic body next to his in the Pharaoh Suite of the St. Regis Hotel, their usual love nest overlooking the great pyramids.

And now she wanted an introduction to the most infamous antiquities broker in all of Egypt, Saladin. Whatever operation she had going, Mahmud wanted to know as little as possible about it.

Nonetheless, he could refuse his mistress nothing. He would provide her with two agents who would escort her to Saladin's ultra-secure villa estate in Garden City, the most affluent neighborhood in Cairo. He had earlier arranged a meeting for her with the man, one who had an obvious penchant for discretion.

AFTER CHECKING in on the intercom at the bottom of the driveway, the driver of the black Range Rover drove through the opening wrought-iron gate entrance, then sped up the long single-lane road to Saladin's villa perched high atop a hill in Garden City.

Two brawny Mukhabarat agents emerged from the vehicle and opened the back door. Sarah Geffen stepped out, fashionably attired in a dark blue Maskit pantsuit with a matching headscarf. Though wearing a head covering was not required of women in Egypt, men preferred it when they did, especially for reasons of piety or, in Sarah's case, to convey a sense of sophistication.

The visitors were met by an aide who led Sarah through the lush, expansive garden atrium of what was obviously a home of great wealth. The two agents returned to the car, its engine running to keep it cooled in the desert heat.

The illicit antiquities market must be thriving these days, Sarah mused as she was escorted into the library where Saladin himself was waiting, standing by a large, arched window overlooking the Nile River.

"Welcome to my humble home, Mrs. Geffen," Saladin said, his outstretched arms gesturing her toward a comfortable, dark-red leather armchair. He was wearing an extravagantly lustrous gold Stefano Ricci couture jacket with Mandarin collar and black slacks with gold slippers. He took the matching armchair across from his guest.

"I do not see many clients in my residence, but you have the honor of being the first Mossad agent here," he said disarmingly. "If it were not for our mutual friend, Director Mahmud of the Mukhabarat, you would likely have had a much more difficult time getting in at all. But how is our friend Waleed, hmm?" His baritone voice carried with it the hint of someone who knew more than he should, given the circumstances. It was clear he knew of their affair, at minimum.

Sarah was polite, but to the point. "He's fine, thank you. I understand you have a particular set of Israeli parchments given to you by Abu Tariq. I am here to take possession of them."

Saladin looked at her as if he hadn't understood her properly. "I beg your pardon?"

"I would like you to hand over property which was stolen from the Israeli government. Abu Tariq gained that material illegally and, as my government's representative in this matter, I intend to recover the parchments and return them to Israel without delay."

Saladin laughed out loud, his white teeth punctuating his long, curly black beard. "And what about my client, who is expecting a great deal of money for these, not to mention my commission? And frankly, I do not bother myself with the origins of materials I take in for placement."

"I'm afraid Abu Tariq is dead," Sarah said flatly. "I just got word from a reliable source on the ride here that he was killed by a black desert cobra in a Cairo alley."

Saladin's demeanor changed instantly. It was less one of sympathy, however, than of outright opportunism. He now had sole control of what may well be the most important religious artifact in all of Christianity. Something worth in the "many millions" of U.S. dollars, as Tariq had estimated—and now no one to have to share it with.

"I see," Saladin muttered thoughtfully, stroking his beard. "Well, that is a pity. But I fail to see how you intend to confiscate the parchment manuscripts, Agent Geffen, since I still intend to sell them to the highest bidder. This is what I do, you see. Even you cannot deprive a man of his livelihood." He smiled confidently as he folded his hands and set them on his lap.

"You must know, even here in Egypt, Mossad can make your life very difficult. Need I elaborate?"

"And you must realize that with a snap of my fingers I can have you beheaded where you sit in a matter of moments," he said coldly and without hesitation. "Do not threaten me, Agent Geffen."

Sarah had not expected such a bold retaliation, but she did not doubt him. She tried to mask her concern with a passive face. "Too many people know where I am, Saladin, and who I'm meeting with. But there is no need for such ultimatums that won't end well for either of us. I'm sure we can come to some accommodation here. Perhaps we can cover your standard commission. Would you be amenable to such a provision?"

"Well...since poor Abu is no longer my client, it would seem to me that ownership now passes to the possessor. So, in all candor, we are no longer talking about a mere commission, but full market value."

Sarah slowly shifted in the leather armchair, an uncomfortable warmth circling her neck as her temper flared. Then she abruptly stood up.

"I suggest we both give this some thought over the next twenty-four hours, then meet again to arrive at some mutual resolution," she said. Saladin pressed a button on the table next to him, then stood.

"I cannot see how another meeting can resolve anything, frankly, but should you come up with…oh, say ten million dollars in that time frame, then I would be most happy to resume our discussion. In the meantime, however, I will contact certain clients I know who would find these manuscripts most desirable."

The doors to the library opened and Saladin's aide appeared.

"Escort the lady to her car," he said bluntly. "Good day, Agent Geffen."

CHAPTER
THIRTY-FOUR

Now back at the hotel, Hana nervously paced her room, considering all available options to find and liberate Michael, Karl and Aaron from whatever situation they may have found themselves in. She had no clue at all where they might be or even how to find out. She also feared that even asking at a local police station might subject herself to arrest. The overwhelming feeling of isolation and the fact of not knowing was eating at her.

Hana realized she needed a clear head to make sensible decisions, but a maddening sense of desperation kept gripping her. Her normal state of mind thrived on being in control; it was as natural to her as breathing. But she was one woman alone in a terribly uncontrolled situation, and it felt as if all potential avenues available here—in archaically patriarchal Egypt—were closed to her.

Obviously, she could not turn to Sarah, wherever she

was...*whoever* she was. It was now clear as day that *she* had engineered that little performance. *Damn her and whatever misguided motives drove that woman!* The sense of betrayal was formidable—but again, Hana had to keep her head about her.

I wonder if Yossi knows... she thought. Given his past heroically cooperative efforts on their behalf in Argentina, Hana couldn't imagine he had a deceitful bone in his body. She would call him first, if only to either eliminate or engage him as a resource.

Then what? My grandfather? The pope? Or...wait...yes, that option might actually work! But first...

With determination, she grabbed her phone and called the number Karl had given her for Yossi Geffen in Tel Aviv. The call connected, and the onetime Israeli commando and current Mossad agent answered.

"Yossi, this is Hana Sinclair. I'm here in Cairo and, well, we've got a serious problem."

"I'm sorry to hear that, Hana," he said with genuine concern. "How can I help?"

"First, let me explain the situation..." She recapped everything that had occurred since Yossi had passed on to them the details of that tapped call between Khalid Zadani and Abu Tariq. Finally, she got to the scene in the Khan el-Khalili restaurant.

"Yossi, there's only one way those soldiers could have known about Michael having that ancient parchment from the National Library—Sarah betrayed him. She *had* to have called the authorities at the same time she had the artifact itself delivered to Michael in the restaurant! It was a setup, plain and simple. As I think back on it now, Sarah did show several vague signs of duplicity. I just let them pass. I'm sorry to have to break it to you this way, but I see no other excuse. So…what do you think?"

There was a long pause at the other end of the call. Then she heard what she took to be an emotional sigh of frustration, even defeat.

"Hana, to be honest, I've had my own suspicions about my wife since a short while after we got married. Little things. Things only a trained agent might recognize. And it shatters me to have it confirmed now. Sarah always spoke of never having enough money, teasing me that she should have married up. I see now she wasn't joking. And if what you said about those parchments being worth millions is true, then I wouldn't put it past her to have worked out a plan to acquire them on her own. *Dammit!* This is devastating!"

"I'm so sorry, Yossi," she said earnestly. "She's double-crossed all of us, but I know you're the one who has the most to suffer over.

"But, speaking of suffering, we must find out where those soldiers took Michael, Karl and Aaron. Is that something you might be able to learn? I'm out of options here myself."

"Yes, I do have a contact in an Egyptian intelligence unit. Let me call him now. I will call you back, Hana. Do not worry, you can trust me. We will find the guys and get them back to you as soon as possible. Shalom for now."

"Remi Shapiro, my old friend…shalom! Do you recognize my voice?"

After a pause, Remi exclaimed, *"Saladin?! My god, it's been a long time! Please, tell me you've got some irresistible artifacts my boss can't live without, because frankly, I could use a big win right now. I've had the worst time trying to close a deal on some parchments that came into my hands, but now they've vanished and keep eluding me. A long story I won't bore you with."*

"Then you are in luck, my friend. I have come across what may well be the most important discovery since the Dead Sea Scrolls—perhaps even greater than those, in fact. Yes, these parchments, four of them, are absolutely fresh to market. Your Mr. Darwin *must* make an offer on these soon, as no one has seen them yet. The IAA has not even registered them. I was told they came directly out of a cave in Wadi Murabba'at recently. But we must act fast, as forces are—even as we speak—conspiring to acquire them by unreasonable means."

"Then *yes!* Of course. I've learned to trust your judgment over the years in such matters, Saladin. I doubt money will be an object, since Pastor Darwin's museum needs big attractions to keep it relevant and thriving. So, tell me more about these parchments of yours."

As Saladin related his description of the parchments, Remi got an uneasy feeling in his stomach. Then he heard the words, *"…and an exceedingly rare manuscript written by St. Paul himself!"* and nearly retched, his exasperation was so visceral.

"Saladin! Those are the same parchments I had *in my very hands* four days ago! They were stolen from me here in Jerusalem. I was tasered by someone sitting behind me during an event in the Old City, and whoever it was stole my backpack, the bastard. Oh God, the terrible irony!" As he said these words, it crossed Remi's mind that perhaps it was one of Saladin's underlings who had tasered him, only ramping up the irony.

Saladin was surprised at this turn of events, but unmoved by his old friend's predicament. He was, after all, a businessman. And such a fabulous treasure as he now possessed did not come along often. No, not often at all.

A superstitious man, Saladin briefly considered that perhaps there was a curse on these materials. All the more reason to move them quickly.

"I am very sorry to hear this, Remi. But whatever the awkward circumstances, I have obligations to my clients to act on their behalf. I cannot concern myself with how certain materials came into their possession. Do you see my quandary?" He smoothly blamed his "predicament" on the seller, not revealing that Saladin himself was in the unique position this time of being the current owner. "Surely you did not already pay for them, did you?"

Embarrassed by the question, Remi could hardly admit he'd originally stolen them from Khalid Zadani's hotel room.

"No, thankfully...but, well, it's another long story. So, what are you asking for them?"

"Ten million dollars U.S., in bearer bonds or trans-ferred to my bank in Singapore. The manuscripts have already been provisionally authenticated by the highest authority, the curator and head librarian of Saint Catherine's Monastery in the Sinai. The St. Paul document on its own would forever change the foundations of Christianity, Remi. Nothing else like it exists. You can come take possession of them here in Cairo or I can have them couriered to you in Jerusalem. But time is of the essence. I suggest you decide within twenty-four hours, even sooner."

Saladin knew he was facing an uncertain deadline with Sarah Geffen's imminent and likely aggressive actions, whatever they might be, hovering over him at that very moment. The specter of a swarm of Mossad agents invading his villa was hardly appealing—though something about her demeanor gave him the vague impression she might be working alone. Nevertheless, he had to act on the assumption that she had potentially hostile resources in her favor. It was only prudent. He cursed himself for not having taken her head when he had the chance.

Remi did not flinch at the price. Darwin had paid more for other artifacts, and in fact his museum had a half-billion dollars in inventory as it was, although the provenances of many of its scrolls, tablets and other artifacts were believed to be sketchy.

"Alright, I'll arrange for the bank transfer once I get approval from Pastor Darwin. And yes, I will come to Cairo to pick them up myself. I should be there tomorrow, though I'll confirm everything with you shortly. Thanks, old friend, and please, don't let those parchments out of your sight. I can't bear losing them again."

"HANA, I'm afraid I have some bad news," Yossi said after she picked up the ringing phone. "Possibly very bad."

"I'm sitting down. Go ahead."

"Michael, Aaron and Karl have been taken to Scorpion, a supermax prison in south Cairo. Without due process, they have been dealt with as prisoners, with no pending arraignment or trial date set. That's how it is with the Egyptian legal system, especially when someone is picked up for presumed theft. They are treated like convicted criminals from day one. And I'm afraid Mossad won't be able to assist in their recovery, Hana. I fought like hell to make the case, but the politics of it are too volatile. I'm so sorry."

Hana lost it. As she listened to Yossi speak his first words, tears streamed down her cheeks and her stomach clenched into a tight knot as the worst possible images formed in her mind. Michael, the man she loved...her beloved cousin Karl...and Aaron, who only wanted a good time with his new friends—all in a heinous Egyptian prison? *How could this happen?!*

"Are you still there, Hana?" Yossi asked tenderly, hearing her emotions spill out.

"Sorry, Yossi. I'm having a hard time processing this," she sniffed. "So, nothing you personally can do to help? I feel so alone now, something I'm not used to."

"If there were anything I could do, anything at all, I'd be on a plane in a heartbeat. At the moment, I am out of options, but I will try to think of something.

"I understand. I do have one idea I'm hoping beyond

hope may work. If I need your help in its execution, can I count on you?"

"Absolutely, Hana. I'll move heaven and earth to undo what damage my wife has caused. I've just dealt with that matter here with the powers that be. She's now been declared persona non grata by Mossad and has been cut off from all official resources. Sarah is now a rogue agent."

CHAPTER

THIRTY-FIVE

F
ather Michael Dominic felt trapped in a frightening, horrific dream, as he, Karl and Aaron were thrown into an obscene prison, then shuffled from one squalid processing cell to the next as brutal guards shouted curses at them in Arabic and repeatedly whipped them with rugged leather straps long stained from past bloody beatings.

But this unspeakable nightmare was no dream. All three of them had been transported in a putrid prisoner van packed with common criminals to the dreaded supermax penitentiary called Scorpion Prison, the shame of south Cairo. In the words of a former warden, *"It was designed so that those who go in don't come out again, unless dead."*

Major Fareed and his soldiers spared no sympathy as Michael's explanations and pleadings fell on deaf ears, almost as if their arrest and imprisonment had been predetermined. Nothing he could say or do would

GARY MCAVOY

move his captors, and given the deservedly abominable reputation of Egyptian prisons, he had a sinking, gut-level fear that there would never be a way out of this real-life nightmare.

One glimmer of hope grew in his mind: Hana. She had seen it all happen in the restaurant and smartly stayed back, removed from the provocative confrontation as it was occurring. Surely, she would do whatever it took to find and rescue them.

But how? What could a woman alone do in—likely from her perspective—such a barbaric, male dominated Third World country? The callous bureaucracy alone would be daunting, and Hana didn't speak Arabic.

Thinking about it only made him more depressed. *How did he ever end up in such a dreadful situation?!*

Sarah. It had to be her doing. Sending that blind package by messenger when she was due back shortly was all the proof Michael needed that she had her own agenda now...probably had all along. The Mukhabarat was acting on her orders. Maybe they owed her a favor, or she made some arrangement with them. *Why didn't I see it?! How could she have conceived such a deceitful and cowardly act? Was Yossi in on it, too?*

MICHAEL, Aaron and Karl were stripped of their clothes and forced to put on ratty, dark-blue underwear and matching prison uniforms. Standing in a long line of other inmates being processed for incarceration—with no kind of legal due process—they watched as the men in front of them had their heads forcibly shaved.

Michael's turn came, and by then he felt thoroughly demoralized, as if he were losing part of his humanity, watching clumps of hair fall off his shoulders and onto the filthy floor by his toes.

It might be impossible for anyone to forgive such inhumane treatment. But as a priest, as a human being, he must try. He recalled a parable, when Peter asked Jesus, "Lord, how many times shall I forgive my brother when he sins against me? Up to seven times?" And Jesus answered, "I tell you, not seven times, but seventy seven times." Michael was struggling with even this once.

He looked at Karl and Aaron, both of whom were looking as forlorn and dispirited, given the horrors they were all experiencing. They, too, had assumed that the odds of getting out of this were not very good at all.

"*PRONTO*, office of the Holy Father. This is Father Bannon."

"Hello, Nick. It's Hana Sinclair."

"Hana! What a pleasure hearing from you! Shall I put you through to His Holiness? He is available at the moment."

Hana was always surprised by the freedom of access she enjoyed with the pope because of her grandfather being one of the pontiff's closest friends and advisors. In this instance, though, she thought it wiser to have the pope's personal secretary relay details of the situation.

"No, I think it would be more appropriate if I speak

with you first, then you can pass on what the pope needs to hear. Nick, Michael's in terrible danger. So is my cousin Karl Dengler, one of the Swiss Guards, along with a close friend of Michael's, Dr. Aaron Pearce from Loyola. We're all here in Cairo, and to be honest, things are pretty dire.

"Without going into long and drawn-out details, let's just say we were all unexpectedly betrayed by an agent of Israel's Mossad, and now Michael, Karl and Aaron have been imprisoned here on false charges. As you might imagine, I have little personal influence in Egypt, and of course as a woman here, not much respect where it will count on trying to free them.

"I do have one idea which I think may have merit, and I'll pursue that next. But I thought it important to let the Holy Father know, for obvious reasons. And if he has any influence in a Muslim country, well, it's an all-hands-on-deck situation. But keeping him at a bit of a distance from what I'm about to try…well, that is why I am relaying the information through you."

"Goodness, Hana. I am so sorry to hear this. I can't imagine what you're going through. You absolutely did the right thing in calling me. I'll explain things to His Holiness right now and see if there are any political expedients we might come up with. I can say with no doubt he will be deeply disturbed by this news and will do whatever he can to free Michael and the others."

"Thanks so much, Nick. And I'll let you know if my interim plan works. Take care."

Hana's next call was to Karl's partner in the Swiss Guard, Lukas Bischoff, who was on duty at the Vatican.

"Lukas, I'm afraid I have some bad news. Michael and Karl have been arrested in Cairo on spurious charges, but—"

"Arrested? *No!* How is that possible, Hana? Do you know if they're okay? What can I do to help?"

"To be honest, I really don't know their current condition. But as I was about to say, I think I have a plan that might work, though it's a long shot. And before I ask you something, you must trust me and not ask questions about why or how I know this. All right, Lukas?"

The young guardsman paused, concern for Karl wracking him. "Okay, go ahead."

"Do you have your commandant's personal cell phone number? I know Colonel Scarpa is in Jerusalem, and I need to reach him. That's all I can say right now, Lukas. Do you have his number?"

"Yes, of course. He gives it to all the guardsmen. Got a pen?" Hana pulled out a pad of paper from the hotel desk and wrote down Scarpa's number.

"Thanks. All you need to do now is stand by and pray. I'm doing my level best to get them out of prison and will keep you advised."

"They're already in prison?!"

"Yeah, I know. They do things differently here, Lukas. I'm trying not to think about it myself, else I'd make myself crazy with worry. I'll talk to you soon, all right? I have work to do now."

THIRTY-SIX

Having delivered his prisoners to Scorpion the day before on what proved to be a factual tip from Mossad agent Sarah Geffen, Major Kamal Fareed of the Mukhabarat had arrived at his office the next morning when his secretary handed him two messages. The first was from his confidential source at Mossad headquarters in Tel Aviv, saying only:

Agent Sarah Geffen Now Persona Non Grata
Do Not Engage In Any Official Capacity

Well, he considered, *a most surprising change of events. I wonder what brought that on?*

The second message was from Sarah herself, asking him to call her.

Curious to find out what might have caused her to be ostracized by such a venerated agency, he couldn't resist returning the call. Intelligence personnel lived on acquiring information, including gossip about internal affairs. He made the call.

"Sarah, this is Kamal Fareed, returning your call."

"Thank you, Major. I wanted to follow up on yesterday's arrest to see what you did with those thieves. Are they being held, or…?"

"Yes, of course. They have all been taken to Scorpion Prison, where they will remain until a decision is made as to their status. I don't see that happening anytime soon, frankly. But I am grateful for your tip. It certainly helped raise my profile with my superiors. The other parchments stolen while in-transit from the Dar el-Kotob Library in Cairo to the National Library have yet to be recovered, so the priest and his two friends will be interrogated today or tomorrow to learn where they have hidden the rest of the documents.

"I have one question for you, though, Agent Geffen. I received a communique from my source at Mossad saying you are now 'persona non grata.' May I ask what happened?"

Sarah nearly dropped the phone, she was so shocked. She couldn't believe what she just heard.

"What are you talking about, Major? That's ridiculous! I have—*Wait*…did you just say '*the priest and his two friends*'? There should be four, not three. How many did you arrest at the restaurant?"

"Just the priest and two other men." He checked his notes. "Yes, Father Michael Dominic, Sergeant Karl Dengler, and Dr. Aaron Pearce."

"No *woman?* There was also a woman with them! You did not arrest the woman?"

"There was no woman, no. But we were happy to have caught the ringleader with the library parchment, especially him being a Catholic priest. The others were just collateral."

Sarah now realized why she had been blackballed from the agency. Hana Sinclair must have somehow eluded the soldiers and made phone calls exposing her. *That obviously means Yossi knows, too! Damn that* zonna! she cursed. *Bitch.*

Well, it had to happen sooner or later, she reasoned. It was the sooner part that worried her, though, since she had still intended to rely on her Mossad credentials and capabilities to complete her plans. But now she was on her own.

With Saladin not budging in acceding to her intimidation, and with her expulsion from Mossad depriving her of resources to back up her threats, Sarah saw the writing on the wall. She would have to abandon her plans to get the parchments. But at least she still had the all-important silver scroll. That alone would fetch a small fortune.

CONFINED TO A CRAMPED, fetid cell with Karl, Aaron, and one other man who looked to be an Arab in his seventies, Michael ran his hands across his nearly bald scalp, the uneven stubble testament to the careless shearing each of them suffered when getting shaved.

As the guards were delivering breakfast, they slid what passed for food through a horizontal slot in the cell door, most of which fell onto the floor. Each man received a small piece of cheese, a few beans, and a wedge of hard bread, likely several days old. There were no beds in the cell, only low concrete platforms, each cushioned with a large, flattened cardboard box and one tatty wool blanket. All inmates were deprived of the basic necessities for comfort or hygiene—there was no soap, shampoo, combs, toothbrushes or toothpaste; and books, newspapers, prayer rugs, paper and writing instruments were all banned.

Hearing Michael talk with his colleagues in English, the older man shyly sidled up to him, asking, "Are you American?"

"I am an American, yes," Michael replied, "but I currently live in Rome, in the Vatican. I am a Catholic priest, a Jesuit."

The man's eyes opened wide, and he smiled mercifully. "Praise be to God! I too am Catholic, a Maronite! I taught history at the Collège de la Sainte Famille here in Cairo. It is a French international school for boys, founded in 1879 by your order, *the Jesuits!* But the Egyptian government did not agree with my curriculum and I have been here now for such a long time. They call me a political prisoner, if you can imagine that.

"It has been so many years since I have had the privilege of a priest at my side, Father. Would you please hear my confession?"

Surprised, Michael was suddenly and gratefully reminded of his calling and its concomitant obligations. For a precious moment, he was removed from his appalling circumstances.

"Yes, of course. What is your name?"

"My name is Hassan," he said proudly, as if it were the only precious thing he possessed.

Michael took the old man's shoulder and guided him to a back corner of the cell, where they had a bit more privacy. In barely a whisper, he began the rite of Confession, making the sign of the cross. Hassan's eyes filled with tears as he realized the intimate sacredness of the moment, something he had given up on long ago. Speaking in a low voice, he gave his confession to the young priest, who himself was gently weeping now, overcome with raw emotion.

CHAPTER
THIRTY-SEVEN

Having finished his business in Israel and continuing his Middle East tour of regional mithraeums, Colonel Niccolò Scarpa's next stop was at the Mediterranean port of Alexandria, Egypt's second largest city. It was also where one of his most thriving mithraeums was located, serving the largest military installation in the Middle East, the Mohamed Naguib Military Base, named after an Egyptian army officer who became the country's first president.

As he was casually speaking to a small group of fellow soldiers, his cell phone hummed. Turning away from the group, he answered it.

"Colonel Scarpa? This is Hana Sinclair, sir. You may recall we met at the St. Onuphrius Monastery with my cousin, Sergeant Karl Dengler?"

"Of course, I remember you, Hana. And Karl was of tremendous help to us then. How is he?"

"Well, Colonel, That's just it. We find ourselves in a truly awful situation here in Cairo, and you are the only person I can think of who might help. Let me explain…"

Scarpa listened to her story. Hana left nothing out, so he would have all the facts in order to prepare him for her request.

"…And that's my reason for calling you, to hopefully—"

"Hana, say no more. I know exactly what's needed now, and I'm fully prepared to help rescue Sergeant Dengler and the others. This will take some quick planning, but I think we'll be prepared and ready to strike in a day or so. As it happens, we do have a large contingent of Mithraists in Cairo, even many who work at Scorpion Prison, as I recall. No doubt this could be a dangerous mission, but our members are loyal and true, and have taken an oath to perform without question at times like this.

"I am currently in Alexandria, about two hours away from Cairo and the prison itself. But I will stay in touch with you, Hana. Stay put and pray for the best." He ended the call.

Her instincts rewarded, Hana was overcome with relief. Though she did not know the colonel well, she knew Karl idolized his commandant. And her cousin was not easily influenced, all of which made her feel more optimistic that Scarpa and his conscripted troops had not only the ability but the inclination—as well as the means—to pull off whatever operation he might be devising.

REMI SHAPIRO HAD JUST LANDED at Cairo International Airport with the new bodyguard he hired in Tel Aviv, a man whose résumé included experience as a Mossad agent and who came highly recommended by the discreet security agency Remi frequently used.

As a precaution against yet again losing the precious parchments he intended to acquire from Saladin, he would take no more chances this time. The bodyguard seemed capable enough, and certainly looked the part: tall, muscular, and supremely confident. Plus, he was a fellow Jew. His name was Yossi Geffen.

Fortunately for Yossi, Remi never put the name together with the woman who punched him in the hotel room. After all, remembering someone's surname in such a violent moment was hardly a priority.

"As I mentioned on the plane, Yossi, Saladin is an old friend. But he has a paranoid streak and thus a lot of security, so don't be alarmed by all the guns."

"It takes a lot more than guns to alarm me, Remi. I am not worried at all."

"Good. The money transfer will be completed for this transaction by the time we arrive. So, it should be a simple matter of picking up what I came for and getting back on the plane for Tel Aviv. It's almost eight o'clock now. Saladin said he should have things ready by noon, so we've got a few hours to kill. Anything you'd like to do in the meantime?"

"Well, if you don't mind, I do have a little side business I'd like to attend to while I'm here. Off the clock, of course. Why don't I meet you at Saladin's villa about quarter to twelve? Would that be all right?"

"Sure, not a problem. I'll grab some breakfast at one of the local cafés and we'll meet up at his residence in Garden City at eleven forty-five."

HAVING ENGINEERED his being hired by Remi consequent to monitoring his phone calls—while coordinating his assignment for the job under the aegis of the secretly Mossad-owned security agency Remi had been guided to employ—Yossi was now able to deal with Sarah and her duplicitous exploits in Cairo.

And once Remi had the purloined parchments—which rightfully belonged to the State of Israel—it would be no problem for Yossi dispossessing him of the manuscripts and turning them over to the IAA once they were back on Israeli soil.

But first, he had to find Sarah. His tracking monitor of her cell phone—standard for Mossad units in case of special assistance situations—showed that she was about twenty kilometers from the airport, apparently staying at the Kempinski Nile Hotel in Garden City, not far from Saladin's villa. Obviously, she had been in contact with Saladin to acquire the parchments herself. Knowing her as he did, Yossi assumed she would have used the intimidation of her Mossad influence to try manipulating her target to yield the manuscripts. But as Remi told him he had arranged for Darwin's transfer of millions into Saladin's account, Saladin still held the parchments, and now was just waiting for Remi to conclude the deal by picking them up.

Then what would Sarah's plan be? he wondered. Given Saladin's tight security, she couldn't be planning to steal them—unless she figured she could just seize them from Remi once *he* acquired them. Well, in that case, she'd be in for a big surprise.

He needed to get to her sooner, though attempting to arrest her in Egypt and return her to Israel would be nearly impossible.

Then he remembered she had recently acquired the legendary silver scroll from Remi. He had no doubt now that instead of turning it in to IAA or Mossad as would be expected, and as she'd told him, she'd held onto it for herself. So, what to do? Try to intercept his wife at the hotel? Wait until his return to Tel Aviv and grab her there? If he attempted anything here in Cairo, it would surely tip her off, making it that much more difficult to recover the highly desirable silver scroll back in Israel.

He decided to wait until Tel Aviv, when the element of surprise would be in his favor.

THE MUWAFFAQ SALTI AIR BASE in Azraq, Jordan—home to the Royal Jordanian Air Force—also boasts a substantial U.S. military presence as host to several MQ-9 Reaper drones and other top-secret equipment and regional strategic operations.

In fact, the United States had invested heavily in the airbase for years, pouring hundreds of millions of dollars into its infrastructure while establishing intelligence, surveillance, and reconnaissance facilities in the war against ISIL—the Islamic State of Iraq and the Levant. Jordan had been a trusted ally of the United States for decades and having a central military installation in the Middle East was key to U.S. policies.

On his arrival that morning by reciprocal military transport from Alexandria, Colonel Niccolò Scarpa and his lieutenants were treated as honored guests by the base commander and were shown great courtesies as they made their case for borrowing one particular piece of equipment for a purportedly classified mission—a Sikorsky UH-60 Black Hawk helicopter. Though aircraft costing six million euros are not usually "loaned out," the base commandeer was not only a good friend of Scarpa's, but the *pater* of a Jordanian mithraeum.

Of the specialized variations Sikorsky had sold to the Royal Jordanian Air Force, Scarpa chose a secret version of the UH-60 with modified low-observable technology, enabling it to essentially evade Egyptian radar, with extra blades on the tail rotor, harsh angles, flat surfaces, and other noise reduction measures, making the aircraft much quieter than conventional models. Such efficiencies could give them an upper hand when breaching Scorpion Prison from the air.

Scarpa was depending on it.

The next phase of his plan was rounding up ten exemplary combat soldiers for the mission—fourteen being the Black Hawk's maximum personnel capacity, accounting for onboarding rescued individuals. Scarpa traveled with an entourage of four of his best men from

Rome, so he only needed a few more from the local mithraeum's membership, not a difficult task.

Having composed his unit for the mission and gotten a map of Scorpion Prison and the surrounding vicinity, Colonel Scarpa explained the impending operation to his team.

They would launch the rescue and recovery raid the following day.

CHAPTER
THIRTY-EIGHT

At eleven forty-five, the dark gray Škoda Kodiaq Yossi had rented drew up to Saladin's villa. Seeing a taxi idling at the curb with Remi sitting in the back seat, he motioned to him to join him in the SUV; they could drive up the villa road together.

Approaching the house, three armed guards were waiting for them. Stepping out of the vehicle, both men were frisked for weapons. Yossi reluctantly yielded his Beretta 70 service pistol, making a mental note of who took it from him.

They were escorted into the home's garden atrium by Saladin's aide, who led them through the house to the library with its arched-windowed view of the Nile River. Remi was enthralled by the luxurious appointments as he took in the room. Yossi was more circumspect, feeling slightly vulnerable without his Beretta.

"Welcome, gentlemen," Saladin said as he walked

into the room. "May I have some tea brought in for you?" Both men declined.

"Remi, will you introduce me to your colleague?"

"Ah, sorry, of course. This is Yossi Geffen, my body-guard. I'm not taking any chances of losing these parchments again."

At the mention of the name Geffen, Saladin's eyebrows arched, and he glared at Yossi.

"Would you by any chance be related to a Mossad agent named Sarah Geffen?" he asked suspiciously.

Taken by total surprise—since he hadn't known Sarah met with the broker—Yossi steeled himself for reactions by either man. He glanced at Remi, whose face was suddenly dawning with both recognition and fear that he may have made a terrible mistake.

"As it happens, that scheming bitch is my ex-wife," he spat convincingly, visibly disgusted. "We have nothing to do with each other now. I haven't even seen her in months. How do *you* know about her?" He stared hard at Saladin.

Turning the questioning around was a standard defense maneuver when being interrogated unofficially, and the ploy worked. Remi turned to Saladin, too, wondering how *he* knew about the woman who had attacked him and took the silver scroll.

Saladin explained, "This Sarah Geffen person came to me two days ago, insisting I turn over the parchments to her, even threatening me with Mossad's influence. I had the vague impression she was acting on her own, but I have no actual basis for that. Only intuition."

Continuing to distance himself from suspicion, Yossi responded, "Your instincts serve you well, Saladin. I once worked for Mossad myself, and heard from the grapevine that she's been tossed out of the agency, considered persona non grata for exercising self-interest over duty. So, I doubt you have anything to fear from her. Besides, you are obviously very well protected here."

Saladin smiled at both confirmation of his suspicions and the compliment from Remi's colleague, while Remi was pleased to hear validations by his own bodyguard.

"Shall we get down to the business at hand, then?" Yossi suggested.

"I was about to say the same thing," Remi concurred, turning to his host. "Have you received the wired funds from Pastor Darwin?"

"Yes, I have, indeed. Everything is in order," Saladin said, smiling. "And here are your exquisite parchments. I trust you will take proper care of them." He reached into an archival folder and theatrically produced the four manuscripts, laying them out on the long, ebony coffee table, each of them protected in an acid-free Mylar conservation sleeve.

"Excellent," Remi enthused, knowing this would please his boss tremendously. He gathered them up, returned them to the archival folder, then stood to leave, extending his hand to Saladin.

"Thank you for working with me on this. I am so very grateful."

"As am I," Saladin said, returning the handshake.

Because the two men were now heading out of the house and no longer posed a threat to their protectee, one of the guards returned Yossi's Baretta, which he tucked back in his shoulder holster.

During the drive to the airport for their return to Tel Aviv, Remi was beaming, telling Yossi of all the obstacles he'd had to endure to get to this point, including those involving Sarah. Otherwise, it was a quiet drive, with each man left to his own thoughts: Remi, whose high comfort level finally assured him the worst was over. And Yossi, who was planning to seize the parchments once they were back on Israeli soil.

THE LASH of the whip came down brutally hard on the muscled but tender flesh of Michael Dominic's bare back as the guard repeatedly flailed him.

"Where are the rest of the stolen library documents?!" he screeched in Arabic. Then he moved over a meter to his left and gave Karl Dengler the same lashing, shouting the same question. The whip tore through the smaller man's bare skin as he remained stoic, in silent refusal to submit to his captors. One more meter to his left, the guard tore into Aaron's back as the larger man's body arched in pain.

All three of them had been dragged out into the courtyard—what prison guards called the "playground" —stripped shirtless in the hot sun, then handcuffed and hung in stress positions, their arms suspended from a metal grate above their backs.

After a dozen continuous beatings, Michael weakly kept repeating their defense in Arabic: "Why are you doing this?! We know nothing about your library's documents. We were set up by a rogue Israeli agent who lied to get us out of her way. You must believe me."

But the guard would have none of it. The beatings continued as rivulets of blood streamed down their backs, forming red puddles in the dusty tan sand around each man.

A young boy in a red fez came over with two buckets of filthy water and heaved a splash of the scummy liquid over each of their backs. Infection was almost guaranteed.

The guard hung up his whip and disappeared for a while, presumably having gone inside the nearest detention building to rest and refresh himself from the strenuous work of torturing other human beings.

Hanging by their trusses in the scorching heat, the water on their bloody backs both refreshing and painful, Karl turned his head to the priest, his face sweaty and tortured.

"What are we going to do, Michael?" he wheezed. "I'm not sure I can take much more of this."

"I know, Karl," he replied in his most assuring manner, despite his own agonizing condition. "All I can say is pray to God they believe me sooner than later."

Aaron, bigger and stronger than the others, was more optimistic. "I think I might be able to wriggle out of this brace," he muttered, twisting his wrists in circles as he tried in vain to free himself from the cuffs. "And once I do, I'm going to kill that masochist with my bare hands."

"There's too many of them, Aaron. They'd be on you in a New York min—"

At that moment the growing sound of a loud, whirring motor filled the air, the ground shaking as it got closer. Sand blew in a huge vortex around them as the gigantic body of a Black Hawk helicopter roared over the building, hovered over the three bound prisoners, then landed right behind them in the playground between the H-shaped detention buildings.

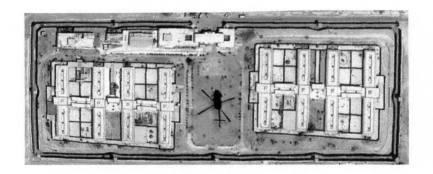

CHAPTER
THIRTY-NINE

A squad of men in full combat gear with Heckler & Koch G36 assault rifles aimed and ready poured out of the helo, four setting up corner defensive positions around the bird as another four took offensive stances to neutralize guards on land and in the towers.

Colonel Niccolò Scarpa jumped out of the cargo doors—one guard at his side for command protection—and instantly saw Michael and the others trussed up on the playground, stripped to the waist. The sight of their bloodied bodies infuriated Scarpa.

Several of his men were returning fire from some guards in the high, round, fortified towers overlooking the prison grounds, but there were far fewer hostilities than they expected, due to Scarpa's region-wide order that fellow Mithraists, especially those serving at Scorpion Prison, turn a blind eye to the planned incursion and lay down their arms.

Scarpa and two soldiers helped free Michael, Karl and Aaron from their shackles, throwing emergency space blankets over each man to protect them from the blistering sun as they led them back toward the Black Hawk.

"Wait," Michael protested. "There's one more man in my cell, here in the first building. I want him to come with us. His name is Hassan. He's in the first wing. Turn right and go to the fifth cell down on the left. Get the key from any guard."

"I'll show him where it is," Aaron said, shaking off the space blanket. "I want a word with that guard, anyway."

Two armed soldiers accompanied Aaron as the three men entered the building. Encountering a pair of guards who were rushing at them from the hallway, the soldiers dispatched each one with a single shot. His intimidating height and build having its intended effect on other fleeing guards, Aaron trudged down the hallway until he found the guard who had whipped them cowering behind a battered Coke machine. He stared the man down.

"*Sayyid, please!*" the guard pleaded in English, his hands held over his head, terrified now that the tables were turned. "*I was only doing my job!*"

"Give me the key to the cells," Aaron growled with a dark menace, his hand held out.

The guard hurried to produce the key from his belt ring and handed it to the former prisoner, who now towered above him.

Aaron pocketed the key, then reached down,

grabbed the guard by his throat, and lifted him up high against the wall, his fury unrestrained.

"You are one miserable fuck. If I had more time, I'd give you a taste of the whip myself. But as I only have a minute…"

Aaron pulled back his balled fist and let it slam into the guard's face—once, twice, a third time, all in rapid succession. He let the guard fall onto the fetid concrete floor, his face a bloody mess. Aaron kicked him in the gut repeatedly, cursing the man until the two soldiers pulled him away. Aaron was panting, his uncontrolled rage beyond anything he had ever felt in his life. As he was walking away with the soldiers, he suddenly twisted around, pulled back his leg, and thrust it into the guard's head. "And *that's* for Michael and Karl, you sick bastard!"

The three of them went down the corridor to Aaron's former cell to fetch Hassan, who was fearful at first sight of two soldiers with guns and a very bloody Aaron.

"Come with us, Hassan. We're being rescued. You're a free man now."

The Catholic Arab couldn't believe his good fortune, and with eyes wide, followed his new friend out of the cell, down the dank corridor and out into the bright sunlight, where a terrifyingly large combat helicopter was waiting for him. Scarpa's soldiers helped him aboard.

The Black Hawk's rotors spun up to full speed as the rest of the soldiers jumped back into the cargo bay while a medic attended to the wounded priest and his friends. As it lifted into the sky above the notorious prison yard,

Michael looked back down, silently swearing never to return to Cairo again.

Scarpa handed him a comms headset, which he fastened over his ears. "Now do you see the power of the Mithraist movement?" the colonel asked the priest.

"I never doubted it," Michael said, doing his best to smile. "Hey, how did you know we were here in the first place? I never thought we'd ever get out of that hellhole."

"Your friend Hana put things in motion," Scarpa replied loudly over the steady rotor noise. "She called everyone. Even the pope, I think. That woman can really get things accomplished. She found out from a Mossad friend of yours that you'd been taken to Scorpion. So, we put together a rescue team with men and equipment borrowed from the Royal Jordanian Air Force. And of course, our own motto is the same as your country's Marines: *Leave no man behind.*"

"I don't know how to thank you, Colonel. Anything I might do for you in return?"

Scarpa paused for a moment, then looked into Michael's eyes. "Father, I realize you are very close to the pope. The only thing I might ask is that you refrain from mentioning my relationship with the Mithraists. His Holiness might take it the wrong way, or be concerned that my loyalties are divided, which I assure you they are not. The Swiss Guard is always first and foremost in my life. I firmly believe that soldiers every-where deserve to be supported, and this is one proven way we can do that."

"Colonel, you have my word on that. Though I don't

believe the Holy Father would mind at all, since what you are doing has an honorable and historic mission. Perhaps you might choose to tell him yourself one day, when the timing is right. And if I can help lay that groundwork, you have but to ask. I'm incredibly grateful you rescued us from that awful place."

The two men looked at each other knowingly, a shared camaraderie that would likely last for a long time.

"It might interest you to know, Father, that we found a great deal more silver at the St. Onuphrius Monastery, much of which we split with the nunnery, and the rest of which went into our modest treasury. We tried in vain to locate many of the other landmarks described in the silver scroll, but they had either already been looted long ago or were buried in places impossible to reach now. A lot of earth movements and blowing dirt and sand can happen over two thousand years, not to mention the development of roads, new homes, office buildings and apartment houses. As-yet undiscovered finds of great significance likely are forever buried now. It's a pity, really, but we did our level best. And thank you again for lending us Sergeant Dengler. He has a brilliant future ahead of him in the Swiss Guard."

CHAPTER
FORTY

E arlier, knowing the rescue operation was imminent, Hana had caught the first flight she could get from Cairo to the Queen Alia International Airport in Amman, Jordan. From there, she took a hired car sixty kilometers east to Azraq and the Jordanian air base where Michael, Karl and Aaron were due to be returned.

On arrival, she hastily presented her *Le Monde* press credentials to the base public relations officer and explained her role as a colleague of Colonel Niccolò Scarpa. Thinking ahead in his planning, Scarpa had left her name with the PR officer prior to departure, expecting Hana might arrive before they got back, gaining her provisional entry until the colonel's Black Hawk returned to base from its classified mission.

Then she waited. Settled in on a sofa in the base commissary, looking out over the nearby helo pads, Hana was fraught with tension as she anxiously rubbed her hands together and nervously swept her hair back. She couldn't bear the not knowing, wishing Colonel Scarpa had at least radioed ahead and given her an update. As a result, she was left thinking the worst, that Michael and Karl, and even Aaron, had been...*No*. She left the thought unfinished.

BEFORE LONG, the unmistakable sound of a Black Hawk's powerful General Electric T700 engine was heard approaching the landing pad. Even with the helo's special silencing apparatus, the sound grew deafening the closer it got. The pounding *thrum* of the rotors combined with the resulting vibration of the building was comforting to Hana, who realized that she would at least know *something* in a few more minutes. And that was better than waiting.

Grabbing her bag, she ran out the commissary door, down the hallway to the exit leading to the tarmac and slammed into the crash bar that opened the metal door. As the helo rotors spun to a stop, the cargo doors were pulled open and several armed soldiers emerged from the bird. As she stood at the gate barrier, Hana checked their faces, trying to gauge the success of the mission by their countenances and feeling hopeful. Like the true soldiers they were, their expressions held no hint of their emotions.

Then her heart lifted as she saw Michael step out, wrapped in a shiny silver blanket, wearing an olive camo t-shirt beneath that and scruffy blue prison trousers as he limped toward her with his head down.

Hana nearly cried as she saw Michael's shaved head, imagining that was probably the least of their vile treatments. Still, it was a shock.

Behind him, Karl was being carried out on a stretcher, so bad were his injuries. Despite his own condition, Aaron insisted on helping to carry Karl's stretcher and place it on a gurney that had been rushed out to the helo pad by two medics from the base infirmary. Behind them she saw a frail, somewhat disoriented man, also dressed in blue prison trousers, being escorted by two of the soldiers.

Michael reached the gate first, and only then did he look up to see Hana standing there, tears in her eyes. Letting the blanket fall from his shoulders, he wrapped both his arms around her, silently wincing as they embraced, but feeling comfort for the first time in so many days, comfort he honestly had believed would forever be denied him as an innocent inmate in that most notorious of all Egyptian prisons. No words needed to be spoken.

As Karl's gurney passed her, Hana broke away to greet her cousin and hold a warm hand against his cheek. "Are you okay, Karl?"

The young guardsman looked up at her, a thin smile curving his lips. "As okay as I can be now, but I'll be up again soon. And I'll expect the same hug you just gave Michael."

"You'll get that and more. Looks like you're in excellent hands now," she said, glancing at the attentive medics. "I'll drop in and see you later."

Standing by, Aaron—also in a camo t-shirt and blue

pants—watched Karl being wheeled away. Hana turned, slung her arms around him, and pulled him into a warm, gentle hug. "Thank you so much for taking care of my boys. Mainly a feeling I had. Don't ask how I know. But you seem to be the caretaking type, Aaron. You're a good friend to them. To all of us."

Blushing, Aaron grinned. "We would have been in a lot more trouble had Colonel Scarpa and his team not rescued us. You can't imagine how vile and inhumane that place is. It should be permanently shut down on humanitarian grounds."

Taking his arm, then Michael's, Hana walked them both to the infirmary, where they would be thoroughly examined and preventively treated with antibiotics against the potentially contaminated water that had entered their wounds.

But now, they were free.

CHAPTER
FORTY-ONE

Before boarding their Aegean Airlines flight in Cairo Airport's Terminal 3 for the ninety-minute trip to Tel Aviv, Yossi had made every accommodation on Remi's behalf, acting not only as his bodyguard—or rather, covert protector of the parchments—but his personal aide as well, handling tickets, baggage, Customs, and the various airport personnel involved. Reinforcing his presumed contractor status in Remi's eyes was prudent until they were back on Israeli soil, though he felt a bit deceitful playing the part, knowing official confiscation of the manuscripts would be the ultimate outcome. There was even the possibility of an arrest once they were in Israel. But he found Remi to be pleasant enough company and actually took pity on the litany of misfortunes he had endured as Remi described them during their drive to the airport.

As the jet lifted off the runway, Yossi looked at his watch. It was just past one o'clock. His thoughts turned to Sarah and where she might be, what she might be doing.

WITH THE SILVER scroll officially secured in a specially marked diplomatic pouch—along with a personal security device normally banned in-flight—Sarah Geffen passed through Cairo's airport security in Terminal 2 without issue and was the last person to board the nonstop Egypt Air flight to Tel Aviv a little before one o'clock.

She had used one of several diplomatic passports she had secretly acquired over the years—under assumed names, of course—knowing Mossad would surely have registered her real name on a no-fly list at this point. Such a standing safeguard as backup passports was not uncommon for those dealing in intelligence tradecraft, and given her current motivations and the challenging situation she now faced, Sarah was especially grateful for her prescience. The false documents and extra cash she had brought would be essential in maintaining her cover for just a while longer.

IT WAS AROUND two-thirty when both flights arrived simultaneously at Ben Gurion International Airport in Tel Aviv. Aegean Airlines has a permanent base at Terminal 3, and as Yossi looked out the window, he saw their jet was being parked on Concourse C, with the jet bridge for Gate C3 being extended out to the aircraft door.

Egypt Air had no routinely assigned terminal at Ben Gurion, so incoming flights were routed to whichever terminal was convenient to the airport's operating schedule. On arrival, Sarah's flight was assigned to disembark at Gate C8, also in Terminal 3.

After retrieving her diplomatic bag from the overhead compartment, she lined up to leave the aircraft with other passengers in coach, her ponytail tucked beneath a baseball cap. It was only a couple of minutes before she reached the door, and as she walked up the jetway, she reached into her bag and pulled out a pair of sunglasses, donning them before entering the concourse.

As passengers queued up to disembark the Aegean aircraft, Yossi fetched both his bag and Remi's from the overhead compartment and took their place in line. He laid out the plan in his mind. Once they were clear of the terminal and had gotten a rental car, he would break cover with Remi, identify himself as a Mossad agent, take possession of the parchments in the name of the IAA and the State of Israel, and detain him for possible arrest. He still felt bad about having to do so, but that was the protocol.

Emerging from the jetway with Remi in front of him, Yossi scanned the crowd, as was his instinctive custom when surrounded by large groups of people. He was looking for anyone out of place, perhaps standing, waiting, staring at him a bit longer than might be normally expected, then averting his or her gaze. He had no reason to believe he was being sought by anyone; it was just in his nature.

Then he saw her. His wife Sarah strolling down the main aisle, coming from one of the gates at the far end of the concourse. Though she was wearing shades and a baseball cap, he would know her body and that assertive gait anywhere.

Inconceivable! he thought, stunned at the serendipity. Then he spotted the telltale strap of a diplomatic tag on the bag she carried, presumably containing the twelve plates of the silver scroll.

He had to act! He had to stop her and seize the bag she was carrying, something she would likely prevent from happening any way she could—even violently if it came to that, public space be damned. But doing so meant he'd have to leave Remi unattended. And if Remi saw him interacting with Sarah—who he'd already had a nasty run-in with in Jerusalem—he'd definitely hightail it out of the airport and out of Yossi's control...*with* the precious parchments.

What to do?

WALKING TOWARD THE CONCOURSE EXIT, Sarah was unusually tense, on high alert for any suspicious activity, knowing she was now a wanted agent. She relied on her counterintelligence training to spot anyone waiting for her, looking for her, or following her. Behind her sunglasses, her eyes scanned left, then right, then ahead, repeatedly. As she casually strolled along the concourse, she used angled shop windows to see if she was being followed. It would only be a matter of minutes before she reached freedom in the back of a taxi.

Then she suddenly froze mid-stride, almost tripping as she saw the tall, unmistakable profile of her husband a few meters behind her in the window reflection of a bookshop she was passing.

Miz-day-en! she cursed under her breath as she continued keeping pace. Her mind raced as she considered her few options. She knew Yossi wouldn't hesitate to take action in the airport, flashing his Mossad credentials as he made an arrest, his powerful arm choking her out as airport police rushed to his aid. No, she couldn't allow that.

She casually zipped open her diplomatic pouch and reached inside for the contraband item she had placed there before leaving the hotel in Cairo.

As she was passing an empty row of seats in the waiting area of one gate, she felt Yossi approaching from behind. He was just reaching out to her when suddenly she turned and leaned into his body, as if hugging him. Instead, the stun gun she had in her right hand sent 50,000 volts of electricity through his entire nervous system, stopping him in his tracks. As he convulsed, she guided his large frame down onto one of the seats on the aisle, held the gun on him for a few more seconds of charge as she bent over him, largely ignored, then abruptly walked away at a fast clip.

Looking back from the direction Yossi had come, Sarah suddenly spotted Remi in a red polo shirt, standing in the center aisle, staring wide-eyed at his bodyguard's slumped body several feet away. *This was her chance!* Turning in his direction with her head down, she approached the hapless man, who was protectively holding a green backpack while guarding Yossi's camo duffel bag at his feet.

Blending in with the flow of the surrounding crowd, she turned, came up behind him, and as she reached for the backpack strap, discreetly plunged the stun gun into his lower back. Remi was sufficiently disabled to release his hold on the strap, letting it fall into Sarah's grasp.

As he dropped to the ground amid the gasps of onlookers, Sarah had already vanished into the surging crowd.

FORTY-TWO

With two Swiss Guards at his heels, Pope Ignatius walked swiftly from the Apostolic Palace to the Domus Santa Marta guesthouse and Michael Dominic's apartment. The young priest had just arrived back from the Middle East and, having been appraised of his injuries and treatment, his father was desperate to see him.

"Michael, my dear boy. What have they done to you?" the pope asked, running his hand across his son's shaved head. He sat on the edge of Michael's bed as the guards waited outside the door.

"I'm truly fine now, Father. Holy Father. I'm still not sure how to address you."

"When it is only you and me, *father* is fine, and preferred. Even *papa*, if you like. I am also known as Papa Ignatius, after all." Though his face was etched with concern, Enrico Petrini smiled as only a loving father could into the face of his son.

Michael laughed. "Somehow, I think *papa* would be crossing some kind of line. But I do like it, and it is how your flock addresses you. Okay, *papa* it is, then."

"So, tell me everything that happened in Israel and Jordan. And only Egypt if you wish to discuss it. I so regret there was nothing I could do from here, Michael. For several arcane reasons, the pope has little influence in certain Middle Eastern countries."

"That's all right...Papa." Michael looked up at his father with such love, grateful to be in the warmth of his company, here in the safety of the Vatican. "It's a long story, so make yourself comfortable..."

THE POPE SAT in awe of every detail his son related, cringing at the Scorpion Prison scene he described. He reached out to hold Michael's hand as the young priest calmly related every detail of their collective pursuits: Simon's initial discovery of the scrolls and their translation; Aaron Pearce's arrival and their planned trip to the Holy Land to inspect the silver scroll; of Ishak Ramzi's murder and Mossad's involvement; of the discovery of St. Paul's parchment...and so many of the details of others involved and events both known and yet unknown.

In particular, as-yet unknown was the fate of both the silver scroll and the attendant parchments discovered by the two young Arab boys. Michael had to admit he still had some confusion about that, as Yossi had last indicated he would try to retrieve the scroll from Sarah while chasing down the televangelist's agent, Remi Shapiro, and recovering the parchments he had.

By the time Michael was finished, the pope shook his head at the sheer complexity of it.

"Of course, most of all I would like to see that presumed St. Paul parchment," the Holy Father admitted. "This has the potential disruptive impact of a discovery like the James Ossuary. I am not the first—nor am I likely to be the last—sitting pope who will have to deal with such challenges to Church doctrine and tradition, whether true or falsified. Or to be called on to fulfill his role as Defender of the Faith. Fortunately, we have all the resources of faith, history, and science to support us in an effort that is likely to require years of analysis and prayer, with scholars offering new interpretations of existing Scripture, confirmation of what we already know—or the introduction of whole new sacred textual tracts we have yet to see."

"Well, Your Holiness, I do have digital images of the silver scroll and all the parchments. I'll have them prepared for your personal review immediately, and from there you can determine the next courses of action."

"That seems the prudent course for now, Michael, yes. So be it, then."

HANA AND AARON had gotten off the same flight from Amman as Michael and Karl, and while the latter two took a taxi directly to the Vatican—with Karl now well on the mend—Aaron and Hana shared a cab to their respective apartments, which were fairly close to each other in the Trastevere section of Rome.

As they rode along in the back seat, their conversation turned to Michael. As a researcher, Aaron was astute, and he hadn't missed the warmth of Hana's reception for Michael at the airbase in Jordan.

"It's clear to see that you and Michael have a special bond, Hana, something you're both handling with grace and dignity. And I respect that. If things were different, you'd be the perfect life companion for him. And I suspect he'd want that, too. But all three of us know that's not something he's likely to break his vows for. Though if ever there comes a time when Michael can make different choices… Well, at least we know where your heart lies.

"Though we haven't stayed in touch for a while, we've been close friends for a very long time, and Michael Dominic is one of the most honorable men I've ever known. Are you getting my drift?"

Hana was somber as she weighed what her new and trusted friend was saying. She thought back wistfully to Marco, and their separation because of both him having to raise his daughter in Paris, and her move from there to Rome for her new job.

"Yes, I caught that drift a while ago, Aaron. I admit it: I *do* love Michael. And I realize that's an impossible situation. We've already had a couple close encounters of the forbidden kind, but neither he nor I would be ashamed of anything that's happened. We both respect his vows, period."

Aaron nodded in understanding and reached out to pat her hand reassuringly. "I knew you'd be able to handle this with grace and dignity, Hana. You two are friends, and that's how it will stay for now. But if ever there comes a time when Michael *can* make different choices... Well, at least we know where your heart lies already."

Hana smiled appreciatively at Aaron's words of comfort and encouragement as the cab pulled up to her apartment building. "Thanks for understanding, Aaron. I know it wasn't easy for you to drop into the middle of this mess between Michael and me like that. But the truth is always better in the end and your friendship means more than I can say."

Aaron took a deep breath and suggested, "I don't know if this is something you've considered, and please forgive me if I'm out of line, but given the, uh, certainty of Michael's position, would you like to have dinner with me sometime? I'm sure Michael would not mind at all. He might even be happy with the idea."

Hana smiled at him and looked into his gentle gray eyes. "I'd love to," she said. "You offer people the security and serenity that I'm drawn to so strongly, and I'd love to get to know you better."

A mutually understood smile passed between them, and they said goodbye with a warm hug and a gentle kiss on each other's cheek.

As Hana walked up to her apartment, fetching her

keys from her bag, she smiled, feeling much lighter now that her long held secret had been revealed, without judgment or criticism from Aaron.

Quite the contrary, in fact.

EPILOGUE

It was a week later when Yossi's phone rang. Sitting in his office at Mossad headquarters in Tel Aviv, he picked up the receiver.

"Hello, husband," the voice said. Yossi paused a moment.

"Sarah, my lamb," he purred, his saccharine tone edged with a slight hostility. "Where have you been? You're missed by so many people here."

"I'll bet I am," she said wryly. "But don't worry, our paths will not cross again. I have but one question for you: where are the parchments?"

"Ah. How soon was it before you realized you'd been duped, I wonder?"

"It was pretty quick. Once I got into the taxi at the airport, I discovered Remi's bag contained the usual dreck a man might carry. But curiously, the parchments were missing."

"Ah, yes, the parchments. I had checked those with a couple of bags we didn't carry on. They were securely hidden and are now in the safe hands of the IAA, where they shall remain. As for the silver scroll...well, let's just say you should watch your back at all times, my love. As you yourself must know, Israel does not take kindly to the misappropriation of its cultural legacies—especially by its own agents.

"I also understand that Colonel Scarpa sent out a great number of searchers using digital copies of the original documents you hold, and at this stage, most of the treasure seems to have already been looted or is even now unrecoverable. The IAA will put out a statement to that effect in the next few days, so good luck trying to sell it beyond its historical value. Which alone might tide you over for a while, *if* you locate a gullible buyer. But you will be found, Sarah. Know that."

Furious at his being both unflinchingly principled and likely accurate in his assessment, Sarah cursed herself. Without saying goodbye, she disconnected the call.

She had only a few days, then, to find a fence here in Morocco, and try to pass off the silver scroll's treasure map as still being viable.

But her prospects did not look good. At this point, the silver scroll may well be *fakakta*.

IN THE PRIVATE shared room of their barracks, Karl had returned to the loving embrace of Lukas, who not only missed his partner's absence but berated him for taking such reckless chances with hunting for buried silver—despite it being under the authority of their commandant—and especially for doing whatever it was that landed him in an Egyptian prison.

He continued to nurse Karl's wounds from the whipping for several more days, but the scars would remain.

"Hey, whatever happened to that silver bar Colonel Scarpa gave you? You holding out on me?"

Karl laughed. "No. As it happened, we helped rescue another prisoner at Scorpion, a Catholic teacher named Hassan, who found political asylum in Jordan. As he had nothing to start his new life there, I gave him the silver bar. He needed it much more than I did." He put his arm around Lukas and pulled him in for a warm hug.

"I have everything I need here," Karl said.

"REMI! Where the hell are those parchments you promised me?" Pastor Darwin was back in Dallas, now on a tear on the phone with Remi in Tel Aviv.

"Well, Pastor, apparently it was just not to be. I'm now convinced of that. I had them, and then I didn't, and then I did, and finally, they were ripped away from me once again by that same Mossad agent. You might as well not spend another minute thinking about it since they are both gone now and irretrievable.

"But there is another manuscript I've heard about

that may be obtainable. One from the great Italian astronomer Galileo. It seems an exhibition is coming to Loyola Law School in Chicago soon, and with it, the original Vatican documents of Galileo's trial.

"Here's what I'm thinking…"

~

FICTION, FACT, OR FUSION?

Many readers have asked me to distinguish fact from fiction in my books. Generally, I like to take factual events and historical figures and build on them in creative ways—but much of what I do write is historically accurate. In this section, I'll review some of the chapters where questions may arise, with hopes it may help those wondering where reality meets creative writing.

SPOILER ALERT

If you prefer to sustain the illusion of fiction as presented in the book, it is suggested you stop here and not read what's real and what's not.

GENERAL

As in all my books, vehicles, trains, airports, transportation schedules, restaurants (and their menus), locations, time zones and travel times are all consistent with reality. As much as possible, events take place in real time, using actual locations and mentioning local buildings and businesses where suitable. Avid readers have often commented that they have come across specific places I describe in their travels, making their experience that much more realistic and enjoyable.

PROLOGUE

Every word in the Prologue is historically accurate and verifiable. The constant plundering of caves is an ongoing problem for the Israel Antiquities Authority (IAA), whose role in preserving biblical history through archeology and working proactively to prevent looting is highly commendable.

CHAPTER 2

There are indeed only sixty-five licensed antiquities dealers in all of Israel, and each ancient manuscript discovered for permissible sale on the open market must be registered with the IAA. As I mention in the book, this is one reason for the proliferating black market and its often-underhanded dealings.

CHAPTER 3

The process of cutting the silver scroll here has actually been done before, on the very Khirbet Qumran copper scroll as described in this chapter. This was done in 1956, since the scroll was too rigidly rolled up to be able to read and translate. After six years of trying to figure out how to do it, scientists ultimately chose a special circular saw and a dentist's drill to cut the scroll into 23 panels, which are now displayed at the Jordan Museum in Amman.

The 23 Copper Scroll panels at the Jordan Museum in Amman

CHAPTER 7

It is stunningly true that, as of this writing, there are still some *thirty thousand caves* in the Judean Desert yet to be explored and excavated for what the Essenes and other early cultures may have left behind. Think about that.

Everything about the Mithraists here is historically accurate—except their existence today, which is fictional. From the first through the fourth centuries, when it was disbanded, Mithraism was truly the main rival to Christianity, given the proliferation and influence of the Roman soldiers who made up its membership.

CHAPTER 8

The ancient mithraeum temple constructed deep beneath the ruins of the Circus Maximus in Rome is still intact, and available to visit on tours.

The actual handshake greeting of the *syndexioi*—members of a mithraeum—are sadly lost in time, so I have contrived what might be a suitable alternative to a secret handshake, based loosely on the similar Freemason's greeting.

CHAPTER 9

The descriptions of the locations of gold and silver are accurately paraphrased from the Khirbet Qumran Copper Scroll, and represent actual places where the Essenes (not the Mithraists, as used in the story) are said to have buried their treasure. And yes, the estimated value as described in the Qumran Copper Scroll is upwards of $3 billion. Treasure hunters have been searching for the bounty for decades; as far as is known publicly, nothing has yet been found.

CHAPTER 10

Though our silver scroll for the story is fictional, there is factual basis for its existence. The Khirbet Qumran Copper Scroll is an authentic find, part of the Dead Sea Scrolls discovered in 1947. In that scroll, reference is made to a separate *silver scroll*, which—in addition to having the same descriptions on where the great treasure of the Essenes had been hidden—reveals that the silver scroll expands on those details, providing further clues as to the treasure's location. To date, that silver scroll has yet to be discovered.

Simon's description of the value of that copper scroll's treasure, $3 billion, is based on today's scholarly estimates.

CHAPTER 11

The IntactPhone is an authentic device developed by an Israeli firm, CommuniTake Technologies. It is the most advanced cellular phone of its kind, and the Israeli government must indeed approve every purchase to prevent it from being used by hostile forces.

CHAPTER 12

Catalogued as Nahal Hever Cave 8 in Israel's Judean Desert, the nickname "Cave of Horror" was given after the skeletons of forty men, women and children were discovered inside, all Jewish refugees from the Bar Kokhba revolt of c132–136 CE.

Just a small observation here, but I found it curious that in Israel people *do* eat green salads for breakfast. So keeping with his character, I figured I'd make Pastor Darwin a little vexed by the uncommon custom.

CHAPTER 14

The sixth-century Madaba Map in the Church of Saint George is, as shown, fully authentic, and is still to this day brilliantly resonant with images depicting Jerusalem prior to its destruction in 70 CE. The notes about the map confirming the locations of the Cardo Maximus—the main North-South royal road in Roman and Byzantine Jerusalem—and the Nea Church, as well as another road running through the city, are historically correct.

CHAPTER 17–18

Although Roman Emperor Commodus was believed to have been a strong supporter and a likely member of Mithraism in the second century, I have constructed the mithraeum beneath Jerusalem's Western Wall in my imagination. I assume there is not one located there—but one never knows…

And there actually *is* a long network of underground tunnels and cisterns beneath Jerusalem's Western Wall, still in use today.

CHAPTER 24

The "Jesus Family Tomb" in the East Talpiot neighborhood of Jerusalem is indeed a genuine tomb, long believed by many authorities—notably Dr. James Tabor, a Biblical scholar and professor at the University of North Carolina at Charlotte—to contain the ossuaries of Jesus and his family, attributable mainly to the unique epigraphs inscribed on each bone box. And collectively this is quite compelling, since they identify what is very possibly the family of Jesus Christ. Much has been written on this controversial matter, and the interested reader is encouraged to explore more on the topic.

The parchment "confirming" the fact is, of course, from the author's imagination. However, those Hebrew names identified in this chapter are the actual inscriptions that appear on each ossuary.

CHAPTER 35

The conditions described for Scorpion Prison in Cairo are as authentic as my research can confirm, including the statement by its former warden (Major General Ibrahim Abd al-Ghaffar) which was accurately quoting him as saying, *"It was designed so that those who go in don't come out again, unless dead."*

There is a moment in this chapter where Hana is shown to have unusually intimate access to the pope. For new readers questioning this, I refer you to previous books rather than give out any spoilers as to why Michael's predicament would be of interest to the pope.

If this is the first book of mine you've read and you wish to read more, please start with *The Magdalene Deception* and go on from there, where things will be made clearer.

CHAPTER 38

It gave me no pleasure to describe the torturous treatment Michael, Karl and Aaron suffered under from the guards at Scorpion Prison, especially knowing it was based on research of actual beatings that occur in reality at the notorious penitentiary. Human Rights Watch and other humanitarian groups report on such violent subjugation even today, mostly carried out on political prisoners.

CHAPTER 42

Again, if you are new to my books and this is your first read—in my third book, *The Magdalene Veil*, it was revealed to Michael Dominic that his father was his lifelong mentor, Enrico Petrini, currently Pope Ignatius.

EPILOGUE

Remi Shapiro and Pastor Gabriel Darwin are destined to make another appearance in the next book in this series, *The Galileo Gambit*. To make sure you receive notice of forthcoming books, please sign up at garymcavoy.com/contact/

MORE ON THE DEAD SEA SCROLLS

For those interested in how the Dead Sea Scrolls are handled and preserved, I would refer you to a brief but excellent article by Joe Uziel, head of the Dead Sea Scrolls Unit at the Israel Antiquities Authority. See garymcavoy.link/rbbDpk

AUTHOR'S NOTE

Dealing with issues of theology, religious beliefs, and the fictional treatment of historical biblical events can be a daunting affair.

I would ask all readers to view this story for what it is—a work of pure fiction, adapted from the seeds of many oral traditions and blended with the historical record, at least as we know it today.

Apart from telling an engaging story, I have no agenda here, and respect those of all beliefs, from Agnosticism to Zoroastrianism and everything in between—except where charlatans are involved. I cannot abide good people of faith being preyed upon, as seems to be especially common here in America.

Thank you for reading *The Jerusalem Scrolls*. I hope you enjoyed it and, if you haven't already, I suggest you pick up the story in the earlier books of **The Magdalene Chronicles** series—(especially) *The Magdalene Deception*, then *The Magdalene Reliquary* and *The Magdalene Veil*. After that trio of adventures, the same characters and a few new ones are featured in my **Vatican Secret Archive Thriller** series, so far comprised of *The Vivaldi Cipher*, *The Opus Dictum*, *The Petrus Prophecy*, *The Avignon Affair*, and this latest entry, *The Jerusalem Scrolls*. And be watching out for *The Galileo Gambit*, next one up.

When you have a moment, **would you consider leaving a review on Amazon**, Goodreads, Facebook and perhaps elsewhere you find convenient? Reviews are crucial to a book's success, and I hope for The Magdalene Chronicles and the Vatican Secret Archive Thriller series to have a long and entertaining life for readers.

You can easily leave your review by going to my Amazon book page for *The Jerusalem Scrolls*. And thank you!

If you would like to reach out for any reason, you can email me at gary@garymcavoy.com. If you'd like to learn more about me and my other books, visit my website at www.garymcavoy.com, where you can also sign up for my private Readers Group mailing list.

Kind regards,

AUTHOR'S NOTE

Gary McAvoy

ACKNOWLEDGMENTS

Throughout this series I have had the grateful assistance of many friends and colleagues, without whose help this would have been a more challenging project.

I am indebted to Dr. James Tabor, whose ground-breaking work in biblical archeology, and in particular the "Jesus Family Tomb" in Jerusalem, was the inspiration for this novel and which proved essential to my research. Dr. Tabor is a biblical scholar and Professor of Ancient Judaism and Early Christianity in the Department of Religious Studies at the University of North Carolina at Charlotte. He is considered one of the world's foremost authorities on ancient Late Second Temple Judaism and early Christianity.

My editors, Sandra Haven-Herner from Reedsy and Kathleen Costello from GrammarToGo are both keepers for every book I've done and every book yet to come. Any author would be honored to have their help and expertise.

As always, to my hand-selected beta readers team who never lets me down with their careful review of early material and invaluable feedback—thank you all. Ben Cheng, Andrea Cooper, Yale Lewis, Don Reiter, and

Lisa Knapp Treon: you are MVP standouts for your contributions on this one.

ATTRIBUTION FOR THE COPPER SCROLL PANELS PHOTO:

Osama Shukir Muhammed Amin FRCP (Glasg), CC BY-SA 4.0, via Wikimedia Commons

Ingram Content Group UK Ltd.
Milton Keynes UK
UKHW040055270723
425834UK00002B/5/J